W9-DID-959

The *Ethical* BUSINESS WOMAN

KATHLEEN BALOTA

PAGE PUBLISHING, INC.
New York, NY

First originally published by Page Publishing, Inc. 2016

ISBN 978-1-68289-539-9 (pbk)
ISBN 978-1-68289-540-5 (digital)

Printed in the United States of America

ACKNOWLEDGMENTS

I would like to thank David Michie and Captain Pete Ferentini, from MarineMax in Naples, Florida. They gave me valuable insight into yachts and yacht sales along with some liberties to use Captain Pete's name in my book.

I would like to acknowledge the various trademarked names mentioned in this book. Names were taken off the Internet as part of public knowledge or are popular TV shows or TV personalities, so I will not mention each individually.

I would like to acknowledge several friends: Laura Lukas, who encouraged me to read more. Chris Salopek and Mary Ruscher, my quilting friends who told me to take up a new hobby in retirement. I know they meant sewing or quilting, but their words planted the seed for me to write this quilt of words.

Finally, I would like to acknowledge my family, who always inspire and support me. Without your love and understanding, I wouldn't have tried to write this book.

CHAPTER 1

The Sales Convention

Francine was excited to put on her new Antonio Melani dress with its coordinating tan-red-and-black jacket. When she saw the suit on a recent visit to downtown Chicago, she balked at the three-hundred-dollar price tag, but it was the power outfit she needed for the annual sales conference. She paired the dress with her high-heel Michael Kors shoes and matching handbag. Francine looked at herself in the mirror and smiled. She was usually very hesitant about admiring herself. She had a lifetime of living in the shadows of her beautiful sister, so self-admiration was very difficult for her. Today was different. She felt confident and professional for the venue while keeping a very feminine, classy look that could transition well for the evening conference reception.

The sales conference featured products from Magnacraft Corporation, which was the company that employed Francine for the past ten years. At thirty-four years old, Francine was one of the younger sales representatives. Magnacraft's product portfolio included items used in manufacturing plants, such as fixtures, hoists, and conveyance equipment, as well as technical support resources. Francine had gained sales experience in all the product lines and had exceeded sales goals for the last six years. Her efforts were rewarded two years ago when she was promoted to a senior sales manager role. The pro-

5

motion entitled her to participate in the company profit sharing program, and although the sharing percentage was small, Francine looked forward to becoming a senior sales executive. That position was given a substantial salary and bonus package that allowed those employees to live quite comfortably. Some of the more tenured sales executives had homes with in-ground pools, drove exotic cars, and in general, lived the good life.

The good life was Francine's goal. She wanted a lifestyle comparable to her sister's and brother's success. Today might be that day. It was rumored that there would be a promotion announced during the opening sales meeting at the conference. The recipient was not privy to the announcement so as to not ruin the surprise moment, but the rumor was that Francine had the highest sales dollar amount, the largest number of new clients for the company, and the highest customer satisfaction percentage from customer surveys. Yes, today was going to be Francine's day—finally.

Magnacraft Corporation's headquarters was located in the general Chicago area, and most of the sales reps, including Francine, worked and lived close to that office. Rather than holding the annual sales conference in a conference room on site, Magnacraft rented a larger conference room and adjoining display room at a prestigious local hotel. The extra room allowed the company the opportunity to invite their key distributors and potential customers to attend the latter part of the conference. The strategy was to have a kickoff employee-only meeting to go over sales forecasts, financial information, and other internal employee information, followed by an instructional tour of the product display areas for sales reps to familiarize themselves with all products in the portfolio. The tour served as a practice round for salespeople to polish their speeches for the upcoming distributor and customer visit.

The distributors and potential customers were invited at noon for a well-portioned lunch with open bar. Sales reps would be spread around the tables to keep conversation focused on Magnacraft's product value. After lunch, a well-rehearsed and uplifting speech from Magnacraft's president would be given to all attendees followed by opening the doors to the display hall. In the evening, a lavish dinner would be provided, again with open bar. All sales representatives, sales managers, and sales executives were required to circulate among customers to strengthen the relationship. The results of this one-day event have been overwhelmingly effective, with very high distributor loyalty to Magnacraft's products.

For the sales employees at Magnacraft, this event was a real treat. They were each provided with a hotel room the night before and the night of the event. The overnight stay allowed the sales team to relax and not worry about their commute, home responsibilities, or driving under the influence. This year's sales conference was especially special because it was at the Hilton Hotel in downtown Chicago.

Francine carefully checked her makeup and hair prior to leaving her hotel room for the opening conference meeting. She had fashioned her light-brown hair into a loose upsweep so she wouldn't have to worry about it frizzing into a helmet head. Francine had suffered all her life with hair that could grow outward exponentially if subjected to humidity, and September weather in Chicago could change quickly.

Francine took one final look in the mirror and was satisfied with her appearance. She grabbed her purse and headed out the door to the hotel elevator. When she arrived at the conference room downstairs, she quickly scanned the room to find a table close to the stage. She had planned on sitting with her colleagues Sara Johnston and Jim Ruscher. Sara and Jim worked with Francine on several sales campaigns, and the three of them ate lunch together when they were in the sales office. Francine saw her friends waving at her across the room, but as she walked toward their table, her boss, Mike Purser, stepped into her path and said, "Francine, we've been waiting for you to arrive. Please sit at the table with me, John Delully, and a couple of other people. We have a table front and center."

Francine's pulse quickened. Surely this was another sign that she was getting the promotion.

"Sure, Mike. I'd be honored to sit with you and John," she said eagerly.

She quickly motioned to her friends Sara and Jim that she was sitting elsewhere and then walked to the front table. Francine felt everyone's eyes on her as she walked, and she purposely kept her head straight forward as not to seem too important. When she got to the table, she carefully hung her purse over the chair's back and sat down next to Mike Purser. John Delully, the vice president of Magnacraft, was standing next to his chair while talking to another executive. He nodded to Francine as she sat.

Francine settled into her seat and glanced at the beautiful flower arrangement on the table. She was impressed with the elegance of the table settings as she noticed Mike Purser's brown leather-bound notebook and his Magnacraft conference folder kit. She then glanced at the setting where John Delully, the VP, was sitting and noticed an impressive satchel that Francine imagined contained some type of writing table plus his conference folder kit. Other people started to take seats at the table when a feeling of panic hit Francine.

"Oh, crap! I forgot my folder and conference kit in my room," she muttered.

She quickly got up and hurried out of the room to retrieve her materials. Her thoughts were whirling as she realized that everyone was watching her leave, and she hoped that her outburst was not heard by anyone. *Did I say that or think that?* she thought to herself. In any event, she knew that by the time she returned to her seat, the conference would have started.

"Why me?" she whispered to herself as she sped her walk to a run.

Francine retrieved her conference materials, and luckily, the conference speaker was not at the podium when she returned to her seat. She quickly seated herself and removed her notebook from the conference kit. She felt beads of perspiration on her forehead. She thought, *Please, forehead, don't drip on my folder,* as she gulped down a full glass of water to cool herself down.

The table of eight was now fully occupied, and she quickly greeted the other people seated at her table, which included another company executive and four sales team associates. Francine thought that the table seating was an odd combination of employees. She quickly dismissed the thought.

The conference finally began. Joe Miller, the president and founder of Magnacraft, sprinted up to the podium and greeted his sales workforce. Joe was well liked by the employees for his easygoing personality and great smile. Joe was the epitome of the American Dream. He came from a humble upbringing and worked hard to transform a small equipment shop into the corporation that Magnacraft was today. Although his friendly demeanor was admired by everyone, all employees were aware that Joe's nature turned very tough and matter-of-fact when it came to business. It was better to pass Joe in the hallways and say hello than to be summoned by him into a meeting and barraged with questions.

Joe presented a frank forecast to his employees. Business was good, and the company had met corporate expectations for the year. However, Internet competition had dramatically decreased sales in most product lines. Joe stressed the importance of customer relationships in keeping other core businesses. He made a candid plea to all employees to listen to their customers to find what service the company may provide that could make the customer's job easier.

"Responsiveness to customers is the key. Products are commodities that can be purchased through multiple sources, but personal service lies with our sales staff. Sales relationships are an art. Seek out their needs and find creative, fast ways to help our customers. Without doing these simple things, the profession of a sales representative will become extinct. Think about that and take advantage of the opportunity you have with your existing customers, including all of those coming to our conference and product display today."

Wow! What an impact his words had to the conference members. The room was silent, without even a jingle of a coffee cup. Francine listened to these words sincerely. She knew that she was one of the few sales reps that really tried to understand the customer's needs. She knew Magnacraft's products well but owed her success to understanding the business of each customer in her portfolio. Understanding the customer's business took time but led to increased product sales. She often wanted to go a step further, to understand the personal frustrations of her customers and to sell additional stock management services to her customers so they could concentrate on their own core business.

Hmmm, maybe I can implement a stock management program into Magnacraft's service portfolio after I'm promoted to sales exec. This is going to be a great day, she thought as she jotted a note.

There were a few more speeches and presentations from other Magnacraft executives, followed by a scheduled break. The last speaker hinted at a special announcement from Magnacraft's human resources VP. Francine took advantage of the break time to meet with her colleagues and friends, Sara and Jim, outside of conference room.

"That speech from Joe was very scary," said Sara. "Jim and I have recently lost several customers who prefer to do their purchasing online. Heck, we have our own online website, but customers prefer to go to the cheapest supplier regardless if their items are junk and they have to replace them."

"Isn't that the truth," replied Jim, "Cheap and fast is what customers are after. Their internal scorecard doesn't reflect if the items have been replaced frequently, just cheaper. We're screwed. We're dinosaurs."

He looked directly at Francine and said, "You don't have to worry. You'll be a sales executive soon, probably today, and you'll be telling us to work harder. You won't have to worry."

Francine was taken aback by her friend's words. She never stopped to think about the job relationship change after she was promoted. Jim was right. Sales execs managed the sales reps for that product line. They didn't frequently have to contact customers. Their only contact with customers was when something went wrong, or to entertain customers.

Hmmm, Francine thought, *I would miss the interaction with my customers.*

The scheduled break ended, and the sales force was summoned back into the conference room. It was time for the human resource VP to speak. Francine was anxious for the promotion announcement because she had not been told definitively that she had gotten the promotion. Her anxiety quickly changed into nervousness. Francine's stomach felt like she just drank a cup of pure acid. Her back felt damp, and her hands were clammy, but she sat properly upright in her chair with hands folded on her lap and a slight, interested smile on her face. She learned throughout her experience to be a consummate professional, even when nervous. "Never let them see you sweat" was her motto. Unfortunately, she had to use that motto with customers, with her family, and today, with her coworkers.

The conference room quieted as Nora Sanders, a peculiar woman and the vice president of human resources, walked up to the podium. Nora was a competent woman, but Francine felt she had the demeanor of a robot. Francine felt sorry for her. Nora probably was a very nice person, but years of personnel bureaucracy with all the various dos and do nots had made Nora afraid to show emotion. Francine could not recall one occasion where she ever saw Nora having a good time socializing with her coworkers. Nora's appearance looked great in her beige cashmere suit with a red accenting scarf, and she smiled dutifully to the audience as she began her presentation talking about the various accomplishments in recruitment and training programs.

The moment finally came when Nora announced that there was going to be a new person added to the executive ranks. She continued, "Due to our lower sales forecast, the newly formed position will not be a full sales executive rank but rather an *intern* sales executive. The new position will allow that person to learn the job responsibilities that come with being an executive at Magnacraft, and when the sales climate improves, the internship will turn into a full sales executive position with all the benefits that an executive enjoys." Nora smiled and scanned the room to let the words sink in to the conference participants.

Francine had to think about those words quickly. She was disappointed to have to wait a little longer for her goal as a full-fledged sales executive but understood the position of the company. She wondered if she had to get up to say an acceptance speech or just stand up and nod a complimentary thank-you. *Oh yes*, she reflected, *I'll just have to stand up*, as she relaxed a little in her chair.

"This year," Nora explained, "the woman being promoted has made continual accomplishments to Magnacraft. Her knowledge and

11

professional skills make her a consummate choice for an executive position. We are very pleased to announce that our newest intern sales executive is Karen Warnette. Please welcome Karen into our executive ranks."

What! *Karen Warnette!* Francine's inner self screamed.

Francine's mind became frantic with disbelief as she thought, *Karen has never made one cold customer sales call. All she did was be involved in various projects that other people ran, especially my projects.*

Francine felt herself become clammy all over her body. Nausea from the morning coffee acid overtook her. She vomited her stomach acid into her coffee cup as she heard a less than overwhelmed audience clap as Karen said her thank-you.

"What a crock of crap!" someone muttered at a table behind Francine.

There were several gasps in the audience, to the dismay of the executives.

To some other coworkers, the scene of Francine falling into her table setting and vomiting was more entertaining than the recent announcement. Francine thought to herself that she would take comfort in that thought later. For right now, embarrassment overtook all her emotion. Francine's friends, of course, quickly moved their attention to Francine's way when the announcement was made. They thought Francine was the shoe in. Sara quickly got up from her table and hurried toward Francine to help. Francine's boss also was trying help by holding Francine's head off her place setting.

Francine heard someone say, "How embarrassing for Francine."

She wondered if the comment was about the vomiting or the announcement.

Sara helped Francine stand upright, threw a napkin over Francine's contaminated coffee cup, and wrapped one arm around her as they hurried to the women's restroom. Once there, they just looked at each other, stunned. Francine said, "Let's not talk about it now, but tonight, after the customer reception, I'm going to get seriously involved with a bottle of bourbon, and I'm hoping to count you in."

Sara laughed and said that she was happy Francine only said *a* bottle. They giggled until Francine's tears started to flow. Then only a hug from her dear friend Sara could console her.

Francine desperately wanted to go back to her hotel room before the customers arrived, but she knew that she needed to return to the conference room to be professional. She knew that every sales rep hoped that they would be getting promoted, and although she may have been the person that everyone thought was receiving the promotion, all the sales reps would be saddened that the promotion wasn't for themselves. There would be lots of shallow congratulations given to Karen Warnette from each one of the sales team.

What bothered Francine and what now consumed her thoughts was the question, why did her boss ask her to sit at that front table? She wasn't the type of person who was confrontational, but she was dying to know the answer. Francine walked directly back to her seat at the table and apologized for getting ill in front of them. She thoughtfully congratulated Karen, who was seated next to the VPs.

Mike Purser nonchalantly tapped Francine and asked her to help him with some pamphlets. Francine walked with him toward the wall when Mike asked, "You thought you were getting the promotion, didn't you?"

Francine, with all the poise she could muster, looked directly at Mike and said, "Actually, I did. And knowing now that I ranked number one in surpassing the company goals, I would now say that I deserved the promotion."

Mike did not have a response and only nodded and lowered his gaze. He had always liked working with Francine, and he knew that his profit sharing depended on his sales team. Francine consistently came through with sales and new accounts. Francine continued, "Mike, why did you ask me to sit at the front table?"

Mike led her into a small room adjoining the conference room, and Francine noticed that Nora Sanders was sitting at a small table in the room.

"Please sit down, Francine," Mike said as he took a seat next to Nora.

Francine sat accordingly and nodded at Nora. Mike said, "We asked you and several of your peers to sit with the upper management team as a final recognition for what you accomplished during the past year. Your contributions to Magnacraft have been substantial, and we thank you for your years of service. But regretfully, we will be letting you go effective immediately. Nora has some paperwork to give you, and then our security team will lead you back to your hotel room to pack and check out of the hotel."

"What? Final recognition?" said Francine. "Is this a bad joke? Why?"

Francine felt her stomach acid churning again. Her face and body felt flushed and hot. She could not quite comprehend what was happening.

Nora Sanders took control of the conversation. She slid some paperwork toward Francine and in, a very matter-of-fact way, said, "Francine, we are making personnel reductions and unfortunately have decided that you are not executive material. Therefore, Magnacraft cannot continue to invest resources into your development. We thank you for your past service, and the paperwork I am handing you outlines the termination procedure and resources available to you to procure a new position elsewhere."

Francine was numb and waited for when Nora would say "Any questions?" But that time didn't come. Instead, a nondescript man in a suit arrived to escort Francine away.

"Wait a minute," Francine demanded. "I've met every challenge, surpassed individual sales goals, and brought in several millions of additional customer sale dollars in new contracts to Magnacraft. You have got to be joking."

No one answered. Nora just sat and stared at her, and Mike just kept looking at the floor. Francine continued in a very shaky voice, "Mike, you know I led most of the team strategy sessions. Heck, the new prodigy, Karen Warnette, didn't have one solid idea to offer nor brought in one dollar of new business. This is a sham."

Mike replied, "I understand what you are saying, and I am truly sorry, but Karen is the type of policy administrator that we see as a Magnacraft executive."

Nora said, "Mike, stop! You have no authority to make explanations on executive profiling." She turned to Francine and said, "Thank you, Francine, for your past service to Magnacraft."

Francine stood up, her tears welling up in her eyes, and said, "This is outrageous. Every sales rep will be shaking in their boots when they hear about this. They all are going to be worried about being terminated since they all know that I had the best sales record. And my success with my customers has been because of a sincere, trusting relationship. That relationship led to increased sales business for this company. My customers are coming here today. What are they going to think when they hear I was fired?"

Nora said, "Well, they won't hear that because the paperwork you received stated that you left Magnacraft to pursue other opportunities. Breach of that explanation to your coworkers or your past customers will terminate your severance monies and your reemployment service opportunities."

Francine's head was spinning, and her stomach was aching. She so badly wanted to say, *To hell with your buyoff! You fired me for no cause,* but the practical side of her quickly glanced at the paperwork in front of her. Her severance package was about three months' salary, or about $18,000 gross. Knowing she had only about $8,000 disposable income in her savings and checking accounts, she knew she needed the money. She pulled the paperwork closer and signed the severance agreement as tears ran down her face.

Francine walked blindly to her hotel room, escorted by an unknown security person, with thoughts about her customers who were going to attend the conference displays and the dinner tonight.

Who will be their guide in my absence? What will they think? What will everybody think when I don't show up? she thought.

Francine's only hope was that her coworkers noticed that she got ill in the meeting and didn't recover well to attend the balance of the event. She definitely did not want her "leaving" to be the topic of everyone at the conference today.

When she finally arrived at her room, she told the guard that she would need a few minutes to pack and calm herself. He nodded and took a seat at a bench by the elevators in the hallway. Francine entered her room and carefully closed the door behind her. As she locked the door, she felt a flood of tears running down her face.

Francine darted into the bathroom and sat on the side of the tub and let the flood continue.

After a few minutes, she stood up and rinsed her face in the sink. She walked into the bedroom area and retrieved her personal cell phone from her purse. She sent a text to her friend Sara Johnston: "Hey, girlfriend, leaving for home. Have flu. I'll talk to you tomorrow." She read her text before she pressed Send and felt satisfied that word would get around the conference.

"That will be sufficient for today," she said aloud.

Francine quickly packed her bags and was escorted to her car by her security follower.

"No need to check out," he related to her. "Everything is being taken care of."

His statement didn't do anything to comfort her. She realized that the Magnacraft executives wanted to ensure she wouldn't make a scene in front of any of their customers.

Francine truly was a great salesperson and a great employee. Francine worked hard to cultivate her customer base. She had a motto of being "firm, fair, and not too familiar." She gleaned this motto after hearing a professional speaker early in her career. She loved working for Magnacraft and thought their products were superior to the competition in terms of quality and dependability at a fair price. She also loved the people at Magnacraft, including the relationships she made with the people she met in Magnacraft's tooling and assembly plants.

Francine had several large accounts with national distributors, including Standard Product Distribution Company (SPD), with their main distribution warehouse in the Chicago area, and Total Distributors Company, with their main office and distribution warehouse in the Indianapolis area. These two distributors accounted for over 50 percent of the total sales dollars in Francine's portfolio, and both companies were sought by every salesperson in the Midwest. They chose Francine because of her open and fair negotiation of terms as well as her quick responsiveness.

Francine arrived home about noon with a throbbing headache. She hoped that she would not run into any of her neighbors. She did not want to talk at the moment, but even worse, she did not want anyone to see her reddened face from tears. The ride from downtown Chicago to northern Chicago took about thirty-five minutes, but Francine couldn't even remember the drive.

She loved the walk-up townhouse she rented and initially felt comforted as she walked around her rooms. She was angry and hurt. As evening came and the wine she was drinking was taking effect, her anger transformed to sadness, embarrassment, and fear. What is her next step? Who can she confide in? How can she possible tell her family? The questions just kept coming.

Francine wished she had a family that would be comforting and nonjudgmental. But the Pacques were not known to be a family that Francine could lean on. Her parents, Bertrand and Gertrude, were good-hearted people, but they shared a very small outlook on how people should live. They owned a small and profitable accounting firm in Kenosha, Wisconsin, handling the accounting needs of many of the businesses along the highway corridor between Chicago, Illinois, and Milwaukee, Wisconsin. Between tax season and monthly accounting for their clients, Bertrand and Gertrude did not have to advertise their services. They worked a ten-to-twelve-hour day, six days a week, and spent their off time taking care of their home. Francine's parents believed that marriage was all important and that spouses have to act as a team to support the breadwinner in the relationship. They did not understand why their thirty-four-year-old daughter was not married or why she worked in a typically male-dominated field of sales. There were many instances where they chastised Francine about her life and job. *No, I'm not going to tell Mom and Dad about losing my job. They would probably make me work for them in some capacity until they found a suitable spouse for me,* Francine thought.

She thought about confiding to her brother or sister but also decided not to take them into confidence. Francine's brother and sister were incapable of giving guidance and empathy to Francine. Both of them were the popular stars of their high school. Francine's brother, Gerard, was a star football receiver. He was loud, boisterous, and extremely good looking. His athletic six-two physique and good

17

looks made Gerry the guy that every guy wanted to be and every girl wanted to date. Chants of "Pack it in" where common to hear during the school football games, and that handle was used often in media football chronicles and in the school hallways. Gerry wasn't a scholar, but his grades and athletic feats led to a generous college scholarship that led to a bachelor's degree in sports administration. As everything always turned out roses for Gerry, he received multiple offers from schools around the Midwest. He accepted an offer with Northwestern University and still worked there today.

"Of course," Francine said aloud, "Gerry married a beautiful girl he met while in college, who gleefully gave up her dreams of a career to be a homemaker for her husband. They have three beautiful children who idolize their father."

Some sisters might want to have an ultrapopular brother in high school, but to Francine, who was not beautiful, athletic, or very forceful when she was growing up, Gerry was a nightmare. He consistently teased her and nicknamed her something that she still cringes when she hears—Fanny Pack. Gerry thought the play on her name was ingenious, and so did her family. The nickname followed Francine from grade school until today. When she complained about it, and she did numerous times to her family, her parents just would say that she was too sensitive.

"Yes, I am," she would reply.

Usually, her parents would just continue commenting on their son's humorous talents.

"Oh, he's just hilarious," Francine would sarcastically reply.

There would be no comeback reply from her parents. Occasionally, they would just look at her and shake their heads. Gerard was a star in their eyes and hearts, so was her sister, Genevieve.

Genevieve, or Princess Vivian, as Gerry nicknamed her, was an extremely beautiful woman. She was a beautiful child, with striking blue eyes and streaming golden hair. As she grew into a teenager, she somehow skipped that gawky period that all young women go through. No, Genevieve transformed into a butterfly without the caterpillar stage. She was radiant, with pouty, full lips and a thin but curvy figure. She was nice too. Everything came easily to her in life.

Genevieve was so popular in school that no one even questioned whether she would be homecoming or prom queen. It was a done deal as far as anyone would think. Genevieve was smart but not really interested in furthering her education after college. She had so many suitors that her parents had to monitor all phone calls coming in to her. After high school, Genevieve worked at a local Chicago modeling firm, and her pictures were frequently seen in newspaper and local magazine ads. She worked as a model for about five years until she married a successful young lawyer, Matt Mulvane.

Matt was the son of a prominent Chicago family, and for a wedding present, they presented them with keys to a substantial home in the Lake Forest area. Genevieve had a beautiful life, with a wonderful husband, and now with a beautiful son and daughter.

Francine's reluctance to confide to Genevieve was because Viv would not understand it. Whenever Francine tried to confide anything to her, Viv would look back at her in a bewildered way. She would ask Francine what she did to provoke issue, whether it was a romantic breakup or a personal problem. Genevieve just didn't understand since everything came so easily to her. Sometimes Francine would question whether some ancestor performed a future blessing to Gerard and Genevieve as the first- and second-born. Francine was the third-born. She decided to go to bed and pretend today didn't happen.

CHAPTER 2

The Employment Agency

Morning brought reality to the practical side of being unemployed. Francine's severance pay would cover her bills until the end of the year, but she needed to be gainfully employed by November to be safe. Being that it was already September, she only had less than two months to find another good-paying job. Francine made a mental note to call the employment agency tomorrow. Today she would research sales positions and opportunities listed on the Internet so she would be more informed of job positions, requirements, wage ranges, etc., prior to going to the agency. She fought the urge to call her friends and vent her situation, but something inside her head told her to assess the situation first.

Francine noticed that it was a beautiful, crisp September day as she peered out the window. She forgot her problems for a short while as she watched a mother with her two young children walking down the street. The children were running and kicking up the leaves that had fallen on the sidewalk as the mother lovingly laughed and ran alongside them. Francine thought, *Why isn't that me? How come my sister, brother, friends—heck, everyone has a family, a home, a life.* She felt the tears come down her cheeks. Francine decided to close the window blinds so she wouldn't get distracted again.

20

The day passed faster than Francine expected. She did job research during the morning and was surprised to find few experienced sales positions. She did find many entry-level sales positions, but Francine was an accomplished salesperson, and she needed a sales position commensurate with her experience. She also needed the higher salary that a senior salesperson would receive. She thought about some of her current purchasing choices, such as the Audi automobile she leased and her beautiful clothes collection. Not to mention the boxes of shoes and handbags she had accumulated since living in Chicago.

She thought, *I have to look good to look successful, and I deserve it.*

She felt justified for a minute before she grabbed her cell phone and cancelled her spa appointment for this coming Saturday. The next call went to the employment agency, and she made an appointment for the following morning.

In the afternoon, Francine made minor adjustments to her résumé. She had a habit of periodically updating it, as suggested by self-development seminars she occasionally attended. Every time she did an update, she thought that it was a waste of time. She never planned to leave Magnacraft until retirement. Now she understood the importance of a periodic update. *If I had to create this from scratch after yesterday's traumatic day, I would have been too shook up to do a good job,* she thought.

Francine faintly smiled as she remembered that she kept a home backup file of her sales presentations, sales pitch notes, and customer background information. She would never use any of the information against Magnacraft, but to have some material gave her some satisfaction. She felt ready for her appointment with the employment agency tomorrow.

Francine decided to take a long, leisurely bath along with a large glass of wine prior to going to bed. She was anxious for the day to end. Sleep did not come easily that night.

The employment office that Magnacraft contracted as part of the severance package was located in Rosemont. Francine carefully dressed in a dark-blue business suit with a soft-blue patterned blouse and low navy sling-back shoes. She carried her purse and a briefcase containing copies of her résumé and examples of some sales presentations. She had never been to an employment agency before, but her severance literature had explained that the agency was focused on professional employment placements and that "necessary" information regarding Francine's past positions had been provided to them. Francine crinkled her nose when she read the word *necessary. What does that mean?* she asked herself.

"Hello, I am Francine Pacque, and I have a 10:00 a.m. appointment," Francine told the attractive young female receptionist.

"Yes, welcome, Francine," the receptionist replied. "I will let Mr. Terrance know you are here. Please have a seat and have some coffee if you like."

Francine made a mental note that she liked this place already. She seated herself and decided to forego the coffee. She didn't want any more acid stomach episodes.

After a few minutes, a man in his midforties walked into the reception area.

"Good morning, Francine. I am Nick Terrance, and I am assigned to your account," he said.

Francine thought, *Hmmm, "your account." Sounds like he's a salesman and I'm the customer.* She held out her hand to signify that this was a business meeting.

"It is nice to meet you, Mr. Terrance. May I call you Nick?"

"Yes, please do," Nick replied. "And may I call you Fran or Fanny?"

"No! Francine, please," she retorted as she thought, *At least he didn't call me Fanny Pack.*

During the next few hours, Nick and Francine reviewed her educational background, résumé, and visual presentations. Nick commented several times on the impressive deliverables that Francine achieved, and although she could not share specific sales numbers or presentations from her past employer, Magnacraft, for proprietary reasons, Nick said that he would be able to advertise her skills to prospective employers.

"I am going to pair you up with another client of ours from a different industry so you two can practice your interview skills. But first, I want you to review a list of potential interview questions.

Think about your answers, then write your answers down so that you will be comfortably prepared for future interviews. When you and your partner feel comfortable being interviewed, some of our staff will sit in and critique," informed Nick. "Does that sound agreeable to you?"

"Yes," answered Francine, "but when do I see the listings of potential employers? I'm anxious to get a feel for the available job market."

Nick shuffled in his chair slightly and answered, "Well, Francine, it is a very tight market right now. There are many salesmen and saleswomen currently interviewing for a small amount of jobs. Our employer client list is large and contains many of the global names you would recognize, but they also have ongoing quotas to search for prospective new people. They frequently interview clients but less frequently actually hire them."

"What? You have to be kidding! All companies want and need good salespeople, and Chicago should be full of jobs," Francine cried out. Suddenly her stomach ached, and she felt a rush of heat through her body.

"Oh my god, I never thought it would be difficult for me to land another job!"

"Please, Francine, calm down," replied Nick. "I'm only stating that it is a very tough market and there is no guarantee on getting a job commensurate to your past position. There is very high competition for a small number of positions."

Nick continued, "Also, please remember that it is getting close to the end of the year, so most companies will not hire a new employee until after their fiscal year-ends. Almost all companies tighten their belts during the final quarter so they can meet their financial goals. It is expensive to hire a new employee due to their salary, benefits, training, and learning curve."

Francine knew that all too well. She and her other colleagues always had to work the hardest during the final year-end quarter. She also knew that sales were usually down in her industry during that same time. She remembered the stress that she and the other employees at Magnacraft had during those final months. It was even hard to procure a pen from the stationery cabinet as every discretionary expense was questioned.

Francine's heart sank as the realization that she may not get a new job by November or even by December or later. *Why did I lease that new Audi?* she thought.

She thought about her closet, questioning if there were any clothes or accessories she could return to the store. Unfortunately, she knew too well that she would be so excited to purchase something that the tags would be removed and the items worn the very next day. Her stomach was now in a full-blown knot as she realized she was in deep trouble.

She retreated to a cubicle that the employment agency assigned to her and started reviewing the potential interview questions. The questions on education, past employment, and future goals were easy, but the questions that tried to uncover her hidden personality were not. She laughed, despite her stomach ache, at some of the questions like, "If you were an animal, which one would you be and why?" Her personal favorite was "Describe your innermost feelings relating to your last employer."

"Ha!" she blurted.

She could go on and on with that subject, from the love she felt for the people and the products to the betrayal at what she thought would be her golden moment. Francine continued to work on the list and jotted notes down so she could refer quickly during the practice interviews with her partner.

Francine decided to get some fresh air at lunch and visit one of the local diners. She walked in the brisk, windy air for about two blocks before finding a suitable diner. She was glad to feel her cheeks chilled by the wind and thought that her color would look better than the dour face she had in the morning.

She turned on her cell phone when she sat down in the diner booth and noticed eight texts from colleagues at Magnacraft wondering if she was feeling better. She wasn't surprised that her absence after the announcement was the work gossip. Two of the texts were from her good work friend Sara. Sara Johnston and Jim Ruscher were the coworkers Francine planned on sitting with at yesterday's conference. Francine noticed that there was also a phone message from Sara.

"Hi, Francine, I'm worried about you. Yesterday was too weird with you being seated at the front table, hearing the promotion announcement, and then you getting sick. I hope you are feeling better, but please, girlfriend, please call me as soon as you can."

With a big sigh, Francine dialed Sara's personal cell phone. The ring was immediately answered.

"Francine! Hi! I am so happy you called me back. Are you OK?" Sara asked.

"Hi, Sara. No, I'm not OK at all. My professional life is in shambles, and I cannot talk to you about it," answered Francine. "I am not returning to Magnacraft, and that is all I can say right now."

"Oh no," Sara replied. After a long moan, Sara said, "Can you tell me if you got mad and quit? None of us would blame you after hearing that Karen got your promotion. No one could believe it, and no one liked it either. It was the talk at the bar after the customer display and dinner was complete. How could they do that to you?"

Francine replied while her voice was cracking. It was immediately obvious to Sara what had happened.

"Sara, I can't talk about it. Right now I'm at an employment agency to get another job. I just can't believe it." Francine stopped to blow her nose. "I gave everything to that place, and now I'm finished. And to make it worse, the job market sucks! I'm probably going to have to start at an entry-level position for some depressing company."

Sara replied, "I'm so sorry, Francine. I don't know what happened, but let me know if I can do anything for you." After a pause she said, "Can I meet up with you for dinner or a drink? Or if you just want to sit around your place, I'd be glad to give you company."

The words helped Francine. She knew that she could count on her friends Sara and Jim. Francine replied, "That would be great, but I need to get myself back together first. I just need some time to cool down and reflect and relax. Thank you. It means a lot that you offered," Francine said weakly.

There was an awkward silence for a short time until Sara asked, "Francine, everyone is asking me about what happened yesterday. What should I tell them?"

Francine thought for a few seconds and said, "You know, I don't like being a victim, and I can't really talk about what transpired. But I know that Magnacraft will say that I left to pursue other opportunities, and that's going to be true. So I say that you tell them that you don't know all the details but that I was thinking of leaving the company and decided to do it. They'll all think it was because I was mad about Karen Warnette getting the promotion and I just upped and quit."

Sara said, "That sounds good, but they will all ask where you are going to work. What should I say?"

Francine thought for a few seconds and replied, "You know, tell them that I decided to take a few months sabbatical in the South before I start my next position. Tell them that I have several offers but you are sworn to secrecy. That should quiet them down."

Sara laughed and said, "Are you kidding? Most of them are so stressed out from work and family that when they hear you are going on a long vacation, they'll just tune out and think about how nice that would be."

The girls giggled a little until Francine's lunch arrived at her table.

"I've got to go now, Sara. Thank you so much. Let me give you a call in a couple of days, and we can plan to see each other then."

After several good-bye remarks between the girls, the call ended. It was the first time Francine smiled since the betrayal, and it felt great.

Francine returned after lunch to the agency and went into the ladies room to redo her hair, which was completely ruined in the Chicago wind. After freshening her makeup and giving herself a spin in the mirror to ensure that everything was in the right place, she commented to herself, *a girl doesn't want to walk out with toilet paper attached to her shoe.*

She strode back to her cubicle to find a very good-looking man sitting in the side chair.

"Hello, are you Francine Pacque?" the man inquired.

"Yes, I am. Hello. Are you my study buddy?" Francine responded.

In the few seconds that transpired as she walked into her cubicle, Francine noticed that the man was about her age, approximately six foot tall, and had thick but slightly shaggy hair.

Please be my study buddy, Francine secretly thought.

He threw his head back slightly as he laughed and said, "Yes, unfortunately, I am."

Francine, quick with her wit replied, "You are unfortunate to have to study with me?"

"No! No!" the man exclaimed. "I'm just unfortunate to be in this position to have to be here. I'm sure you feel the same. Don't you?"

"Now I get it," Francine replied.

She extended her hand and introduced herself. As they shook hands, he said, "I'm Brian Sherman. It's nice to meet you, Francine."

Francine smiled and settled into her chair, but she was aware that her pulse quickened. She was glad that she combed her hair and applied more lipstick after lunch. Brian was a stud! She quickly made a mental note of his traits: six foot, 180 pounds of lean muscle, nice brown hair, brown eyes, and angular nose with a matching masculine angular chin. Francine glanced to see if he was wearing a wedding ring. She noticed Brian's gaze changed as he realized she was checking him out. Francine refocused her eyes on his face, but she thought a man like him had to be used to attention. She was glad she only looked at his finger.

Brian said, "I understand that we can use one of the small offices to work on our interview skills. Are you ready?"

Francine replied that she was ready and grabbed her information, but as she walked to the conference room, she became aware that Brian was not reciprocating at checking her out. *High school all over*, Francine thought. *If Genevieve was here, he'd be carrying her books already.*

They settled into a small conference room and began getting acquainted. Brian said that he was a civil engineer and usually hired as a contracted position for a particular job. A contracted position was a temporary short-term job without benefits such as insurance or 401Ks, but the pay was high, so the individual could afford to purchase benefits on his or her own. He explained that contract jobs were common in his line of work, and when the stretch of highway he was responsible to oversee was complete, his employment ended. Brian said that many civil engineers got employment through employment agencies, and in fact, this agency found him his last position.

In their exchange of information, Francine found out that Brian was single. *Jackpot*, Francine thought. *Maybe this employment agency business is not so bad.* She smiled to herself, thinking how quickly her thoughts changed from her problems.

Brian and Francine worked on their interview skills for several hours before notifying Nick Terrance that they were ready to be critiqued. Nick asked them to go into a small conference room, where he and several other employment consultants would critique them. They were allowed to hear each other's interview if they both consented. Brian asked if there would be sensitive questions asked about wage criteria and benefits. If so, he would rather be alone. Nick Terrance informed them that the mock interviews would be somewhat brutal as to prepare the client for potential questions, so personal questions such as benefits and wages would be included. Brian briefly looked in Francine's direction while he considered the potential questions, then he turned back to Nick and said he would like to go solo. Terrance suggested that Brian be first for the mock interview.

Francine thought, *So much for ladies first*, although she was privately relieved to have a little more private time to gather her thoughts.

Francine was a little puzzled as to why they wouldn't benefit from hearing each other's interview since they were in different fields of work. She returned to her temporary cubicle and started to review her notes. Soon she was daydreaming and reliving the traumatic day she had at the sales conference.

"How embarrassing," Francine whispered to herself while she glanced around to see if anyone was within earshot. "First, it was bad enough not to get the promotion, but then upchucking at the front and center table. Oh my god! Second, to get fired on top of it all and get escorted like a criminal out of the hotel. Disgusting! How am I ever going to get over this one?"

She stared blankly at the desk and continued, "What am I going to tell my family? They already think I'm a loser. Well, Mom and Dad don't think that way, but I'll get that same old 'What did you do?' speech followed by 'Your brother and sister don't seem to have any problems. Why can't you be more like them?'"

Francine closed her eyes and said softly, "Believe me, I wish I would be more like them. I've wanted to be like them my whole life."

Francine still had her eyes closed and head tilted downward when she heard, "Francine, it's your turn." She popped up to see Brian looking bewildered at her. She thought, *He probably thinks I was taking a nap.*

"How did it go?" Francine asked Brian.

"Fine. They gave me some valuable tips on things to include during my interview. It was good!" Brian said with a smile. "They are waiting for you in the conference room."

Francine collected her interview material and went to the room.

"It's almost five o'clock already. See you tomorrow, Brian," she said as she walked to the conference room.

Her practice interview lasted about an hour. The team asked Francine standard interview questions during the first mock interview, and Francine's preparedness had them impressed. The second interview was more difficult because they did a panel interview, where each person asked Francine questions. The flow of the panel interview was more difficult as some of the panel focused on different aspects of her career, education, and personal objective. Each interviewer had their own personal rhythm when asking questions, and Francine had to adjust her cadence and tone when answering each interviewer.

At six o'clock, Nick Terrance said, "It's getting late, so why don't we call it a day. We will do the full critique and suggestions in the morning. Francine, I just want to say how impressed I am with your delivery. You listen well to the interviewers and answer very completely. Well done, Francine."

"I'm a salesperson. Listening to my customers is why I am a good salesperson. I hope that doesn't come across as overconfident or conceited, because obviously I'm about as low as I could be right now. But my customers have always told me that I was a great listener. Thanks for the compliment. I will see all of you tomorrow," Francine said as she stood up and shook all three interviewers' hands. "Shall I meet you in this room tomorrow morning?"

"Yes, how about meeting us at nine o'clock?" Nick answered as the other two interviewers nodded in agreement.

They all said their good-byes, and Francine left the conference room and returned to her cubicle to get her coat. When she walked into the cubicle opening, she was startled to see Brian sitting in the side chair.

"Brian! I thought you left an hour ago," Francine said.

"I was going to leave, but then I thought you may want to go out for a drink and maybe catch some dinner," Brian asked pensively.

Francine thought quickly and realized she didn't have anything on her calendar or anyone waiting for her. Francine's heart started to pound faster, and although she wanted to answer him demurely, she blurted out, "You bet. Let's get out of here."

They exchanged some dining recommendations and settled on sharing a Chicago-style pizza. Brian knew of a pizzeria several miles away, so they drove their respective cars and met at the restaurant. Francine felt emotionally tired from the events of the last two days, but she was happy to have something to look forward to this evening. It had been a while, six months actually, since Francine had been on a date, and although this wasn't really a date, she was going to dinner with a good-looking single man.

Her thoughts went back six months to the breakup she had with Steve Braming. She and Steve had dated on and off for three years. Steve was an actuary for an insurance firm. Her parents, especially Francine's dad, liked Steve very much, but Francine suspected it was more an appreciation for Steve's math ability that impressed her accountant father. Steve was an average-looking thirty-four-year-old man with a good job and good sensibility, but Francine never had any wildly-in-love feelings for him. He was safe, kind, and predictable. Francine wanted more adventure than Steve would ever provide. They both knew they were not the right one for each other and, six months ago, called off their relationship for good. Francine didn't know why she was thinking about their breakup now, except that she anticipated a thrill by meeting Brian for dinner. It was a thrill that never existed with Steve.

She parked at the restaurant and carefully checked her makeup and hair in the car mirror. She applied a little more mascara and her new lipstick and felt ready for adventure. Francine found Brian sitting in a booth with a pitcher of beer and two glasses already on the table.

"Francine! Here!" he shouted and waved to get her attention.

Francine quickly moved into the booth and said, "This was a great idea. Thanks for asking me to join you."

Brian laughed while saying, "You better wait until you see if you like the pizza before you thank me. Here, let's toast to our new jobs, wherever they may be." He poured Francine a mug of beer and handed it to her.

"To our new jobs, and to our new friendship," Francine toasted.

They drank several big gulps. Francine thought beer never tasted so good.

They spent the next hour eating, drinking, and getting to know each other. Brian had been married and had a son, now six years old. He explained that his engineering jobs usually took him to different locations around the country where highways and bridges were being constructed. Most times those jobs took months, and his ex-wife couldn't handle being alone. He shared that his wife ended up getting cozy with a man that lived in their apartment complex. One thing led to another, and one day, after he returned from one of his jobs for a weekend, he found a half-empty apartment, except for his personal things. His wife had already moved in with the neighbor. Brian said that she left a note explaining all the gory details.

"What did you do?" Francine gasped.

"Well, it was a shock. My life was instantly devastated. All I could think about was my son, Johnathon, and how some other man was holding him, not me. Then, I had the same vision about my wife! It took me a while to calm down before I called her cell phone," Brian said.

As he talked, his eyes turned glassy, and Francine knew it was still hard for him to talk about it.

He continued, "My ex answered on the first ring. She had been watching for my car and knew I was home. She was crying as she tried to explain.

"She said she never wanted to hurt me, but she just didn't want a life with me on the road. She said she was lonely, young, and things just happened between her and the other guy," Brian said and then stopped and looked downward to collect his emotions. "Anyway, it was already done. She had made up her mind and was already moved out. She's been really good about me seeing little Johnny. So we got divorced." Brian shifted his gaze to the tabletop. He was clearly thinking back to that past situation.

Francine said, "Brian, I'm so sorry. How long have you been divorced?"

"It's been four years already. Little Johnny was only two when it happened. It sucked, but I'm not mad at her anymore. She deserved more than a husband that was gone all the time, but she also knew my line of work before we got married. I guess she didn't know how it would be until after we had Johnny."

Francine hesitated but then asked, "So is she still with that guy?"

"Yeah, they got married as soon as the waiting period after a divorce passed. They have two other kids now and a house in Crystal Lake," Brain answered. "I'm glad that at least Johnny has a brother and a sister. Half-brother and half-sister, that is. Johnny is a happy kid, and I can see that his mother is happy too." Brian continued, "So enough about me, tell me about you now."

They sat for another hour as Francine told Brian about her last serious relationship. She also shared her background about growing up in Racine, Wisconsin, and then moving after college to Chicago. He asked her if she had any siblings, and Francine told him about Gerry and Genevieve. She even shared some of the gory details about her brother's constant verbal bullying and her sister's constant "perfectness." They laughed when she shared her high school nickname of Fanny Pack.

"It's not funny," Francine said as she continued laughing.

"Oh, au contraire. It's really funny," Brian said.

"I shouldn't have told you then. That name followed me every day through the hallways of high school. I was so embarrassed. All of my brother's friends and most of the school called me that. Please, please don't call me that name too," Francine pleaded.

"OK, have it your way," Brian teased, "but if I get mad at you sometime, it may just pop out of my mouth."

Francine gave him her most evil look. They both laughed and then agreed that they should be getting on their way home. Brian gave Francine a brotherly hug before walking to his car. All Francine could do was think about him. *Boy, I'd like to have his shoes under my bed.* She giggled, got into her car, and drove home.

As Brian drove home, he thought to himself, *I like this girl. She's funny, talented, and not too into herself. She's pretty too. I wonder if she would like someone like me?* His eyelids raised in hopeful anticipation of things to come. He continued to drive home and shifted his thoughts back to his problem of finding a new job.

CHAPTER 3

Nighttime Demons

Nighttime always brings the demons, Francine thought as she lay in bed.

Reality had hit her, and the thought of eventually running out of money loomed on her mind. She also hadn't told her family about her job loss and groaned at the thought of telling them. Francine phoned her parents every weekend, so she had several days before she called. As she thought about it, Francine decided that she didn't have to tell them anything yet. It would be easier to tell them after she found other employment. Then she could just tell them that she changed employers, not that she was let go. If she told them she was fired, there would be too much explaining on her end and too much lecturing on their end. She made a mental note not to share her unemployment news.

She thought about Magnacraft and how much she would miss working there. She wished she could trash-talk the company, but besides her severance paperwork forbidden any negative talk, she truly didn't dislike the company. She thought about the human resources VP, Nora Sanders. She always admired Nora although Nora never befriended anyone. Francine wondered if that was typical of someone who worked in human services.

Are they like doctors, who cannot be drawn in by their patients in case their patients don't have good outcomes? Are human resource people susceptible to the same issue if one of their coworker friend's services are no longer required? she pondered.

Francine turned onto her side and pulled up her blankets as thought about some of the scenarios where it could have been very difficult if a friend relationship existed for a human resource employee and they had to discipline or terminate their friend. She decided that she could not do that type of job. She decided not to hold a grudge against Nora Sanders.

Her thoughts flowed to Karen Warnette, the young employee who received the intern sales executive position that Francine thought she had earned. Karen was a graduate of the Wharton School of Business, which is a difficult school to be accepted at, much less graduate with honors from, as Karen had achieved. Karen had interned at a Fortune 500 company during the summers prior to graduating. Francine remembered how excited the Magnacraft staff was that Karen accepted employment at their company.

Karen was a tall thin young woman who had an aristocratic look to her features. She was very attractive, even pretty, but not too pretty that the men couldn't concentrate. Francine pictured her sister, Genevieve, if she worked at Magnacraft and laughed.

Viv could stop a man from breathing, if not from working. Good thing Viv is a stay-at-home mom, she thought.

She determined that the unique characteristic Karen Warnette possessed was an aloofness to her coworkers and an absolute dedication to pleasing the Magnacraft staff. Francine thought about the first sales campaign that Karen was assigned to follow and learn from the tenured sales team of Sara Johnston, Jim Ruscher, and Francine. The sales campaign was for an adjustable fixture platform that could be used to mount equipment and be adjusted ergonomically by the person using the equipment. Magnacraft had other adjustable platforms, but this technology used adjustable motor controls rather than gears for adjustments. It was state-of-the-art, and other competitors did not possess the patent.

The team was happy to have a new intern join them and warmly welcomed Karen into the team. Karen took copious notes on the equipment functions but had nothing to contribute when the team brainstormed ideas and formulated their sales presentation. The sales presentation was scheduled to be presented in Magnacraft's main sales conference room to all the sales executives and John Delully, the vice president of Magnacraft, for final critique.

The customary manner of making team presentations was to divide up the presentation so that each person of the team presented some of the information. Francine, Sara, and Jim were very aware that Karen Warnette had never presented anything of this magnitude, so they spent a lot of time coaching Karen for her portion of the presentation. Karen had learned to be a good speaker during her days at Wharton, and she talked slowly to make sure her enunciation was clear but her cadence was slow and deliberate. Francine and the team worked with her late into the evening before the presentation so that she would deliver some life into her presentation. The team explained that in the field, customers got distracted by their phone, e-mail, problems, etc., during sales presentations, so it was extremely important to not become boring. By the time they left for the night, Karen had a much better speech delivery.

The sales presentation was early the following morning. The team set up their display and presentation on the video screen, while their boss, Mike Purser, watched them with pride. When the executives were seated, Jim Ruscher stood up to start the entry sales pitch. As he started, John Delully stopped him and said, "Mike, we're anxious to see how our new sales hire is progressing, so we would like Karen to make the presentation."

This was a bit shocking to the team and definitely not the norm, but Jim sat down, and we all gave a smile and "good luck" nod to Karen.

Karen presented the material quite well for being a new hire. Of course, she only had to read what the team had put together, but she delivered the presentation well. A discussion and critique of some additions to the presentation were given by the execs, and the team took notes on the suggested revisions. The group was about to adjourn when John Delully said, "Karen, you did a fabulous job on this presentation. Were you able to give some of your Wharton knowledge to the team?"

Karen answered, "Yes, we had extensive training on new sales techniques at Wharton and was able to add my touch to enhance the presentation."

The three other teammates looked at one another in surprise and disgust. She added nothing, and the team worked on her presentation skills late into the night. It was an unbelievable betrayal to Francine, Sara, and Jim. But the three of them did nothing to rebuke her as that seemed like a rude and heartless thing to do to an intern. As the execs stood up and shook Karen's hand in congratulations, Sara, Jim, and Francine left the room in silence.

As Francine thought about that presentation day, she wondered if she would have handled it differently today. She doubted that she or Sara or Jim would have done anything different. *Salespeople are a different breed than executives. We have to be warm and engaging or we won't have customers for long*, Francine thought.

"So does that mean that executives have to be heartless?" she said aloud.

"No," she answered firmly.

Francine knew some outstanding executives, including her ex-boss, Mike Purser. John Delully was also outstanding and admired by everyone. She realized at that moment that she should have taken a cue from John Delully when he said that remark to Karen. He was announcing, in a roundabout way, that she was one of them, the executives, not a salesperson.

Francine thought to herself that not everyone could be the head guy. It takes a lot of other employees to make a company, and every single one of them want to be that head guy. She realized the importance of finding your niche and being good at it. Karen probably knew from the first day she was hired that her path was to become an executive. She didn't have to become one of the team of sales; she needed to become one of the team of executives. Although Francine would never forget that day when Karen didn't recognize the entire team, she also realized that Karen was new to the executive team as well. It didn't make Francine feel better, but she accepted it a bit better.

"Maybe I'll feel different when life turns around for me, but for now, 'Shame on you, Karen Warnette,'" Francine stated.

Then, as in every restless night, Francine's thoughts went to her past. Those days of adolescent teasing and being the brunt of her brother's jokes kept her awake. She thought of a past crush she had on a junior classman, Curt something. She was thrilled at his advances to her and was hopeful that he would ask her to the prom. He finally did approach her on prom, but it wasn't to ask her but instead to ask if she could introduce him to Genevieve because he wanted to ask her to prom. Francine remembered telling him that Viv was already going to prom with someone. Curt muttered something in disappointment and turned and walked away. She never talked to him again. She never went to prom either.

Morning came with a new feeling of hope. Yesterday's appointment at the employment agency went well, and Francine was anxious to hear of her job prospects today. She also was eager to see her new friend, Brian. Francine took extra time preparing her ensemble. She chose an Ann Taylor dress with a contrasting jacket. She took out her four-inch black killer heels and put them carefully on her feet. She looked at herself in the mirror and smiled approvingly.

"Today is going to be a great day," she said aloud, as if she were trying to talk herself into a good mood.

CHAPTER 4

A Job Opportunity

It was another brisk, windy day as Francine walked from a parking garage into the employment agency. The same attractive receptionist greeted her and informed her that she could go straight into the office for the duration of her time at the agency. Francine went into her cubicle and saw Brian talking with some other clients at the coffee break area. She wanted to talk to Brian a bit before the interview training resumed. Francine planned to walk over to the group at the coffee machine, but Nick Terrance called to her and said that they were ready to resume her consultation. She waved to Brian and made a disappointed face toward Brian as she followed Nick into the conference room.

Nick and the same two consultants were in the conference room. After they exchanged pleasantries, they started the critique of Francine's résumé and interview. The group worked for about an hour tweaking several interview answers, but all in all, they were very impressed with her delivery. Nick asked the two consultants if they cared to leave while he went over some job prospects with Francine, and they left the room.

Nick handed a stack of prospective jobs to Francine. She was thrilled at first when it appeared that there were many opportunities. But after reviewing the job openings with Nick, she realized that the

39

sales jobs were entry-level positions. Nick explained the job market drop to Francine as he had already done yesterday.

"Sales positions were being reduced by online shopping. It is just that simple," Nick stated.

Nick had several other professional buyer jobs to offer Francine, but if her love was in sales, it was going to be slim pickings. She would probably have to start entry level and work her way up. Francine quickly became depressed as she knew that entry level jobs were low paying and usually commission only. Francine knew she had established a pretty high standard of living, and an entry-level job wouldn't cover her fixed expenses. She determined this wasn't going to be the great day she thought it was going to be.

Over the next two weeks, Francine submitted several dozen résumés to companies. Some of the résumés were what Francine called in the sales business as cold calls, or unsolicited résumé submissions. She went on three interviews, and one of those companies was interested in Francine joining their teams but with entry pay.

Depression and anxiety set in as October was near and still no job. Francine had stopped going daily to the employment agency as she was able to access their employment database remotely. Instead of her beautiful wardrobe and high-heeled shoes, Francine opted for pajama pants and a T-shirt paired with fuzzy ankle socks. Her hair was usually fashioned into a ponytail and her makeup, well, there wasn't any need on wasting makeup. She spent her morning drinking coffee and eating cookies followed by an hour or more at the computer looking for work. Then the TV would be turned on. *Judge Judy* was a must see, as well as *The Ellen DeGeneres Show*. Nighttime viewing was varied from reruns of the *Big Bang* to watching endless episode of *Housewives of Atlanta, LA, New Jersey*, and so on.

"At least there is some 'action' in my dull life when I watch *Housewives*," Francine commented while eating popcorn.

Francine's cell phone rang one morning. She reluctantly looked at the caller ID and found that it was Lucas Peterson, one of her clients from Standard Products Distribution Corporation (SPD). She hesitated before answering the call but then thought Lucas didn't know she wasn't working at Magnacraft and needed some item.

"Hi, Lucas, it's nice to hear from you," Francine said as she walked to her kitchen in her fuzzy socks.

"Hi, Francine. Hey, look, I wanted to call you earlier when I heard you weren't at Magnacraft anymore, but I didn't want to bother you," he said pensively.

"You're never a bother, Lucas. How did you know I left Magnacraft?" Francine asked.

"A guy named Luis Ortega called me to say he was handling our account. He seems like a good guy, but he was reluctant to give any details on where you were. I didn't know if you went to a different company, was sick, or won the lottery and quit," said Lucas.

The two of them laughed before Francine answered, "Well, I wish I could say that I won the lottery, but that's far from the truth. The truth is that I left Magnacraft and I'm currently looking for other opportunities."

"Oh, gee. I'm sorry to hear that. You were the best rep to work with. You helped me a lot," he remarked and continued, "Oh, man. I hate to hear that."

"Yeah, it stinks, but I'm confident that Luis will do a great job. He's really nice and has a big family, just like you do. Before long, you and he will be good friends," Francine replied.

"Well, it doesn't change the reason I called. It's about time that we had lunch together. I planned to talk some business with you, but let's put that aside and still meet for lunch. My treat," Lucas announced.

"This I have to see," Francine laughingly said. "After all the lunches I bought for you on behalf of Magnacraft. I'd love to meet with you, and my calendar is free as can be."

"How about tomorrow at noon at Outback?" he asked.

"I'll be there, minus my high heels. I hope you'll recognize me," Francine replied.

They said their good-byes and hung up.

The following day, Francine showered and dressed in her casual but still fabulous jeans and a simple black sweater. She wore a pair of walking boots over her clean fuzzy socks and hoped that Lucas recognized the "simpler" version of herself.

When she arrived at the Outback Steakhouse, Lucas was already at a table along with Joe Silverman, SPD's chief financial officer and a person that Francine had done contractual business with on multiple occasions.

"Hi, Lucas. Joe! How nice to see you," Francine said as she extended her hand to shake with both of her past clients.

"Hello, Francine, I hope you don't mind that I tagged along. I ran into Lucas, and he said that he was meeting with you, and it seemed like a good reason to get out of the office," Joe explained.

"Of course it's fine," Francine lied.

She actually was looking forward to commiserating a bit with her old friend Lucas.

They ordered soft drinks and lunch, and the men updated Francine on their families. Lucas shared school pictures of his four kids and proudly shared how well all his children were doing in school. The conversation eventually turned to Francine, who was not looking forward to the discussion. Besides not having any substantial job prospects, she knew she had to be careful on what she said about Magnacraft as well.

"It's true that I left Magnacraft, but I want you to know that Magnacraft is a great company, and I don't have anything bad to say about its products or its people. I just want to do more than what Magnacraft was willing to try with me. I have a vision that I was hoping to share to expand Magnacraft's business and help our customers. But I wasn't in the right position to get any support on my vision. So I'm looking for another company who will invest their trust in me," Francine said.

She was proud of the way she explained her exit from Magnacraft.

"So, Francine, the rumor is that you were let go. Is that not true?" Lucas asked.

Crap, Francine thought. *He would ask me straight out.* Francine answered, "I would prefer not getting into the specifics, but what I can say is that Magnacraft is very concerned about the loss of business because of customers transitioning to online purchasing. They don't need all of the salespeople that they have, and I was a high-dollar representative. I was their number one salesperson this year, and that is not a secret, so it isn't because of any poor performance on my part."

Francine's answer got Joe's attention.

"Computer online purchasing." He snorted. "That's our downfall as well. As a distributor, we always had a lot of online purchasing, but the competition has grown exponentially. Customers don't really care about ordering items locally or even regionally. It's all about the lowest cost."

Lucas chuckled. "Yes, it's all those accountants pounding in 'lowest cost.'"

Joe frowned but nodded.

Francine felt comfortable with her two old clients and added, "Yes, I agree. That is why, as I thought about my customer base, I came up with a vision to enhance the customer experience. I just have to find the right company to try it."

The three of them finished their lunches and said their goodbye. It was a happy and familiar time for Francine. She drove home and was settling into her couch for *Judge Judy* when her cell phone rang. It was Joe Silverman.

"Hi, Francine, I went back to the office and couldn't get our conversation off my mind. SPD is struggling with our sales as well, and we have tightened our belt accordingly. But it is just a matter of time before we lose market share.

"I had a conversation with our general manager about you. He agrees that you were outstanding to work with and went out of your way to help us financially with your product costs and with implementing a vendor-managed product line for Magnacraft products. If all our suppliers would do that, we would be in much better financial shape."

Joe sighed and then said, "So here it is. We don't have any openings right now for distribution salespersons, but we would be willing to enter into a contractual agreement with you if you were acceptable to increasing our customer base in more business remote areas of the US."

"Really? I'm very happy that you called, and thank you for your offer," Francine answered. Her mind was reeling at the words *new business* and *remote areas*.

"Can I come in and talk to you about this position? I have lots of questions coming to mind."

"Of course! I'm not the person you need to talk to, but Sam Jr. said that you should call him to make an appointment. This is a nonadvertised position. It really wasn't even a position until an hour ago," Joe said. "And, Francine, we are most interested in hearing about your idea to grow the customer experience. I don't know how much you can share on your idea gratuitously, but it is a major consideration in adding this position."

Francine's grin was ear to ear as her mind thought about the positive reasons why working for Standard Products Distribution Corporation would be great. SPD was a major distributor for mechanical tooling, fixtures, and fasteners. They had several product lines, mechanical, safety, electrical, utility, and cleaning products. They were big. Francine quickly thought of the potential. She would even get a chance to sell Magnacraft products, as a middleman, so her past experience would not be lost.

She had questions about her proposed "remote" territory, but she quickly answered, "I will call Sam Jr. immediately, and I can share my vision with him. The vision is based on the salesperson's customer service, so it isn't a secret. It is just something that I am unaware of anyone doing. I would love to be that person to develop it." She spent the next fifteen minutes explaining her vision and how to achieve it. Joe was impressed, and he was eager to give his support.

"Francine, I don't understand all the logistics in what you are explaining, but on the surface, your idea sounds like a win-win. I'm sure Sam Jr. will understand what you are explaining, but my expertise is not in managing inventory. I will give my support of your idea to Sam Jr., and good luck with your conversation with him," Joe stated.

"Oh my god!" exclaimed Francine as she hung up the phone.

She went to her refrigerator to get a cold Diet Coke to celebrate.

"I can't believe it!" Francine shouted out.

She sat on her couch, enjoying her drink while gathering her thoughts prior to calling Sam Jr. She knew she could talk circles about her idea with Sam Jr., but the thought of remote selling was concerning her.

"I would be gone all the time," Francine muttered to herself, "and the remote territory would be mostly mom-and-pop businesses."

She thought about the opportunity that would benefit those family businesses. *Hmmm, small businesses don't have a lot of cash, so the opportunity of becoming a network of businesses sharing inventory and critical spare parts would really be a perfect fit. But I wouldn't be here, in Chicago, much at all. My lease is until June, and there are other issues. Where would I live? How would I travel all over? What kind of life would I live?*

She pondered her future for a moment and then jumped off the couch, saying, "Beggars can't be choosers."

She dialed Sam Jr.'s phone number.

Francine and Sam talked for a long while as Francine explained her vision. Sam Jr. was immediately enthusiastic for her to try out her idea with SPD's products. He explained that her territory could be anywhere that was not being covered by their current sales group; however, their sales group covered all major industrial cities and their outlying area. Francine would have to become a contract salesperson, with only commission percentage as pay, but they would cover mileage for her vehicle. Lodging would be her responsibility. He said he could give a $2,000 advance to cover initial expenses and would give her a trial period of six months. She could decide on when she wanted to start and which direction she wanted to travel.

It took Francine only a few seconds to answer, "I can start on Monday, and I will be going South, at least for the winter."

It was done. Francine had a job. Sam Jr. told her to come to the office tomorrow to go over some paperwork. Her job was contractual, which meant that she would not have benefits and would technically not work for the company but would work for herself. He asked Francine to talk to his human resources person, who would walk her through the forms and could explain what Francine would have to do to set up herself as a "company."

"Thank you, Sam. I really appreciate this opportunity, and I know that I can develop a business model in my territory that can be replicated throughout your business," Francine stated.

"I'm counting on that, Francine. I have faith that you can do it too," Sam Jr. replied.

Francine thought that faith and a little luck was just what she needed. She hung up feeling proud of herself. She quickly called Sara to tell her the good news. Next she called her employment agency study buddy, Brian Sherman. She was anxious to talk to Brian, regardless of her new job.

"Hi, Brian, this is Francine Pacque. Are you at the employment agency?" Francine asked.

"Hey there! No, I actually just left from an interview with a company that I had done a project for a couple of years back," Brain answered. "They have a job starting October first and asked me if I wanted the job."

"Wow! That's great news. Did you accept the job?" Francine asked.

"You bet I did. It is a highway job near Galena, Illinois. I love that area. Have you ever been there?" Brian asked.

"No, I haven't. But I heard that it is beautiful in western Illinois," Francine said.

She was happy to hear that Brian got a job but suddenly felt unhappy that he was leaving. She quickly remembered that she would be leaving soon also.

"I'll be in town for a couple of weeks preparing for the job and probably will take several trips out there to get the lay of the land. Once all the heavy equipment and crews come, I have to know what I'm doing. If you want, maybe you could come out there and visit. I could show you around Galena," Brain said.

His question to Francine was direct, but Brian was nervous while asking her.

Francine's eyes widened with his question. She was thrilled, but the reality was that she would be leaving town about the same time that he started his new job. She thought, *Isn't that the way? I finally have someone interested in me, and now I have to leave town.*

Brian noticed the gap in the conversation and said shyly, "Francine, are you there? I'm sorry if you think I was being too forward. I enjoy your company and just thought a little road trip might be fun. I didn't mean we had to jump in bed together."

Francine smiled at the thought and said, "No, Brian, I wasn't thinking that at all. It's just that I have some good news to tell you too."

She told him about her pending employment and the remote travel requirement that her job would entail.

"You mean you are going to be a traveling salesman in areas where there isn't any companies?" Brian asked.

"You got it. That's exactly my new job," Francine answered.

She giggled at the way that Brian phrased his question and thought about how much she wanted to see him again.

"Boy, and I thought civil engineers had it bad. That's nothing against what you have to do. And you want this job? I don't think it sounds too good," Brian stated.

"Actually," replied Francine, "it is exactly what I wanted."

Francine knew what Brian meant. Most people, especially most salespeople, would not want a job in an unproven, unindustrialized area. But she was different and could not wait to start with her sales strategy.

"Then I think we should celebrate our new jobs. What are you up to tonight?" Brian asked.

Brian grimaced as he asked her. *I hope she says yes,* Brian thought. He hadn't been seriously involved with any woman since his divorce, and he was terrified. But he also did not want to lose Francine as a potential friend…or more.

"How would you like to come over? I'll cook something, and we can have oodles to drink. I'd rather not drive after drinking," Francine asked.

Brian answered, "Sure, but I can't have oodles. I still have to make it home."

Francine giggled. "Well, going home will be entirely up to you."

She was embarrassed at her invitation and wondered what Brian's response would be. The invitation just popped out of her mouth. If she would have thought more about it, she never would have had the courage to ask Brian to stay overnight.

"I'll be right over. What's your address?" Brain said joyfully.

Francine gave him her address and asked him to give her a little time to prepare food. They agreed on a time and hung up. Both of them couldn't wipe the smiles off their faces.

Francine hurried to a grocery store to purchase some steaks, portabella mushrooms, and some fresh salad ingredients. She knew she had some vegetables at home and could make a complimentary side dish of simmered vegetables with the steaks. Her thoughts transitioned to what outfit she should wear when she burst out saying, "My legs! I have to shave my legs!"

The young female cashier looked at her queerly and asked, "Excuse me?"

Francine, realizing her unwanted outburst, answered, "Oh, I'm sorry. I was talking to myself. I have a hot date tonight."

The cashier laughed and said, "Ah ha. I get it."

The two women chuckled, and Francine left to go home.

Francine hurried home to do some prep work for dinner and then take a shower. She let her brown hair flow down naturally onto her shoulders and applied natural-looking makeup. She dressed in the same jeans she had been wearing during the day but found a new light-blue sweater to pair with her ensemble. Comfortable loafers replaced her usual high-heeled look. She hoped Brian would recognize her. After all, she was made up like a professional high-fashion city girl every time he saw her at the employment agency.

At six o'clock on the dot, the doorbell rang, and Francine hurried to the door to welcome her new friend. Brian was holding a small bouquet of flowers and a loaf of bread.

"I didn't want to come empty-handed," he said as he approvingly looked Francine over. "Wow, Francine, I hardly recognize you."

"I wondered about that. I hope I'm not disappointing you," she asked. She could hardly breathe waiting for his answer.

"You look beautiful," Brian said.

They quickly hugged, and Francine led him into her townhouse.

She showed him the main living room and kitchen area and then poured him a beer while she continued prepping dinner. Their conversation was light and happy, as both of them were in a celebratory mood. They sat at Francine's dinette table, which she had made up quite elegantly with a brown table cloth and shimmery orange placemats. She put the bouquet of flowers on the side of the dinette table so they could talk looking forward at each other and without bobbing back and forth around the flowers. Most of the time they talked about their new positions, but the conversation moved to their families and good friends they developed along their paths.

Dinner turned out delicious, and Francine was proud of herself. Living alone, she wasn't used to cooking much. Steaks were relatively an easy meal to prepare, but she was worried about overbroiling them. Brian ate well and threw down several more beers. Francine opted for a glass of wine, which she refilled several times. Brian helped her clear the dishes and wipe down the table. She was impressed that he helped her. She was anxious for what might occur after dinner, but anxious in a good, hopeful way.

They moved to the couch, and Brian motioned for Francine to sit next to him. She carefully sat down close but not touching his body. She was hoping that he would talk for a while and then make a romantic move. Francine noticed that she was more nervous than usual. She hadn't been involved with anyone for a while, and Brian was still almost a stranger, but her attraction for him superseded her fear.

They talked and laughed about their employment agency experience. They both felt uncomfortable there despite their counselors' easygoing manners. Both of them were glad that they didn't have to go back to the agency again, hopefully never. An hour turned into a second hour, and Francine started feeling tired. It had been a long day. Brian never made any move but instead only continued talking.

Francine thought, *What's wrong with me? I practically threw myself at the guy. He's also had three or four beers, so you would think his libido would kick in.* It didn't. Brian talked and talked. She liked being with him, but her romantic feelings were being overtaken by fatigue.

49

"It's been a long, exhilarating day for me, Brian. I'm getting tired," she confided to him.

"Yeah, I am too," he replied. "Maybe I should be on my way home. I didn't have that much to drink, and we ate a big dinner too."

Francine didn't respond verbally. She just smiled at him and nodded. Brian got up from the couch, used the bathroom, and then picked up his coat by the door.

"Thank you, Francine, for a great dinner and conversation. Let's do it again sometime. Maybe when I get back from my canvassing of Galena."

"Sure. Give me a call, and if I'm still around Chicago and not on the road, I'd love to meet up with you," Francine replied.

She was devastated. Sure, she was tired, and he was probably tired too. But she invited him to stay overnight. What a letdown. She knew she misjudged that he was attracted to her.

I never get the guy, Francine thought to herself. *What's new?*

Brian gave her a hug and a short kiss on the cheek before he walked out the door. Francine was dumbfounded. She poured herself another glass of wine and turned on the TV.

"Maybe an episode of *Housewives* is on TV," she told herself. "I could take a lesson or two from those women."

Brian walked to his car and opened the door. He paused for a moment before sitting down in his seat.

"She must think I'm such a loser," he said. "What could I give an upscale girl like Francine? I can't believe her townhouse! That has to cost a fortune. And she has that Audi and all those fancy clothes."

Brian didn't start up his engine while he thought. He wanted to have a serious relationship with her, but he wasn't ready financially. He knew his emotions had healed since his divorce, but he felt insecure around someone as accomplished as Francine.

"I have to keep focused for now. I'll do the Galena job, but I'm keeping my eyes open for a better position in Chicago. I have the talent. I just have to find the right job," Brian muttered.

He thought about his son, Johnny, and how he longed to be in the city to see him more. He thought about Francine's new position.

"She may have to travel, but she'll know that I'll be home when she returns," Brian said.

He turned on his car motor. Depression sank in as Brian knew that he was out of his league. He drove home in a trance.

The following morning, Francine dressed in her normal professional Chicago attire and went to the Standard Products Distribution Corporation main office. She had thought about the offer that Sam Jr. had presented her, and although she still wanted the job, she decided to play a little hardball.

"Good morning, I'm Francine Pacque, and I am here to meet with your human resource manager about my new position here at SPD. But before I do that, I would like to speak with Sam Jr.," Francine explained.

The receptionist knew Francine from past visits and was expecting her this morning. But she took the time to introduce herself and welcome Francine to SPD. Francine shook her hand and thanked her for being so nice. The receptionist said it would be a moment to locate Sam Jr. and see if he was available. Francine stood and waited until the woman gestured for Francine to go through the office door. Sam Jr. was available and could see her now.

Sam Jr.'s office was quite impressive and overlooked a small wooded area. He obviously loved sports, and sports memorabilia from the Bears football franchise, the Cub's baseball franchise, and the Bulls basketball franchise graced his entire office.

"Good morning, Francine. Please sit down. What's on your mind?" Sam Jr. asked.

He walked around his massive desk and sat in an armchair next to her.

"Good morning, Sam. Thank you for seeing me so quickly. This won't take much of your time, I promise. I was thinking about the offer that you gave me so graciously yesterday," Francine said.

"Yes?" Sam Jr. asked.

"I am *extremely* happy to work for SPD, and I have no doubt that your market share will be increased. I also have no doubt that my vision shared with you will work fabulously for the smaller market companies that I will be initially targeting. Replicating this vision in your other territories will be extremely profitable for the company."

Sam nodded and agreed. "The financial implications of your vision have great potential."

Francine continued, "My problem with your offer is that all the risk is on me, and I accept that risk. However, the two-thousand-dollar advance is not enough for me to survive. I'm going to be on the road traveling and renting hotels every night. Two thousand dollars isn't going to last long, even if I find a place for under a hundred per night. I still have my apartment in Chicago, my car lease, plus I have to eat."

Sam Jr. said, "I know that two thousand dollars won't last long, but remember that we weren't looking to add to our sales staff right now. We have budgets to meet, like any company. When Joe and I spoke about hiring you contractually, we felt we were doing you a favor."

Francine answered in her most professional voice as she looked at him directly in his eyes,

"Yes, Sam, you did a tremendous favor for me by offering this position, and I will be eternally grateful to you and Joe for believing in me. But I still have to eat. Also, when I start developing this network of companies, it will take time for the commissions to start rolling in. I will need to develop the inventory list from each company and negotiate what inventory they were willing to carry against what inventory SPD will carry for them. It isn't going to happen overnight, but it will happen."

Sam Jr. thought for a few seconds, nodded, and asked, "What are you proposing?"

Francine remained poised and professional as she answered, "I propose a standard mileage stipend for my car and a minimum of four thousand dollars per month for the next six months plus the commission residuals. Sam, SPD is going to make a bundle on this venture. I think my offer is more than fair."

Sam repositioned himself in the armchair and looked at her for a moment. Then he turned his head as to think privately.

Finally, he rose from his chair and said, "Sit tight, I'll be right back."

Francine sat and waited twenty minutes until he returned to his office with Joe Silverman in tow. This time, Sam walked behind his desk and sat in his massive desk chair. Joe continued to stand and looked at Francine expressionless. Francine's heart was racing, and she thought the men might kick her out of the office as an ungrateful past acquaintance. No one spoke for another minute. Francine wondered if she did the right thing but quickly reassured herself that slowly bleeding her finances would be a disaster. She kept her poker face.

Suddenly, Sam Jr. started laughing aloud. His face was contorted and eyes watering from laughter as he said, "I'm sorry, Francine. I just had to see how you handled under pressure."

Joe started chuckling too. Francine was too confused to change her demeanor and continued to look blankly at both of them. She noticed her stomach was aching and couldn't wait to take an antiacid. She smiled slightly.

Sam Jr. leaned forward and put his arms on his desk while saying, "Joe and I talked about your proposal. This is what we are willing to do. We will meet your demand for a mileage stipend, but you must keep a log of your work-hour miles. Additionally, we will agree to your proposal for four thousand dollars per month for three months, not six. After three months, we want a full report of your progress and will assess if we will continue that wage and for how long. Of course, you will receive the standard percentage commission on anything you sell, and if you don't know already, we also have a bonus policy for adding new companies. The bonus is contingent on their sales dollars, but for your endeavor into a completely new territory, however remote it may be, you may do very well with that bonus policy."

He let his words sink in as Francine processed his offer in her mind.

Sam Jr. jumped into the conversation, saying, "Doris, our HR manager, will be able to fill you in on the various commission levels. So are you are agreeable to our terms?" he asked.

53

Francine looked at Sam and at Joe, and then a smile filled her face.

"It will be a pleasure working with you and for SPD. I'm ready to get started. Thank you very much for your offer."

Both men stepped forward and shook their new employee's hand. Joe patted Francine's shoulder and said, "Good job. I feel sorry for our other salespersons. I don't think they have a chance against you."

Francine smiled as Joe and she walked out of Sam Jr.'s office.

"We are all on the same team. When my program gets set up and they start to replicate it, we are all going to make money, especially SPD," Francine said.

Joe led her to Doris's office and made introductions.

Doris and Francine went through the company's various forms and new employee procedures. Francine was handed a contract, advised of the terms, and signed them without question. Francine was led to a corridor of small offices and cubicles and told that she could pick any cubicle to make her own. There were several offices reserved for when clients visited the main office or when a salesperson needed some additional privacy. Francine was pleased to see an empty corner cubicle with a window available. She quickly claimed that space, and Doris said she would have someone put her name on the side panel facing the aisle. There was a phone, computer, SPD manuals, and stationery supplies already in the cube. Doris said that their computer person would be meeting with Francine shortly to give her the necessary passwords to SPD's documents and inventory lists.

Francine was impressed with SPD so far. They were a warm, engaging group of people. They had standard materials already in cubicles. She expected to spend the next few days on a treasure hunt looking for materials, pens, etc. Francine hurried over to her friend Lucas's cubicle to tell him of her new employment. When she found him, he immediately stood up and shook her hand.

"I already knew," Lucas proudly stated.

Doris quickly sent an e-mail to all SPD employees announcing Francine's new position as a sales specialist for new markets. Francine liked the sound of that title. She felt happy and realized she no longer needed that anti-acid. Lucas said he was asked to introduce her to everyone at SPD that she didn't already know and to take her to lunch.

Francine said to herself while looking toward the sky, "This is a good day. Thank you."

Feeling much better, Francine went to lunch with Lucas and worked with him in the afternoon learning SPD's database. It was a compatible program to the one she used at Magnacraft, so she easily mastered the various screens. She also realized that she could easily make an Excel spreadsheet with lookup tables to capture what inventory was in her future client's stock. She knew that these small mom-and-pop companies would jump at vendor-managed items for fasteners and utility items, but her secret vision she had not shared with anyone except Sam Jr. and Joe Silverman was that she planned to expand vendor-managed inventory to high-dollar, critical equipment.

Critical equipment consisted of any equipment that would abruptly shut down a manufacturing plant's production. They were typically high-dollar items such as large motors, generators, overhead hoists, large gear drives, etc. Critical equipment was unique to each company, but every maintenance manager knew what items were necessities. The reality was that companies could do preventative maintenance to prevent things from breaking or to replace worn equipment, but there were certain items, critical items, that needed a quick reaction plan. The alternative would be to carry an extra piece of that critical item in their stockroom. Those items could be sitting there for years and cost companies thousands of dollars. Large companies could be carrying up to a million dollars to carry critical equipment in inventory, and although they would have immediate use of the item if and when it was needed, sometimes those items became obsolete. It was a big issue for every company. It was a big problem for suppliers too when a customer was down and needed to find a particular piece of equipment.

Francine's vision was to categorize every piece of critical equipment for each company within a certain territory of fifty to two hundred miles. Many of those critical items were the same for different companies, such as motors and gears. With a simple lookup table, Francine felt that she could find and expedite equipment to the needing company. Her unique catch was that someone in her network would have to carry and pay for that extra spare. For extremely high-dollar items, she would negotiate a percentage between the company and the supplier. It would be a win-win for both parties, with neither of them having to claim the entire cost in their inventory evaluation. Francine wanted to be that person who could quickly and easily find the spare for a customer and then arrange special delivery as well. If an item was "borrowed" from another company, a credit would be given to that company until a replacement was provided.

She hoped her sales vision would take off to such a magnitude that she could have zones in her territory, whereas critical equipment would be available within a smaller zone so as to get the replacement to the company in need. It was a great idea and one that she knew would work. The initial work to build the lookup table would take some of her time, but it would also allow her to stay in one destination for a short while rather than constantly travel.

Francine spent the next week learning about SPD, the full product lines they handled, the people at the main office. She spent considerable time learning about other product lines than Magnacraft and set up meetings with other supplier representatives to cultivate a relationship with those people. Francine was almost ready to go on the road, and her personal timeline was to be ready to travel starting October 1.

She contacted a number of her friends and colleagues to inform them about her new position. She explained that she was starting up a new territory for SPD to expand their market base. She genuinely felt proud of her new position and felt relieved to tell others. Her close colleagues from Magnacraft, Sara and Jim, were eager to see her before she started her travel, and they chose a date to meet after work for dinner. Sara and Jim were happy to know that Francine would be handling all product lines through SPD, so they would still be able to share product and people news about Magnacraft with her. Francine assured them that Magnacraft products would be an important player in her product portfolio. She made a note to contact Luis Ortega, the Magnacraft sales rep assigned to the SPD account after her dismissal. Luis would be a key contact for her.

CHAPTER 5

Facing Financial and Family Disaster

Francine felt much more comfortable about her financial situation but still had concern about her townhouse lease. The lease ran until June, so Francine would be on the hook for those monthly payments along with the utilities for the townhouse. She would be on the road most of her time, probably 80 percent of the time, so it would be sitting empty most of the time. She decided that she only had one option, and that was to find a roommate to share expenses.

Francine remembered a prior holiday conversation where her brother, Gerry, talked about the athletes from Northwestern going through university housing. Although she needed to tell her family eventually about her new job, she wasn't ready to discuss it, so to call Gerry was out of the question. Francine turned on her smartphone and typed in "Northwestern student housing." She looked at the variety of websites that popped onto her screen and found one that seemed appropriate.

"It doesn't hurt to try," Francine muttered as she dialed the number. Soon a man answered the phone, and Francine asked if there was someone she could talk to regarding an opportunity to provide housing to a Northwestern student. He put her on pause for several minutes and then redirected her call to a woman named Chris. Francine explained that she was a professional woman and college graduate from the University of Wisconsin. She explained that she lived about fifteen minutes from the Northwestern campus and that she had just accepted a position where she would be on the road for the majority of the month. Francine explained that she would like to find someone who was looking for housing. Preferably, she would like a single female, possibly a graduate student, who would enjoy a quiet environment. She explained that her townhouse was finely decorated and very clean, and Francine would only accept a roommate whom she could trust to maintain her housing standard while she was traveling.

Chris asked several questions, such as the exact address, type of property, price, furnished or not, and so on. Eventually, Chris said that Francine's property sounded like a dream come true, but before they could post her property, they would have to do a background check on Francine to ensure the safety of Northwestern's applicants. Francine provided the necessary information to Chris so the background check could be completed. She also mentioned that her brother, Gerry Pacque, worked for NWU in their athletic department. Chris sounded very happy to learn this as she worked with Gerry quite frequently on providing housing for his athletes.

"It's too bad that you didn't call us last month, before the fall semester started. Our students have all found housing by this time," Chris explained. "But I do have someone in mind. She is a graduate student originally from Japan. She stopped in to see me last week to report that her current housing isn't working out. Her neighboring students party way too much, and this woman is having trouble studying and sleeping. I don't think she would have trouble with the rent you are asking. Let me give her a call. Is it all right to give her your phone number if she is interested?"

"Absolutely," Francine replied.

At about seven thirty that evening, Francine's phone rang. She was hoping it would be Brian as she was still smarting from his abrupt exit several nights earlier. He hadn't called her since that time. The phone number was unknown to Francine, and she hesitated a moment before answering it.

59

"Hello. My name is Lilly Lee. I am calling to inquire about the room you have for rent," Lilly explained.

"Hello, Lilly. Thank you for calling. Were you referred to me through the university?" Francine asked.

"Yes, Chris Schnabel gave me your phone number," Lilly answered.

"Excellent! First, let me introduce myself. My name is Francine Pacque, and I lease a beautiful townhouse quite near to the university. I have two bedrooms and two full bathrooms as well as a large living room, dining area, and kitchen. It's a wonderful townhouse, and it is fully decorated, so you would not need any furniture unless you already own some," Francine explained.

"It sounds very nice. I am particularly interested if it is quiet so I can study," Lilly inquired.

"Yes, it is extremely quiet. I do not like a lot of noise myself. I'm not sure if Chris explained that the reason I am renting a room out is because I will be extensively traveling for my work. So you would actually have the townhouse for yourself probably 80 percent of the time. I plan on leaving October first and will not return until Thanksgiving. Then I will be gone again until the Christmas holiday," Francine shared.

"Oh, I see. It sounds very nice. When can I see the room?" Lilly asked.

"I am very flexible. You can see it whenever you want," Francine stated.

"Can I see it now? I'm very unhappy where I currently live and am anxious to find better housing," Lilly explained.

Francine shared her address with Lilly and found the she didn't reside too far from her. Lilly planned to ride her bicycle to Francine's townhouse. Francine put on the porch light and stood by the doorway so Lilly could easily find her. In a few minutes, a young woman of oriental descent and wearing a large pink polka dot hat rode up to her porch and introduced herself. Francine was impressed with her instantly. She exuded grace with her posture, friendliness with her broad smile, and judging from her hat, she didn't appear to be a wild party girl.

As Francine toured Lilly around her townhouse, Lilly frequently complimented her on the beautiful furnishings.

"You are very clean. That is important to me," Lilly said several times.

It was obvious that she loved the room she would be renting. Francine explained that the entire townhouse would be hers to use as long as she kept it clean. Francine said that Lilly could have friends come and visit but would not allow any parties at her house.

"Oh no, Francine. I am here for an education. There would be no partying. I do have several friends that I made, but they are quiet and good studiers like I am," Lilly said.

They discussed the rent, where Lilly could store her bicycle, and where she could store some of her belongings in the basement. They discussed how they would shop and store their own groceries. Francine thought it was a little overboard but understood that Lilly was used to living in university dormitory, where food was probably taken by others frequently. Their conversation was light, and they easily agreed on the terms. It was a perfect match, and both of them were comfortable. They shook hands, and Lilly handed Francine her first month's rent. She asked if she could move in that very weekend.

"Yes. That would be a great idea. Then we could get to know each other a little before I leave for my job," Francine said.

Lilly stated she would be over at the townhouse early on Saturday with a few items and to pick up the key. Francine agreed and said she would notify her landlord that a roommate would be moving in. Francine knew that her lease allowed an acceptable roommate but wanted to make sure that the landlord was aware.

Saturday came, and Lilly arrived at the townhouse at ten in the morning. She only had her knapsack and one small bag.

"I have to make many trips on my bike. This is all I can carry," Lilly explained.

"Oh my goodness, I didn't think about that. Let's put your bike inside the hallway and take my car back to your apartment to get some more things. I can help you," Francine said.

"You will? Oh, thank you, Francine. I very much appreciate it," Lilly said as she hugged Francine.

The two roommates worked together and had Lilly moved completely by early afternoon. They made a light lunch at the townhouse when they were done and sat at the dining table to get to know each other a bit more.

Soon Lilly said, "I should start studying now. Thank you for your hospitality."

"This is your townhouse now too. There's no need to thank me anymore."

"Yes, but all of these furnishings belong to you, and I appreciate you accepting me as your roommate," Lilly said.

Francine smiled as the young woman cleaned up the dining table and kitchen counter before going to her room to study. Francine could not have found a better person to share her home.

Francine thought, *Getting a roommate went well, but I'm dreading the next item to do.* The item was to tell her family. They wouldn't like that she was going to be a traveling salesperson. She knew she would get a lecture on how she should be married and have some children by now. She also knew that the discussion would shift to how she would ever find someone when she was traveling.

"I know, I know," Francine muttered to herself. "I feel the same way."

There was no other way around it. Francine just had to tell the truth and get it over with. She called her mom and said she was going to drive to Racine tomorrow. Her mother was thrilled to hear Francine was going to visit and asked her to get there in time for lunch. Her mother said she would call Viv and Gerry to see if they were available to stop over too.

"OK, Mom. That would be nice. See you tomorrow," Francine responded.

She hung up the phone and shouted, "Oh great! Now I have to put up with all of them at my throat."

Lilly opened her bedroom door and said, "Francine, were you saying something to me?"

"No, Lilly. Sorry. I was talking out loud. I have to get used to not being alone in here," Francine answered.

Francine scrunched up her nose in embarrassment for her own outburst. She spent the next hour thinking about what she was going to say tomorrow to her family.

The next day came too fast for Francine. She paid extra attention to her hair, makeup, and her outfit because she knew all the eyes of her family would be on her today. *What a nightmare*, she thought.

It was a beautiful, clear fall day, and the hour ride from Chicago to Racine was wonderful. Francine opened her sunroof to get the brisk air circulating around her. She tried not to think about today's conversation with her family. When she drove up to her parents' driveway, she saw that her brother and sister had already arrived.

"Well, here goes," she said aloud. "Confidence is everything."

Francine went through the door with a big smile on her face. "I'm here, everyone. Hello!"

There were hugs and kisses between all the family. Her brother and sister had brought their entire family with them, and Francine was happy to see her brother-in-law, sister-in-law, and all her nephews and nieces. Francine noticed the pride that her parents showed on their faces as they saw their family all together. She knew it was a special time for them.

Her mother made a beef roast with sautéed vegetables and homemade French bread. Her mother was an excellent cook, and the meal was delicious. Everyone ate too much, but her brother was almost embarrassing as he shoveled food into his mouth. Francine thought he was earning his old football nickname, Pack it in, but she didn't want to stoop to his level and tease him.

After the table was cleaned and the children were busy playing in the backyard, Francine said that she had some news to share with them.

Her family looked curiously at her, and her brother said, "What kind of news, Fanny Pack?"

Oh, how I wish I teased him a few minutes ago, Francine thought.

Francine intended to tell them the entire true story, but something stopped her.

"I wanted to tell you that I got a promotion," she lied.

"Really, that's great, Francine," her father said.

63

"How wonderful! Finally, you'll have more money to start investing in a 401K," her mother chimed in.

"Fanny Pack, so who did you have to sleep with to get a promotion?" Gerry asked.

"Gerry! Francine is a nice girl. I'm sure she deserved the promotion," Mom added.

"Francine, that's wonderful," Genevieve added then continued, "I was hoping you were going to tell us that you found a nice boyfriend. Gretchen Dirsch, you must remember her from high school, she found someone. I saw them last week. And Gretchen isn't much to look at. I don't know why you can't seem to find someone."

Matt, Genevieve's husband, added, "Yeah, someone would have to put a bag over Gretchen's head."

Viv touched Matt's shoulder, and they both laughed. Francine was jeering at them.

Only Chrissy, Gerry's wife, offered a simple "Congratulations." Francine was glad she was part of the family. Typically, Chrissy was quiet. She and Gerry had a good marriage, but Francine often wondered if Chris was truly happy. She was alone a lot with the kids as Gerry attended school sport functions.

"Francine, what is your new position?" Father Pacque asked.

The rest of the family was babbling, and Francine didn't know if they were talking about her and her job.

Soon, her dad shouted, "Everyone, be quiet! Let Francine tell us about her promotion."

This was it! This was the time Francine was dreading. She didn't want to be dragged through the dirt with interrogation about her job loss, the lack of finding another high-paying position, her love life, etc.

Francine hesitated for a moment before announcing in a very clear voice, "Thanks, Dad. Well, I was the number one salesperson at Magnacraft this year, and I was honored at their annual conference several weeks ago. I have been developing a new strategy for Magnacraft's products and shared my strategy with them. They loved my idea, and I ended up getting a promotion to a senior sales executive."

Francine paused for a minute to let it sink in. She was surprised how easily the lie was coming out of her mouth.

She continued, "I'm going to be developing a new territory in the South...south of the Atlanta region down to the tip of Florida, to be exact."

"What is this?" her mother gasped.

There were similar comments made by all of them.

"You have to move?" her mother asked.

"Not quite. Actually, I have to move *around* as I will be developing an entire new area. I will be able to keep my townhouse in Chicago, though, so I'll still be back in Chicago often. For sure I will be home for the holidays," she explained.

"I don't like the sound of this, Francine. It doesn't sound like too much of a promotion to me. I don't know why you don't move back to Racine or Milwaukee and meet someone and have some children. I would rather hear about me getting some grandchildren rather than you moving farther away," Mom said.

"Francine, how much money did you get with your promotion?" her father asked.

Francine thought, *How typical,* but she said, "Dad! I'd rather not discuss my wages in front of everyone. But of course I received a good wage increase plus a traveling allowance."

Her family looked at one another to see what reaction they should give her. But slowly they each gave her a halfhearted congratulations.

Some additional questions were asked, and Francine answered them masterfully, although she was making them up as she went along. She decided that she should let them know about her new roommate as well, but she did not want them to think she needed a roommate to make ends meet. So she told them that she agreed to house an intern graduate student from Northwestern University. Her brother sounded impressed that it was someone from his university. Since her brother seemed OK with the roommate, everyone else seemed to fall into line.

The Pacque family dinner and visit finally ended, and Francine got into her Audi. Francine exhaled loudly when as she settled into her seat. As she drove home, she realized how easily she fooled her family rather than have them chastise her for losing her job. Francine felt guilty because lying wasn't something that Francine could remember doing since childhood. But Francine felt relieved and happy as she drove down her parents' driveway. She opened her sunroof and turned up the radio. It was a great ride home.

Francine was going to hit the road with her new job one week from today. She had lots on her mind as she worked during the days at SPD with Lucas Peterson, learning all she could about SPD's products, customer base, and computer system. Her evenings flew by as well as she had to decide on what to bring in her small Audi automobile for an extended time. She knew she would be on the road for about six weeks before returning to Chicago, and she needed to pack a work wardrobe and a casual wardrobe. She had no itinerary, so she had no idea what city she might be in, what fleabag motel she might be residing at, and what she would be doing on her off time.

She looked at her closet and glanced at her beautiful clothes. Francine had acquired an impeccable taste for professional clothes. Her clothes labels included Ann Taylor, Elie Tahiri, Antonio Melani, Calvin Klein, Elaine Fisher, and more. Her shoe labels included Michael Kors, Jimmy Choo, and Prada. Purses and clutches by Michael Kors, Burberry, and Brahmin. It was an impressive closet.

"I don't know which ones should make the cut," she whispered to herself.

She also needed toiletries, hair paraphernalia, some basic food and snacks, some reading books, and some personal comfort decorations (her favorite pillow, some pictures). She looked at her briefcase packed with her work computer and manuals. She also needed to take several boxes of SPD promotional material to give to prospective customers.

A thought came into Francine's head, and she quickly went into the basement. She retrieved a large dark-gray plastic container with a lid. She carried the box upstairs and put all the work items into the box.

"That should work," Francine said. "I'll put the box in the backseat of the car with my work items, and no one will be able to see what is in there. The box doesn't look impressive, so I think my materials will be OK. Then I can just take my briefcase into the hotel room with me each night."

She put her hands on her hips and nodded approvingly.

"The best part will be that my entire trunk will be empty for my clothes. I can purchase clothing bags and take almost all of my things with me," she muttered. "I'll pack my underthings in a carry-on bag and my sweaters and casual clothes in my two suitcases. I'll make it work. It has to work."

She thought for a moments and said, "I'll buy one more container for the backseat to put my other toiletries into. Then I can easily move it into the hotel room." Francine had her plan.

Francine went into the kitchen to get a Diet Coke. As she passed her roommate's room, she saw that Lilly was not home. This was quite usual as she often worked with a study group in the university's library. Francine was wondering if she would get a better chance to know Lilly better when the front door opened and Lilly walked inside.

"Hello, Francine. I hope I didn't disturb you," Lilly said shyly.

"Of course not. I was just thinking about you and wondering if we would have a chance to get to know each other better before I take off on my trip next week," Francine said.

"That would be very nice to have some time together. I have a test tomorrow so I am very busy tonight, but I am free tomorrow night. Would tomorrow work for you?" Lilly asked.

"I think that will work great for me as well. Would it be all right if we ate dinner here at home together?" Francine suggested. "I could even cook something or we could just have a pizza."

Lilly's face lit up. "Pizza is my favorite! Let's have a pizza."

"Great," Francine said.

They spent a time discussing their favorite toppings, and Francine said she would get the pizza on her way home from the office. They gave each other a short friendly hug before Lilly disappeared into her room to continue studying.

Francine sat for a while on her living room couch, enjoying the bubbly taste of a freshly opened can of soda. Her mind was wandering through the list of items she had to do before leaving on Monday.

Somehow, her mind went to her employment study buddy, Brian. *What happened there?* she wondered. *He seemed so interested in me, and we were having such a great time together, and that was it. He just dropped out of my life.* After a couple of minutes debating her next move, she picked up her cell phone and called Brian. There was no answer, only voice mail.

"Hi, Brian, this is Francine Pacque. I just wanted to see how you were doing with your new job. I'm doing well with mine, so far. I leave Monday and am heading South, probably for a month or two. If you get a chance to call me back, that would be great. If not, I wish you well and good luck," Francine said to the voice recorder.

She hoped she wasn't too forward to call him and thought, *For goodness's sake, I'm a thirty-four-year-old woman, not a kid. I talk to men every day at work. Why is it always so hard to talk when it's not business?*

Francine became sad while sitting there all alone. All her demons of losing her job, not having a significant other, and the unknown of going on the road to low potential sales regions were getting to her nerves. *What a loser I am*, she thought. She looked at her Coke and wished she had opted for wine.

The week continued, and Francine worked diligently to prepare for her long trip. She packed her car with the empty gray containers and suitcases to test her packing strategy. She was satisfied on how it turned out. The Audi was not the right car for this type of traveling job, but she had no choice because she had a car lease. *At least I'll be traveling in style and will have a nice car for my off time,* she thought.

Sunday night, she called her mother to say she would be leaving bright and early the following morning. Her mother voiced her concern about Francine traveling alone on the road. Francine assured her that she was traveling in safe areas and in a safe vehicle. She told her mom that she would always be as close as a phone call away. The conversation went well, and Francine hung up on a happy note.

She called some of her other friends before Monday, including her friend Sara, her brother, Gerry, and her sister, Genevieve. Francine never received a return phone call from Brian.

CHAPTER 6

The Ride South

Monday morning was a dark, rainy day. It was unusual to have rain in early October, but there it was. Francine drank a quick cup of coffee and started packing her car. She would have packed it the night before, but she had street parking and did not want to take the chance that her car would be broken into and items stolen. Her packing strategy worked well, and she accomplished packing a large portion of her wardrobe plus her necessary work and personal items. Francine hit the road at about ten in the morning, which avoided the early morning Chicago highway traffic jam.

She looked forward to working in the South during the winter. When she was offered any undefined remote route, Francine could have chosen many places, like the mountains in Montana, the northern area of California, the Upper East Coast, etc. She didn't know why she quickly chose the South except that she always longed for warm weather during the cold Wisconsin and Illinois winters.

She drove on the Chicago bypass and headed for I-65. I-65 would take her south into the Tennessee area. From there, she would decide where to travel next. Today's goal was to get to Nashville. She looked forward to enjoying the sights and cuisine of Nashville for an evening. Her trip was uneventful, and as she turned south on I-65

69

through Indiana, the sun came out. Francine turned up the tunes and cruised. She stopped several times along her way so as to stretch her legs, use a restroom, and get some refreshments. When she was close to Nashville, she noticed a steady stream of hotels along the highway. Francine pulled off on an exit ramp and parked at a gas station. She quickly brought up her smartphone and entered Nashville on one of the travel websites. A list of possible choices came up on her phone. She viewed the list, searching for the cheapest hotel. It was a motel that didn't look too safe. She continued her search until she found an acceptable choice. Francine drove back on the highway and continued several miles to that hotel destination.

Her room was clean and comfortable. She brought in her computer items and one travel suitcase. Francine listened to the news on the television while she freshened up her makeup and brushed her hair. She decided to continue wearing her blue jeans but put on a different tank top with a jean jacket. The jacket had some embellishments on it, and Francine thought it was a good choice since Nashville was the home of country music. She decided to put on her walking boots to finish her look. Satisfied, Francine left her room and headed to the front desk.

"Hi," Francine said to the man at the hotel desk. "Can you recommend somewhere in Nashville, maybe downtown, to find a good place to eat and see the sights?"

"Sure, I can tell you some places to go. I'd recommend going to Division Street. There are a number of bars, and most have music," the hotel clerk said.

"Can you tell me one of their names so I can put it in my GPS?" Francine asked.

"The Patterson House is very popular with the locals and with tourists. I always bring out-of-town company there. It has an old Nashville feel and has good food and drinks. Also, the Red Door Saloon is fun and has the best brats in town," the clerk suggested.

"Thanks for the tips. It'll give me a start," Francine said as she headed out the door.

Francine followed her GPS to Division Street. Her plan was to start at the Patterson House and go somewhere else later for a nightcap. She loved the old charm of the Patterson House the minute she entered the place. Francine was not one who regularly sat at a bar alone and had drinks, but somehow she felt comfortable when she ordered food and sat at the bar. The bartender made it seem as if she weren't alone but rather in a booth.

She ordered a tap beer and asked for a menu. The tables and booths were three quarters full of patrons, and Francine enjoyed the ambiance. Francine noticed a couple talking in the opposite direction from Francine to another man at the bar. Francine overheard several of the phrases as they were talking, and it appeared that they were celebrating something.

Francine was fascinated with the couple because they looked like they came out of a Nashville magazine. The man was about Francine's age, in the midthirties. He had dark tousled hair and a trimmed full beard. He was wearing jeans with boots and had a black cowboy hat, which he carefully laid on an empty car. The only jewelry he wore was a huge silver ring on his right hand.

The woman who accompanied the man was striking. The woman wasn't particularly beautiful, but she would turn any man's head. Right now, she was turning Francine's. She was probably in her late twenties and had thick naturally dark-red hair cut in layers down her back. Blond hair tipping was on the edges of each layer. She wore heavy eye makeup and bright-red lipstick. The woman had multiple tank tops on, one red with a black tank over it. She also wore a long pendant necklace that barely hid her ample breasts. To finish her wardrobe, the woman wore a short jean miniskirt with insets of fluted lace. High-heeled boots finished her ensemble.

Francine ordered the specialty of the Patterson House, the Elvis Panini, and continued sipping her brew. Her food came, and she laughed as she saw bananas and peanut butter as part of the sandwich. The bartender laughed with her and predicted that she would love the sandwich. He explained that it was the most popular dish at the Patterson House. The laughter caught the attention of the couple sitting next to Francine, and they turned in her direction and started talking.

The next hour was very enjoyable for Francine as the couple and she enjoyed another beer and good conversation. They explained that they were celebrating a recording contract that the man received. He was a struggling musician for years but finally was going to have sponsorship and a recording. Francine was thrilled to meet someone in the music business. That life was so different from her life, and she imagined a musician's life of dimly lit bars. The couple was so happy. They hugged and kissed each other several times.

Francine asked the name his record and when it would be available for sale. She wanted to purchase it online. The man said that it would be called "Only You," but he didn't know when it would be available. Francine watched jealously as he turned to his girlfriend when he announced his record's name. *She is a lucky lady*, Francine thought to herself.

The man said, "Yeah, I can't wait to hear it on the radio. That's when some money will start coming in. The music business is hard to break into, and getting into it doesn't pay the bills. I'm lucky because my girlfriend works, and we live together. Soon she hopefully will be living in luxury."

"That'll be nice," his girlfriend added. "We really shouldn't be going out until the money starts coming in. But you know, we need to celebrate too."

They squeezed each other within their arms and gave each other another small kiss.

Francine said she enjoyed meeting them and asked if she could buy them another drink. They accepted, and they spent another twenty minutes together. The man talked excitedly about the music business, various bars he performed at, and the famous personalities he met along the way. Finally, the girlfriend said that they should be getting home, so the three of them said their good-byes. When they left, Francine finished her food and thought about the nice evening she had. She typed the name of the song and the man's name into her Notes app on her phone.

"Did that guy tell you that he just signed a record deal?" the bartender asked.

"Yes! Isn't that exciting?" Francine answered.

"It would be if it was true," the bartender stated. "He's been telling that story for years. I think he probably is a musician, but he's been getting free drinks with that story for as long as I've worked here."

"Are you kidding me?" exclaimed Francine.

Francine immediately thought of her dwindling funds and what a fool she was to buy them drinks.

"I wish you would have told me," she asked, hoping the bartender would feel bad for not protecting her.

"It's part of the bartender code of honor. You have to know when to hold and when to close. I would have said something if you were going to buy them a second drink," the bartender said. "You can have a drink on the house if you would like."

Francine hesitated as she thought about the offer but decided that the last thing she needed was another drink. She thanked him for the offer and left for the hotel. As she was driving home, she thought about how easy it was to deceive people. She thought about how the couple looked the part and then filled their deception with a story.

Francine muttered to herself, "People believe what you tell them. Heck, politicians and the newspapers have been doing that for years."

The drive back to the hotel was uneventful, but Francine thought the evening was very educational. She was happy that she stopped in Nashville.

The next day was a strategic day for Francine. She had to decide what route to take South. She could continue on the normal route through the mountains in Tennessee toward Florida or head to another Southern destination to start looking for customers. Her looked at her map and surveyed the cities south of Atlanta. The Atlanta region was the southernmost city that SPD had a special sales representative assigned. Below Atlanta, it was fair game for Francine.

CHAPTER 7

Louisiana

Francine decided to take a "weather" approach. Since she planned to stay in the southern Florida area during the winter months, she thought it prudent to start finding customers in the Louisiana, Mississippi, and Georgia area first. She brought up some of those state's cities on her smartphone to look up each city's biography. Francine thought that something might guide her decision. She was right. While she was looking up Monroe, Louisiana, she noticed that an agriculture fair was going to be held soon. Agriculture companies use many products that SPD could supply. They might not be a million-dollar customer, but word of mouth was a large part of that culture, and if Francine could get a foothold with some small feed or processing companies, it might lead to future sales with other small companies.

Francine took out her laptop and started looking at websites to find existing companies and existing distributor competition. She began mapping out a route. She had three days until the livestock and agricultural expedition began. That would give her one day to travel and find a hotel for about a week's stay, drive around the town and get acquainted with some locals in various restaurants or stores, and the third day to start making some initial sales visits. The weekend she would dedicate to attending the agriculture expo for additional

74

contacts and potential customers. She called ahead to reserve a hotel room for the next week in Monroe. There were none available. The hotel clerk told her that people traveled to the expo from all around the state, and rooms were reserved months ago. The clerk told her she might have to go as much as fifty miles away to find an available room. At first, Francine reacted badly to the news, but slowly, she started to smile. She had an idea that anonymity might serve her well by staying an hour away from the venue.

Louisiana was hot when Francine arrived to visit Monroe. She thought about all the cold days she had living in the North, and being hot seemed like a treat. Francine was stunned at all the possibilities of business in the area. The city of Monroe had all kinds of businesses and a small but impressive-looking downtown area. Francine was most interested in looking at the area that was holding the exposition in West Monroe. She found a large modern fairground that was bustling with activity as the expo displays were being set up. She located the ticket office building and asked for a flyer. She scanned the following days' agenda, and one item leaped out of the page. Saturday afternoon was a rodeo. Francine had never been to a rodeo, but no one would know that after she did some research. She quickly typed in a search in her smartphone to find the nearest cowboy clothing and boot store. After she located a store, she hurried to her car and left the fairgrounds.

The clothing store had a variety of clothing for men and women. Much of the store was dedicated to cowboy boots and hats. Francine moved to the women's boots section and found an impressive pair of dove-gray boots embellished with studs. The front of the boot had some turquoise stitching surrounding a long decorative tassel. Francine wanted those boots even if she weren't going to a rodeo. She found a pair in her size and then surveyed the other clothing available for both men and women. Her interest in the men's clothing and accessories was mainly educational. Her interest in women's clothing, of course, was purely personal. Francine chose several embellished shirts, tried them on, and purchased two shirts, a pair of studded jeans, the dove-gray boots, a large pair of sunglasses, and several hair adornments. She would experiment with the outfits and her hair back at the hotel.

Francine went back to the hotel and did some research on rodeos. She took her old Magnacraft lanyard and removed the ID card from it. She then went to her computer and found an appropriate background to make an identification badge. After several minutes, a suitable ID badge emerged on the computer screen.

"Hmmm," Francine said aloud, "what would get me into the rodeo?"

She thought for a minute and grinned. Carefully she chose a print font and typed in the words "Cowgirl Gazette, Houston Texas." Below the print, she began to type in her name in a smaller font. She looked at the badge for a moment and then considered whether to use her real name or not. She chose to use a fake name similar to her own. She typed "Ann Peck." Ann was Francine's middle name, and Peck was close to Pacque. If she was caught by someone as a fraud, she could explain that she uses a stage name for work.

Francine inserted some online photo art to make the badge appear valid. She sized the badge to fit her lanyard and printed a copy. The badge didn't quite fit, so she trimmed the badge carefully. The badge looked official.

"If it doesn't work, who will care?" Francine asked herself. "I'll just leave the rodeo."

She was ready with her main prop. She noted that tomorrow she needed to familiarize herself with some rodeo jargon so she would fit in with the other reporters and rodeo personnel.

"Tomorrow will be my first attempt to get new customers. That'll be a big day. There's nothing better than to blow off some steam the following day with a livestock fair and a rodeo," Francine said to herself.

She went back to her computer and studied several companies that she would visit the following day. It always helped to have as much information on the business before making a cold sales call. Francine decided to get a good night's sleep and went to bed early, but anticipation of the next couple of days flooded her thoughts.

Several hours later, she felt her eyes getting heavy, and she nodded off to sleep.

Francine woke up Thursday morning as the sun flooded in through the thin motel curtains. Francine showered and dressed. She chose to wear a black slimline skirt with a white camisole-style blouse and a gorgeous black-and-white bolero jacket. She had purchased the jacket at a boutique in California on a past business trip. It was an extravagant purchase and an unknown designer, but Francine thought the showstopping jacket was worth every penny.

"At least I'm still able to wear my beautiful clothes," Francine said as she dressed.

She took a pair of red high-heeled shoes from her suitcase and her red Brahmin leather purse.

"Perfect," Francine said.

She let her hair fall down loosely on her shoulders. She didn't want to look too "big city" professional and scare off more rural customers. Francine walked into the motel lobby to grab a cup of coffee and some fruit at the complimentary breakfast bar. She noticed that everyone was looking at her. *It feels good to be noticed*, she thought to herself as she exited the hotel and reached her Audi.

Francine headed to an industrial area of Monroe. As she drove to Monroe from Delhi, where she had to get a motel room, she practiced her sales pitch. The industrial area had a number of small factories and business offices. Francine noticed a meat-processing facility and decided that she would try her pitch there first. The building was quite large with several adjoining structures.

"Good morning. I would like to see your CFO if possible," Francine said to the office receptionist.

The young woman looked surprised when Francine asked to see the chief financial officer.

She responded, "Do you have an appointment? I don't remember any appointment on his calendar."

Francine said, "No, I do not have an appointment. But I would like to see him now or make an appointment with him while I am in town."

77

"What business do you have with Mr. Baldwin?" the receptionist asked. "I would have to explain it to him."

"I'll tell you what," Francine said. "It would probably be easiest for me to leave Mr. Baldwin a voice mail and explain. Then he can decide if he is interested. Is there a way to have me leave him a message?"

"Yes. I can do that for you. Why don't you use the lobby phone and call his phone number. It is listed on the card next to the phone."

Francine thanked the young woman, who still looked puzzled by Francine's request, and used the phone. Francine's strategy of contacting the CFO rather than a maintenance manager or operations manager was imperative. Francine knew that relationships ran strong with various business managers, and probably more so in the South. But a CFO's job was to be concerned with money and creating a strong financial system for the company. Francine's strategy was to get a foothold in the critical equipment category.

Every company has certain equipment that must be working or the operation stops. Some of those items are classified as spare parts, such as small motors that can be stocked or easily purchased. Other items, however, are expensive, have long lead times to procure, or have special features. These items are classified as critical equipment. Francine knew from her past sales experience that critical equipment is an inventory issue for her past clients because it is part of their inventory dollars, and the equipment can be on the stockroom shelf for years or until it is obsolete. She was aware of plants that made financial decisions to reduce or eliminate their critical equipment inventory and lost substantial manufacturing time due to not having the equipment after a breakdown.

Francine dialed the number for Mr. Baldwin and waited until the message indicated for her to speak. She knew she would have to speak quickly and capture the CFO's interest before the voice mail message would time out. The voice mail beeped, and Francine started her pitch,

"Good morning, Mr. Baldwin. My name is Francine Pacque, and I am setting up a new business strategy for Standard Product Distribution Corporation out of the Chicago area. My company is willing to stock, at their expense, equipment supplies that your company would deem as critical for running your operation. Items could include such things as specialty motors, drives, gears, hoists, etc. As you know, storing such critical items is expensive for companies, but the lack of storing critical equipment will shut your operation down when the equipment is needed. Standard Product Distribution is taking on the expense and will let you store such items in your inventory or in another company's inventory within a certain range. You would pay when and if you use the equipment. I am the lead for Standard Product's critical equipment venture, and I will be in this area until next week Friday. If you are interested, please give me a call on my cell phone. Thank you. Again, my name is Francine Pacque, and I represent Standard Product Distribution Corporation."

Francine repeated her name, the company she was representing, and her phone number prior to disconnecting the call. *Whew,* Francine thought, *I got it all out before the end of the voice mail. Now all I can do is wait.*

Francine thanked the receptionist and left the building. She drove to the next company located only a few hundred feet away and was parking in the lot when her cell phone rang. She did not recognize the phone number.

"Hello, this is Francine Pacque," Francine said as she answered the phone.

"Hello. This is Jack Baldwin. You just left me a message, and I'm interested in learning more."

"Excellent! Thank you for calling me back so quickly. When would you like to discuss my offer?" Francine asked.

"Well, I always have time to hear about saving some money. Now is as good a time as any for me," Mr. Baldwin answered.

"I'll be right there. Give me five minutes to drive back to your firm," Francine replied. Her chest was heaving because she was so excited.

"I knew the CFOs would like the sound of this," Francine exclaimed to herself.

She returned to the company parking lot, removed her briefcase, and walked in to her first customer.

Francine and Jack Baldwin talked for the next forty-five minutes about the program SPD was offering. Francine explained that a critical equipment list would have to be made by their maintenance manager if one did not already exist. That list would be entered into a spreadsheet that Francine herself would maintain. The list would have all the critical equipment listed for their company, the specifications of that equipment, and any current inventory of that equipment. She explained that she would be adding other company's critical equipment onto the same list, creating a master spreadsheet. She explained that her experience has shown that the same type of high-dollar equipment was used in many industries. "Factories are factories," she explained, "and they have many similar needs."

Francine went on to explain that a zone, or region, would be created between companies within X number of miles. If a maintenance manager calls Francine with a need, she would look at the master spreadsheet to see if another company had the item in stock, and Francine would arrange the transfer of the equipment to their company. If a replacement wasn't found on the master sheet, she would use the resources of SPD to locate and expedite delivery.

The CFO asked about her comment that Standard Product Distribution would stock items at their expense in his company inventory. Francine answered that yes, SPD was open to such a venture; however, the master spreadsheet would need to be completed first. Francine wasn't quite sure of how many companies needed to be on the spreadsheet but would be in a better position after she got several companies signed up for this offer. Eventually, she knew that SPD would stock some items, and she would have to negotiate with the manufacturer of the product, such as Magnacraft, to absorb some of the cost. It would be very similar to a vendor-managed program that many companies had for low-cost commodity items such as screws and bolts.

"Francine, I love the concept, but I have to be missing something. Why would SPD do this? They would be taking on all of the burden. And what is in it for you? I don't know how you would earn anything. It seems like a lot of work on your part," Jack Baldwin asked.

"Remember that the replacement item would be sourced by SPD. That's where they would make their money. Companies don't realize how many times some critical item shuts down their operation. It happens frequently in large plants. The only alternative is to have deep pockets and stock every one of your critical items. SPD realizes this, and so do I. Additionally, after I save your day and expedite something for you, you will start to realize that I provide a service that most others do not. I will complete your list of critical items with the help of your maintenance manager, keep track of your inventories, do all the legwork to find a replacement, and organize the transfer of the item. I know you will find my service level higher than you ever had before. This may lead to additional sales for me and my company. We offer vendor-managed services as well as competitive prices on any inventory item. Here is our brochure of the types of products we cover, and feel free to look up our website."

In forty-five minutes, Francine knew she had a future customer. She may not have sold anything yet, but she had one on her roster. Jack Baldwin explained that he would need to talk to their general manager, and he expected to schedule a presentation with their entire staff early the next week. But as the controller of the money, and with no initial money outlay, it was a win-win for them. Francine agreed and asked to make the meeting early in the week, if possible. She explained that she would like to start compiling the list as soon as possible. They shook hands, and Francine left the building with an extreme feeling of pride.

Francine sat in her car for a moment and regrouped. She did it! She knew her strategy would work. She was anxious for the follow-up presentation and to get started on her spreadsheet. Francine reached for her cooler and was glad to find a semicool Diet Coke in it. She drank some of the can in celebration before driving to her next company.

By the end of the day, Francine had made contact with ten companies. Cold sales calls took a lot out of a salesperson, but Francine could have continued all day except that the businesses were closing for the day. She had various levels of success, with most companies skeptical of some hidden cost but receptive to hear more. She was able to give four companies' CFOs the verbal presentation that she gave Jack Baldwin, left messages for four other CFOs, and only two of the companies flat-out did not want to be involved.

When Francine returned to the motel, she took off her shoes and lay on the bed, ready for a relaxing evening. She checked her phone for messages and found that she had a text from her roommate, Lilly, asking her for instructions to forward her mail. She also had a text from Jim Ruscher, her coworker friend from Magnacraft. Francine started with the text from Lilly.

"Hi. Things are good here, but I don't know what to do with your mail. Looks like one invitation…maybe a wedding? Lilly."

Francine thought she better call home.

"Hi, Lilly, this is Francine. How are you doing?"

"Hi, Francine. Thank you for calling me tonight. I wanted to tell you how happy I am here. Thank you for letting me live here with you," Lilly said.

She meant every word too. Francine treated her as an equal, not as a foreigner or a student. She felt more like a sister to Francine than a roommate.

"I should be thanking you. I'm glad you like it there. How is school?" Francine replied.

"My studies are going very well. I have been receiving high grades and comments from my professors," Lilly shared.

"That's wonderful! Have you had any problems with the apartment?" Francine asked.

"No, everything has been very good. I have been storing my bike in the hallway. I hope that is all right with you. I didn't think you would mind until you come back to Chicago," Lilly inquired shyly.

"I'm OK with that. As long as the bike isn't dripping street water onto the living room floors," Francine answered.

"Oh! No! I have a liner and a towel under the bike. Your floor is all dry," Lilly replied.

"Then I'm good," said Francine. "Can we talk about the mail a bit?"

"Yes, most of it looks like junk mail, and you already told me that you do all your bills online, but there is a formal-looking letter here. It looks like maybe a wedding invitation," Lilly said.

"Can you get it now and open it for me?" Francine asked.

There was a slight conversation pause and then Lilly replied, "I have it right here. I'll open it."

Francine heard the sound of an envelope ripping open and waited for Lilly to read the invitation.

"Francine, I have it opened. Yes, it is a wedding invitation. The names are Brenda Pierce and Ronald Greeson. They are getting married December fifth. Let me read the rest of the invitation," Lilly said.

Lilly read the entire invitation, including the dinner and reception information, but Francine didn't hear her words. She was stunned that another friend of hers, one who had been married and divorced, found someone else and was getting married again. Francine's mind raced back to her college years at UW–Parkside, in Kenosha, Wisconsin. She and Brenda went to school together there and partied on the weekends. *Why does everyone else find someone?* Francine thought. She instantly went into a depressed mood.

"Francine, are you still there?" Lilly inquired.

"Yeah, I'm here. I'm just thinking," Francine replied.

"Do you want me to forward your mail to you?" Lilly asked. "Especially the invitation?"

"No, you don't need to forward it. I probably won't be in town to attend the wedding anyway. Thanks for letting me know. Just put all my mail in my bedroom, and I'll deal with it when I come home, whenever that may be," Francine said. The two of them talked for a few more minutes and hung up.

Although she didn't feel like hearing more news, Francine checked her e-mail and found that she had an e-mail from her sister, Genevieve.

"Hi, sis, I just wanted to send you a link to a trip that Matt and I are going to take after New Year's Day. Isn't that great? I always wanted to go to Tahiti. The kids are going to stay with Mom and Dad, so Matt and I will have a second honeymoon. I'm so excited. We rented a tiki hut on the beach. You will see it when you open the link. Well, that's it for now. I hope your new territory is good. Magnacraft is lucky to have you. Love, Viv."

Francine felt bad lying to Viv about still working for Magnacraft, but if she told Viv, Viv would tell her husband, and it would somehow come out to Mom and Dad. Francine wasn't prepared for that info sharing yet. *A trip to Tahiti. How lucky can one woman be?* Francine questioned. She loved her sister. She just couldn't take another bit of news on how astonishingly lucky her sister was.

Francine wrote back only a few words to Genevieve as a reply.

"Sounds great. Looking forward to the pictures after you go. Work is good. Take care. Love, Francine."

Francine shut down her e-mail and phone and decided to take a nice long bath in the motel tub before going to bed.

"I wish I had some liquor," Francine said as she ran water into the tub.

Her depression lingered until she went to bed as she hoped for a better mood in the morning.

The next day, Francine woke up refreshed, and her thoughts were about hitting more companies up as part of her network. She dressed meticulously in a black pencil skirt with a white-and-black blouse. She kept her hair down on her shoulders and pushed her hair off her face so as to display her large white earrings.

Francine drove to another area populated by small industrial-looking buildings. Her day went well, and she was able to talk to several more CFOs, who promptly referred her to the appropriate maintenance or operations manager. Francine's strategy of "Going to the decision maker, or the money" was working. By midafternoon, Francine had several more companies on board to try out her critical equipment network. She was at a potential customer's engineering office when her phone rang. She recognized the phone number as one of her newly listed companies the day before.

"Hello, this is Francine Pacque," Francine said as she answered the call.

"Good morning, Francine, This is Stan Overmeier over here at Best Manufacturing. You were here yesterday," the man said.

"Yes, I remember you. Good morning, Stan. What can I do for you today?" Francine responded.

"I was wondering if you were only interested in replacing spare parts or if you would be interested in giving us a quote on some things we will need for an expansion we are planning?" Stan asked.

"Yes! Standard Production Distribution handles many of the finest equipment manufacturers. I would love to have the opportunity to quote on some business. When would you like me to come in to see what you need?" she asked.

"There's no big hurry, but we do want to look at our quotes by the end of the month. So if you want to drop by and be included, just come on back this way when you have a chance, and I'll give you the equipment list," said Stan.

They said their good-byes, and Francine made a mental note that she needed to head over to Best Manufacturing during this week. This was what she was hoping. The critical spares might have gotten her into the door, but she needed more purchases to make any money. She grinned and gave herself a congratulatory high five.

The next day, Francine arrived at Best Manufacturing and requested to see Stan Overmeier. Stan came to the lobby a few minutes later and escorted Francine into a small conference room where a large AutoCAD print of a plant expansion was posted. Francine noted on the title block that the expansion was fifty thousand square feet. Estimating that the current plant was approximately two hundred thousand square feet, this was a large expansion. The detail sheets of the drawing showed an expanded manufacturing area, a small maintenance shop, and a small laboratory. Francine was thrilled. SPD distributed a large range of products, and she hoped the quote package contained many SPD products.

Stan went to his computer and printed out several pages. He returned to the table with the printouts and handed them over to Francine. It was a detailed list of all products he needed, and it was large! Francine looked over the list and immediately knew she could provide all the items listed. They discussed some of the items, and Stan said he could provide an electronic list that had detailed descriptions of the items required. *Jackpot!*

Francine thanked him again for giving her an opportunity to quote. She knew that she could give the complete list to SPD, and they would put someone on deciphering the list and put together the quote. But Francine had an idea. She knew some of these products were produced by her past employer, Magnacraft. She decided to give

85

her two friends Sara Johnson and Jim Ruscher a call. If she could avoid the middleman, SPD, and get some of the products directly from Sara and Jim, she could get a better price, plus give her friends some sales. Additionally, she knew that she didn't have time to find the SPD part numbers for such a vast list, and giving the list to the inside salespeople at SPD would also boost the price, so she decided to call her sister-in-law, Chrissy, and see if she wanted to do a little work from home to identify the SPD catalog numbers online. Once done, Francine could input those part numbers directly into her SPD sales catalog and directly provide a quote. The importance of getting this order was huge for Francine, and she was open to taking a smaller sales commission to provide a lowest-cost quote.

Francine called her sister-in-law, Chrissy, from the parking lot immediately after leaving the plant.

"Hi, Chrissy, this is Francine. How are you and the kids?" Francine asked.

"Hi, Francine. Everyone is fine. How are you?" Chrissy asked.

She was excited to hear from Francine; in fact, she would have been excited to hear from anyone. Christine Pacque met her future husband, Gerry Pacque, during college at Northwestern University. Chrissy was a perky and pretty young woman who had planned on being a businesswoman in one of Chicago's many companies. But marriage to Gerard Pacque was difficult due to his long work hours as an athletic department administrator. Gerry was gone frequently in the evenings and on weekends to attend different sports functions. They had a solid marriage and had three children that kept Chrissy busy, but she frequently felt unhappy and unfulfilled.

"I have a proposition for you. I don't know if you would be interested or if you would have time, but would you be willing to possibly do some work for me? It would involve looking up some items that a customer wants to buy and finding the best match in a catalog of a distributor. You could work at your own pace, but I would have to have the list done within a week. Would that be something you would consider?" Francine asked.

She made a face while she made the request over the phone.

"I would just have to look up items on the website?" Chrissy asked excitedly.

"Yes, pretty much like looking up something on Amazon or any other sales website. I would need you to copy the part number, description, and the price down on a list. It is for a quote for a company in Louisiana," Francine explained.

"That sounds easy enough. I surely have extra time sitting around the house. I wouldn't mind at all," Chrissy answered.

"I do have to warn you that it is a long list. And it wouldn't be for free. I can pay you something for your trouble based on how many hours you work," Francine explained.

She couldn't expect her sister-in-law to work for nothing. She just didn't know how she would pay her right away.

Chrissy was beaming. It had been a long time since she did any outside work. She imagined herself sitting in their home office and looking up items on the computer. She only took a few seconds to answer.

"Francine, I would love to help you out. I don't even care about the money. How do we proceed?" she asked.

The two women talked about the detail of the list, and Francine said she would e-mail the list over to her later today. They spent the next ten minutes chatting about themselves and the Pacque family. Francine said she would call her in the evening to talk through the first couple of items so that Chrissy would feel comfortable with the balance of the list.

The week continued, and Francine hit the pavement and worked on her equipment spreadsheet. The spreadsheet of critical equipment was becoming quite large, and she was impressed with its turnout. It was a good week, but her thoughts were now on the weekend. The agriculture expo was opening on Friday night with the rodeo beginning on Saturday afternoon at 2:00 p.m. Francine expected that the news media would show up about 1:00 p.m., but she wanted to arrive a little later so the rodeo personnel would be preoccupied.

CHAPTER 8

The Rodeo

Francine slept in on Saturday morning until midmorning. She woke up refreshed and energized. She was excited for today's activities, but as the morning progressed, Francine became more anxious. She didn't know anything about newswriting or rodeos. She wondered if she would even gain entrance. But as she put on her new studded jeans, a pale-gray shirt embellished with bling, and those gorgeous dove-gray boots with the turquoise stitching and tassel, she became more energized. Francine admired herself in the mirror as she started to put her hair into an upswept hairdo fastened by the glitzy hair clips she bought. She kept some hair strands hanging down to avoid looking too professional.

"This day is going to be fun. I don't care what will happen. At least I'll have an adventure to share with my friends," Francine said aloud. "Today, I'm Ann Peck, fun adventurer."

Francine arrived at the fair exposition grounds at 1:00 p.m. She confidently walked up to the ticket counter and asked the lady working in the booth where the media people should enter.

"The media?" asked the woman. "I don't know anything about that. I'm not sure what to tell you."

Francine jumped in to say, "I'm here to cover the rodeo, but I've never been to this particular fairground before. If you could

88

just point me to where the rodeo is being held, I'll be able to find the rest of the newscasters. Sorry, I probably was supposed to go to another entrance."

The lady shrugged and pointed to the stands where the rodeo would be held. She let Francine through the gates without any other question.

I'm in, she thought gleefully. Francine was already proud of herself, although she knew what she was doing was wrong. She could have paid at the entrance just like all the other people crowding into the fairgrounds. But she justified it, because she had not made any money lately and didn't know when she would start to get some better paychecks.

"I shouldn't have spent all this money on these new clothes," she whispered to herself. "When will I ever wear them again?"

The heck with it! I did everything right and lost my job, I was always a good girl, and I'm single and alone, and I need to get some excitement. It may just be a rodeo I'm sneaking into, but to me, it's an adventure, she thought.

She walked to the bleacher stands and located an area that appeared to be a rodeo staging area for contestants and other rodeo helpers. Francine wandered over to that area and adjusted her lanyard bearing her fake name and fake newspaper credentials. As she walked among the people gathered there, she noticed a local news station was setting up a camera to get some video for Monroe, Louisiana's nightly news coverage. She frowned to see that the newscaster was wearing casual business attire and not a rodeo outfit.

Several rodeo participants were gathered together, talking. A group of young men were in cowboy shirts and jeans and wearing leather chaps for effect and protection. All of them were wearing cowboy hats. One of them glanced in Francine's direction and said to the others, "Well, look at that. I wonder if she is our competition."

The cowboys looked in unison at Francine and immediately started one-liners about her.

"Hey, cowgirl, want to ride my horse?"

"I'd like to wrestle you to the ground. Should I get out my lasso?"

89

One of the cowboys imitated a feminine walk and pushed his chest out like he had a bustline. The cowboys thought they were hilarious and laughed and continued their quips. Francine made a mental note that, apparently, sexual harassment hadn't touched the rodeo community yet.

One of the cowboys, a tall thin man that the group called West, left the group and started to walk toward Francine. Two other cowboys quickly joined West and approached Francine.

"Hello, pretty lady. What are you doing here, and what are you doing later on?" the cowboy named West asked with a very Western accent.

He leaned on the corral fence and waited for a reply from Francine. Francine was very uncomfortable although she enjoyed the flirtation. She extended her hand and said, "Hello, I'm Ann Peck from the *Cowgirl Gazette*. I'm here to cover the rodeo."

"You're what?" the cowboy asked. "That's the first time a pretty lady has done that. Did you guys hear this? She's here to cover our rodeo...from a girl's magazine too. I guess we should have shaved and showered, boys."

The other two cowboys laughed. One of them asked her to repeat where she was from, and after she repeated her information, the three guys took the bait. Francine asked for their names, hometowns, how they became rodeo cowboys, etc. She carefully jotted the information down in her notebook. She asked if she could take a couple of pictures of them. The three cowboys posed for pictures, and then one of them asked if she would like to be in the picture. Francine agreed and quickly posed with the other two cowboys while the other man took their picture. Suddenly, a rodeo representative came up to the cowboys and scolded them for not being in the warm-up area. The rodeo was about to begin.

The rodeo representative looked at Francine and walked in her direction. Francine quickly looked down at her notebook and acted as if she were writing down some key information.

"Can I help you, miss?" the representative asked.

"I'm with the *Cowgirl Gazette*, and I was just interviewing some of the contestants," Francine answered.

"I never heard of it," the man stated while looking at her identification. "What event are you covering?"

Francine felt her face flush. She didn't know anything about rodeos and failed to look up information prior to coming to the event. She thought about rodeos that she had seen in the past, probably on a television show.

"I am particularly interested in seeing the tricks with the horses. You know, jumping over fences and fancy trick riding," Francine answered.

The representative frowned and looked at her ID badge again.

"Lady, I don't know what you're pulling, but did you even look at the events at this rodeo? This isn't a horse show. It's a rodeo with calf wrestling and the likes. Why don't you get over to the seats and stop bothering our cowboys," he said defiantly as he strode away.

Francine didn't know how to reply. So she gave him a dirty look and pivoted quickly toward the bleachers. She quickly walked to the bleacher stands and didn't look back. Francine took the opportunity to find a good seat in the bleachers next to the staging area. She merely held up her newspaper lanyard to the others to slide over. The spectators quickly obliged. As she calmed down in her seat, she felt exhilarated. Although the rodeo representative questioned her ability as a newscaster, she still made it into the rodeo. She smiled and confidently sat at the edge of her seat with her notebook in hand.

The rodeo began promptly at 2:00 p.m. Francine was mesmerized as the contestants showed their skills during the calf wrestling event. She watched intensely when the three cowboys she met earlier were performing. Francine noted each contestant's name and roping time in her notebook to appear like she was an authentic newscaster. Francine also watched the local newscaster as he instructed his camera man to video some of the rodeo for today's news footage. It didn't seem as if he knew anything about rodeos either but wanted some footage of the event.

Francine stayed for the entire rodeo, which lasted about two hours. She left the stands shortly before the event ended to avoid any contact with the cowboys she met earlier. After the event, Francine walked around the exposition fairground and enjoyed some local barbecue. She viewed other livestock and watched some horse judging.

While she was at the horse paddock, Francine became aware of someone watching her. She purposely opened her notebook and wrote some gibberish in it while lifting her eyes under her sunglasses to see the person looking at her.

"Oh, oh," Francine muttered.

It was Jack Baldwin, the CFO from the first company Francine visited in the area. He was standing with his family. It was obvious that Jack recognized her. Francine quickly thought of her image. Was there anything unsuitable? Did she look out of place? She hoped she didn't compromise herself dressed up like a blinged-out cowgirl but quickly realized that there was nothing she could do about it anyway.

Jack Baldwin bent down to talk to his wife while looking in Francine's direction and then walked away from his family toward Francine. She didn't have enough time to take off her lanyard when Jack reached her.

"Hi," Jack exclaimed. "I didn't expect to see a Northerner here at the expo."

Francine was aware that he was looking at her cowgirl appearance from head to toe. She placed her hand over her identification lanyard and nonchalantly pulled it over her head and placed it in her purse.

"Hello, Jack," replied Francine. "I thought I would check out the local attraction since I was in the area. It will help me to get to know the people and area since I will be servicing this area."

She noticed that Jack didn't appear too happy to see her in this attire. *Is that my imagination?* she thought.

Francine continued, "Well, I should be going. It was nice to see you, Jack. I hope you and your family have a good time."

They lightly shook hands, and Jack returned to his family. *Whew!* thought Francine. *That could have gone worse.*

Jack Baldwin returned to his family and enjoyed the rest of the exposition, but his mind kept returning to the strange encounter of Francine in a glitzy cowgirl outfit. He couldn't figure out why the woman he thought was highly professional was parading in a costume, and what was with the *Cowgirl Gazette* ID? He typed in *Cowgirl Gazette* in his smartphone and did not find a matching website.

Hmmm, maybe I made a mistake in trusting this woman with our company inventory information? The sales presentation given by Francine seemed too good to be true. They say when it is too good to be true, it usually is. I better keep an eye on what she is doing with our inventory info, Jack thought. As company CFO, he constantly needed to keep an eye on the ethics involved in sales activities as well as ensuring that the company stayed on budget.

The balance of Francine's rodeo adventure went without any problems, and as she drove back to her hotel, she was pleased with the day. She had fun! She thought a bit about her deception but dismissed it by the time she returned to the hotel. When she got back to her hotel room, she looked at the picture of herself in her cowgirl getup. It was a great picture of herself flanked by two handsome young men. She decided to post it on Facebook and wrote a caption, "Having rodeo fun with my friends." The posting wasn't quite the truth, but who would know otherwise?

Francine took a long bath and went to bed. As she lay there, she thought she would think back to the rodeo, but her thoughts were focused on the upcoming workweek. She knew that beginning Monday, she needed to revisit all her new clients and finish up their critical spares lists and give each of them some personal sales attention. She also needed to get back to Best Manufacturing with a quote on their expansion project. Hopefully Chrissy would be able to find all the items on Best's list. She also needed price information back from Sara Johnston.

Back in Wisconsin, at the Pacque residence, Genevieve and her family was visiting when a Facebook alert came up on Viv's phone. It was a picture of her sister, Francine. Francine looked great with her hair upswept into a fancy hairclip. Viv admired the outfit that her sister was wearing, especially the boots with tassels.

"Look at this, Mom. Francine just sent a picture of her with a couple of good-looking guys. They must be some guys that she knows from Magnacraft. It looks like she's doing great with her new territory."

Gertrude and Bertrand Pacque looked at the photo that Viv was holding out in front of them. They were surprised to see their daughter in such a fancy outfit, but both of them smiled with pride.

"That's quite a getup that Francine has on," replied Bertrand. "But she looks beautiful. In fact, that may be the best I've ever seen her. Usually she's in those stuck-up work clothes."

Gertrude gently hit her husband.

"Bertrand! Watch your mouth. Those work clothes have given Francine a good position at Magnacraft. I do like the way she looks in the outfit in the picture. She looks so girlie. I wonder if she is dating one of those guys in the picture."

Viv laughed and said, "Maybe Francine is dating both of them."

That raised everyone's eyebrows, but Gertrude quickly changed the subject to tonight's dinner menu.

The Facebook pictures did not escape other people as well. Francine's sister-in-law was checking her Facebook page when she noticed Francine with the three handsome cowboys. Chrissy smiled and frowned at the same time because the setting looked so out of place for Francine's character. She showed her husband, Gerry.

"What the hell? What's Fanny Pack up to with that sexy outfit? I don't get the cowboys. Where is she anyway?" he yelled to his wife.

Chrissy just shrugged her shoulders and walked into the kitchen. If Gerry would have seen her face, he would have seen a smile as wide as could be.

The Facebook pictures didn't escape her friends at Magnacraft either. Both Sara and Jim saw the pictures but didn't comment on them to each other until after they heard a *click click click* of high heels approach their cubicle. It was Karen Warnette.

"Hi, Sara. Hi, Jim. Did you see the picture of Francine on Facebook? She was dressed like a cowgirl and had a couple of guys hanging on her. Did you see it?" Karen excitedly asked.

Sara answered, "Yes, I saw the posting."

"Well, what is she doing now? Do you know where she is working? I just can't get over how she looks. She looks so different. Didn't you think so?" Karen asked.

She was clearly upset to see Francine in a different venue, as if it didn't compute in Karen's brain. Sara knew where Francine was working but not all the details, and she surely was not going to share that information with Karen.

"All I know is that Francine said she was going down South for a few months. Vacation, I think. It looks like she's having quite a time, doesn't it?" Sara responded.

Karen gave a little frown and nodded her head. "I guess that's it. I just wondered how our friend was doing."

Karen said good-bye to Sara and Jim and walked back toward the executive offices. Sara and Jim looked at each other and quietly started to laugh.

"I can't believe that she gets Francine's promotion without doing the work, and now she's clearly jealous that Francine is having some fun. Arghh! It's unbelievable," Sara retorted.

Jim said, "Yes, sometimes winning is not enough for some people."

Jim shook his head disapprovingly and turned back toward his computer.

It was evening in Galena, Illinois, as Brian Sherman entered a diner for his evening meal. His week went well with the engineering for the overpass construction he was overseeing. The construction crew he was leading was on target for their schedule, and Brian enjoyed the banter of the crew during the day. Brian even met with the crew twice a week for some dinner and beers at one of the local taverns. But Brian was not happy. He had been alone for the past four years, except for occasional dates. He was ready for a relationship again. He had a job, the respect of his engineering community, and his son was doing fine with his mother and stepfather and family. But he was lonely.

Brian thought of the happy time he had with the woman he met last September. Francine. She was exactly the type of woman he wanted. She was sweet, accomplished, pretty, and funny. She held the same Midwestern values that he shared. She understood the frailty of losing a job and shared the joy of getting a new position as he had done. Brian shifted his gaze down onto the tabletop. Why had he blown it with her? Why didn't he call her or answer her calls? He knew why. He still felt inadequate. His divorce and his latest job loss did a job on him. He was afraid that he would be hurt by the confident saleswoman from Chicago.

His gaze was distracted when the waitress delivered a burger with fries to Brian's table and removed the empty bowl of chili. Brian thanked her and started to eat his fries when he glanced at his phone. He had lot of time to kill before going to bed, so he stopped eating and looked at his phone. It was a Facebook posting of Francine beaming into the camera with three good-looking studs next to her.

"Oh, that's just great," Brian muttered.

He slammed the phone down onto the table and continued to eat.

"Waitress," Brian firmly yelled out, "can you give me another beer?"

CHAPTER 9

The Business Grows

Monday morning came, and Francine revisited the companies that were giving her a chance to develop her spares worksheet. She was reviewing some of the stock at one company when her phone rang. It was her sister-in-law, Chrissy.

"Hi, Chrissy. How are you doing?" asked Francine hopefully.

"Hi! I got your list done. I just e-mailed it to you. I hope I did it right," said an excited Chrissy.

"You what? You have it done already? Let me call you back in a couple of minutes after I get a chance to look at it," exclaimed Francine.

The two sister-in-laws ended their call, and Francine quickly checked her e-mail. There was the file listing all the required items by Best Manufacturing. Neat columns were added next to each item with a cross-reference to the Standard Production Distribution Company part number. Actually, there were multiple entries cross-referenced, as SPD handled multiple manufacturing brands. Each one had the SPD price next to the item. Francine glanced at the bottom of the list and found a grand total for each brand.

"Oh my god! This is a big order. I didn't realize how much each of these items cost," exclaimed Francine.

She quickly called Chrissy back and thanked her for the detailed and quick work. She asked her how many hours she spent on the list.

Chrissy answered that this one was gratis, but she hoped that she could do more work for Francine in the future. Francine said she hoped that she would have more work for her soon and asked if she would be interested in helping her if she needed some stock expedited from one location to the next. She explained that the request could come at any time of the day or night because when a plant was down, her strategy was to give them the best service possible to get the company back into service. Francine explained that she herself would be able to do most of the expediting, but there might be times when she needed some help.

"Francine, I sit in the house as a mom 24-7. I love the kids, but I need more. Our kids would rather be with their friends than with me nowadays. Gerry is always gone or he's watching sports in his study. I would love to feel useful. And if I make some spending money now and then, that would be great," Chrissy explained.

"I'm so glad that you are interested. I would really appreciate knowing I have a backup in case I'm tied up with another customer. Thank you so much," Francine said meaningfully.

Francine quickly called Sara Johnston after she hung up with Chrissy. There was no answer, so she left a message, "Hi, Sara, I hate to rush you, but I am in a rush to get the quote on the items that Magnacraft could provide my customer. I need to get back to them quickly or I'll risk losing the sale."

Francine knew that Best Manufacturer had made alliances over the years with certain manufacturers. She surmised that Best asked her to quote as a formality only. The decision could have been already made. But Francine wanted to be quick to respond with a firm quote as soon as possible.

Shortly after leaving the message for Sara, Francine's phone rang.

"I was just finishing the quote," said Sara. "This is a bargain-basement price. I couldn't do any better for our A-list customers."

Francine was more than familiar with the way Magnacraft bracketed customers. A-list customers were those with the highest sales potential. Sara's quote would be the absolute best price she could offer.

For the next two hours, Francine worked on compiling the quote for Best Manufacturing. She compared the total price from each manufacturer's brand and added Magnacraft's items to the list. By the end of the day, Francine had applied the sales discount she was allowed to give through SPD's sales guidelines and printed off several hard copies of her final quote. At 4:00 p.m., she walked into the lobby of Best Manufacturing and asked for Stan Overmeier.

The receptionist contacted Stan and informed him that Francine was in the lobby with a quote package. He quickly came out to meet Francine.

"You have the quote already?" asked Stan.

"Good afternoon, Stan," Francine said while laughing. "I told you that service is my thing. Here is the quote for your expansion requirements. I chose the best brands that could deliver their items by your deadline with the best price. I also was able to get some items through Magnacraft, the company where I used to work. Those items are at an unbelievable discounted rate. All brands are top-notch, and the manufacturers stand by their products in terms of delivery and service. And of course, I could be the liaison for you so that you would only need to contact one person."

Stan looked at the various pages of the quote.

"I'm impressed, Francine," he said. "Of course I have to review line item by line item to make sure that everything is included, but the list seems to be very professionally done. I should be able to give you an answer by the end of next week, because we will have to review all the offers."

Francine and Stan shook hands, and Francine left. She knew that no one could beat her price. If Best Engineering was really serious in letting Francine provide these items, this project would be hers. The total cost was about $160,000. Francine started to compute her commission in her mind.

Something kept popping up in Francine's mind about traveling directly to South Florida. She had only made one stop, in Louisiana, since she started her new job. Francine estimated that it would take her four months longer to get to Florida if she stopped to find new customers in Mississippi, Alabama, and North and Central Florida.

Florida is a long state, she thought. She wanted to be in South Florida over the winter. So Francine made plans to leave for Florida by the end of the next week.

"Hmmm, I didn't really think this all out so well," Francine said to the walls of her hotel room. "I think the development of a zone in the Monroe, Louisiana, area is good. If any company within that zone has a critical spare that another company may need, I can quickly find it on my spreadsheet. But what about getting it there? Chrissy can maybe handle some expediting from a distributor, but what about company to company if I'm not around? Plus, I don't want to put some greasy part in my Audi."

She thought about her issue as she paced her room. Suddenly, a thought jumped into her mind. She grabbed her purse and drove to a local diner that she often frequented. When she arrived, she quickly looked around the diner to locate Mary, her favorite waitress. Francine smiled. Mary was working the counter.

Mary was a local girl that worked in the diner for the past fifteen years. She was a pretty dark-haired woman who was a local favorite among the male customers because of the low-cut blouses she wore. Mary was a flirt. She joked and flirted with all the truck drivers passing through town and with all the locals too. Everyone liked her, but especially those men, as she bent down to give them a coffee warm-up. Francine frequently noticed how the men glanced at Mary's cleavage.

Mary was married to a local man, Billy, who was her high school sweetheart. They married shortly after high school and had one young son. Francine got to know Mary pretty well over the past several weeks as Mary often sat down in Francine's booth and chatted so Francine would not be alone.

"Mary, hi! When you have a second, come over here. I have something to ask you," said Francine.

While she was waiting, Francine ordered her dinner from another waitress. About five minutes later, Mary sat down in the booth.

"Hi, girlfriend. What's up?" she asked.

"Well, I remember you telling me that Billy was doing some construction work, but I was wondering if he may want to do some side work for me?" asked Francine.

She knew from past conversations that Billy's construction jobs were few and far between, but she didn't want to embarrass Mary by bringing up that information.

"Do you have a carpentry job for him? I thought you were from out of town?" Mary questioned.

"Yes, I am, and I'm going to be relocating to Florida area next week. But I will need to shuttle some inventory back and forth between the companies at some point. I thought it may be something that your husband might be interested in," explained Francine.

Francine could see the excitement on Mary's face, as well and her bosom heaving quickly.

"Let me call him. I'll get right back to you," Mary said.

Francine ate her dinner and tried not to notice Mary as she talked to her husband. It was too comical not to laugh. Mary was jumping up and down while she was explaining the offer to her husband. Shortly, Mary returned to Francine's table and said, "Bill will be right here. He was in the neighborhood, so it only made sense that he come on down."

"That'll be fine," Francine replied.

She was happy that Bill was coming to hear more about the job offer immediately, because Francine needed to get someone in place quickly. She finished dinner and pulled out a map of the area. The map showed all the locations for the companies that agreed to the critical equipment network Francine was creating.

Only ten minutes had passed when a good-looking man walked into the diner, holding a young boy's hand. Francine noticed that the man and boy got out of a large pickup truck when they arrived. Having a truck was a good sign for Francine that Mary's husband may be the man she needed.

"Billy Jr.! Oh, you are so handsome," exclaimed Mary as she picked up the small boy and gave him a hug. She pecked her husband's cheek and pointed to Francine. They walked over to Francine's booth, and Mary made introductions.

"This is my husband, Billy Hanson, and my other love of my life, Billy Jr. He's only three, but he is as smart as his daddy and into everything at home," Mary said.

Francine noticed Mary's pride as she introduced her husband and son. She felt a brief moment of jealousy that she didn't have anyone in her life but quickly dismissed her feeling. Francine noticed that Billy was about thirty years old and looked strong as an ox. He was clean-shaven and quite good-looking in an outdoorsy way. He was wearing jeans with a loose T-shirt with a *Duck Dynasty* logo on it. Francine had heard that the *Duck Dynasty* TV personalities were from the Monroe area, so the logo was not a surprise.

After a few minutes of small talk, Francine asked if she could speak to Billy in private. Mary took Billy Jr. by the hand and led him to the diner counter, where she promised to get him a piece of apple pie with a big scoop of ice cream. Billy slid over to the middle of the booth seat and leaned his elbows onto the table.

"I hear that you may have a job for me. Boy, we would really appreciate it. Things have been pretty slow at the company I'm working at, and Mary doesn't make very much here at the diner," Billy said.

Francine immediately felt bad for them. Raising a family on diner tips and occasional construction jobs had to be difficult. But she really didn't know how much work she could provide for him. She quickly chose her words and continued to think of possibilities as she spoke.

"I do need some help, but I don't know how much help yet. It could grow into a big job if we're lucky. What I have to offer is that I need someone who can pick up some small-equipment items and deliver it to certain companies when needed. Time would be the important thing. I'm trying to create a network of companies in the area that can use each other's critical spare part inventories rather than each one individually carrying all parts. When a piece of equipment is needed, I need someone to hustle it over to the company needing it quickly. There will be times when the item would have to be picked up at the Monroe Airport as well and delivered to a company. Does that sound like something you could do?" Francine inquired.

"That seems simple enough. I have a pickup truck and even have a trailer if I needed it," Billy said proudly.

"What I need you to understand is that the success and growth of this business will be dependent on how fast you can get the part to the company that needs it. It may be in the middle of the night or on weekends. As the companies gain trust in us, they will give us more business. I also will be adding additional companies to the network, so the territory will grow," Francine explained.

"What would the pay be?" Billy asked.

Francine wasn't quite prepared for that question and had struggled prior to Billy arriving at the diner to come up with some wage. She had to remember that she wasn't getting any large paychecks yet either. But she did know that she could charge some expediting fee onto the price of the spare part, so she threw out a proposal.

"Billy, I'm not quite sure of the amount of time you will be required or the frequency. So how about we start with this. I would be prepared to give you $50 for the first hour of a pickup and $15 for each hour after that. That should pay for your gas and your time. Do you think that would be fair?" Francine asked.

She could see the frown on Billy's face as he tried to absorb what Francine just said.

"How many hours do you think it will take per job?" Billy asked.

"I just don't know. It may only take an hour, but it may be several hours if you have to go to the airport and wait for the item to be unloaded. I'm not even sure how often you would be needed to get anything. I'm just starting this program in this area, so I don't have any history to give you a better idea," Francine said.

"Hmmm, I was hoping to get some hours in. It shouldn't be a problem to leave my construction job if I have a pickup or to leave Mary and my son at night or on the weekend. I just hoped it would be more regular," Billy said sadly.

Mary walked over to the table and gave Billy and Francine a piece of pie and coffee on the house. Billy smiled at her, but Francine suspected he was hoping that the pie didn't come out of Mary's check. Francine suspected that it would.

"Just a minute, Billy. Let me think about something," Francine said as she tilted her head back and closed her eyes. About a minute passed when Francine sat upright and started to speak.

"I think I remember Mary telling me that you were good at computers. Does that mean that you spend time on the computer playing games and surfing the net, or do you know any computer programs?" Francine asked.

Billy's eyebrows raised as he proudly said, "I went to the technical school here to learn more about computers. I was pretty good at it. I know some programs like Word and Excel. Is that what you mean?"

"Yes! That's great! I may be able to offer you some other work. My territory is going to be from the Monroe area, in Louisiana, to the southwestern tip of Florida. So I believe I will be traveling between here and Florida monthly. I'll probably be in the Monroe area for a week every six weeks. In the interim that I am not here, I could use someone to go into the companies within my network and check their inventory of critical parts. Since this is my own spreadsheet, no one will be systematically updating the inventory. Each plant has their own inventory system to reorder parts, but since my spreadsheet is to be used as shared critical parts between different companies, no one would update my spreadsheet. What I'm proposing is that you could go into the plants and check the stock against what is on the spreadsheet. If there is a change, you would contact me," Francine explained.

Billy looked at her questioningly. It was apparent that he did not understand.

Francine continued, "Are you free tomorrow? I would like to show you what I'm talking about. This would be a job you could do when you have a free couple of hours from your construction job. I couldn't pay you a lot, but I could pay you maybe $15 per hour? We would have to set a maximum amount of hours you spend per week because otherwise, I'll go broke."

Billy's eyes opened wide. He said that would work fine for him and that the money would really help out his family. Francine looked at the counter and saw little Billy Jr. smearing ice cream all over his face while his mother laughed and grabbed a napkin to clean her son.

Francine felt happy that she was going to be able to do something to help this cute couple out.

Billy and Francine talked about the offer awhile more and agreed to meet tomorrow at Best Manufacturing Company. Francine was looking for an excuse to stop into Best before she left town anyway.

When Francine arrived back at her hotel, she did some calculations to see what she could afford to give Billy in terms of maximum hours. The truth was on the paper. She really could afford nothing more than the pickup and delivery wage, which she could pass onto the customer. As for the inventory job that she just offered Billy, those wages would have to come out of her pocket. Francine stared out the window blankly. She couldn't go back on the offer now, plus she really needed someone to check those inventories while she was traveling elsewhere. *Now what do I do?* she wondered.

"Well, I guess I'll have to sit on the beach for my entertainment when I get to Florida because there'll be no money left for me," she said to herself.

She went back to her calculation paper and put together a budget. She needed to cover her share of expenses for rent and utilities on her townhouse in Chicago, her car lease, her hotel bills, and food. She had only negotiated $4,000-per-month allowance with SPD for six months and after six months, nothing but commission. If she was in the red, she would have to cover her monthly overage with the $8,000 in her bank account. Francine knew that if her new territory and strategy didn't kick in by the end of year, she would have to return to Chicago and look for some other type of work.

"No! I'm not going to be a failure in this job. I know it's a winner. I just have to pray that my instincts are leading me into the right direction," she whispered. She sat in the side chair and closed her eyes, wishing for a nap. *Hopefully,* she thought, *when I wake up, I'll know what to do.*

An hour later, Francine, got up from the chair. She wasn't able to fall asleep because she was thinking about the ridicule she would get from her family if they knew the truth about her new job. They didn't know that she had lost her job at Magnacraft and had taken on this seemingly low-potential territory. They would be shocked and disappointed that Francine didn't take on a more traditional job.

Francine thought about her brother, Gerry, sitting in his office with adoring potential athletes listening to his every word. Gerry wouldn't understand Francine's remote-territory job either. He would say something inappropriate like, "Well, Fanny Pack, if you would just get some plastic surgery and a boob job, maybe someone would want to marry you."

Francine knew he would be kidding, but the words would still sting. She was 100 percent sure that he would say something inappropriate. She didn't dwell on what Genevieve would say because Viv wouldn't say anything mean. She just would not understand why Francine was having any problems, because everything came so easily to Viv. Finally, Francine took a long, hot shower and went to bed. Sleep came easily to her this time.

A jolt of lightning woke Francine in the morning. It was a hot day in Louisiana, and it appeared it would be a wet day too. Francine decided to dress in another one of her fabulous two-piece dresses. She wanted to look professional and successful, as if she didn't have a care in the world. Her dress was pale-blue with some insets of a brighter blue. The jacket was bright blue. Francine fastened her hair in an updo and put on a large white necklace with matching small earrings. She grabbed her briefcase and put on her five-inch heels before leaving the room.

She met Billy at 9:30 a.m. in the Best Manufacturing Company parking lot. She was happy to see that Billy dressed in khaki pants and a striped short-sleeved shirt. Francine knew that he would make a good impression on the factories as her local liaison. After a brief explanation of why she and her associate were at the factory, the receptionist pointed them into the direction of the stockroom. The receptionist said she would inform someone from the staff that they were in the plant.

Francine and Billy went to the stockroom and looked at the various aisles of inventory.

Billy said, "I have to inventory all of this?"

"No, Bill, not all of their inventory. We are interested in only the spare parts that run the factory. Some of those items are called critical parts because if that part breaks down, the plant cannot run. Our spreadsheet lists only those parts," Francine explained. "See those bright-green tags on those parts on the shelf?" Francine asked. "Those are the parts that they identified as critical. You'll find each one identified on your spreadsheet with a description, picture, stock location, part number, brand number, etc."

"Yes, ma'am. I see it now. Let me see if I can find these listed here," Billy exclaimed.

Francine was impressed at how quickly Billy caught on to the spreadsheet. He was equally at ease looking at the spare parts and soon was climbing up stock ladders to look at higher shelves.

"I see what you want me to do. I just have to spot-check to see that each critical part is still there. If it is missing, it was used, and wouldn't be available for another company in the network if they needed it," Billy said.

"That's exactly right. You learned fast. Do you think you could handle the spreadsheet and change quantities or part numbers when you needed an edit?" Francine asked.

"That would be easy for me. In fact, I can see already that I would want to add another column for notes and would want to make a lookup table to sort through the inventories more easily. You know, maybe I could even categorize the companies into subzones, with the ones in the middle location as a home base and maybe subzones for certain distances from home. You know, like a zone for each ten miles or something?" Brian suggested.

Francine smiled. She knew he was the person for the job. Billy would be an asset and could improve her business model.

She nodded to him. "I think that would be a great idea."

A man approached them as they stood within the inventory aisles.

"Hello, Francine, I didn't expect to see you this morning," a voice announced.

It was Stan Overmeier. Francine tensed up even though he was the person she had hoped to run into. She was anxious to hear about her quote.

"Hello, Stan. I would like to introduce you to Bill Hanson. Bill is going to be assisting you and me when I am traveling out of this territory," Francine explained.

Francine was careful to introduce Billy as Bill so it would sound more professional.

The men shook hands and quickly started up a conversation about the area. Since both men were locals, there were several connections between them. The largest connection was Mary Hanson, Billy's wife, who Stan knew from the diner. When their conversation ended, Stan asked Francine to go to his office. He invited Bill as well. Then he left with a smile and walked toward the office complex.

Francine said quietly to Bill, "Well, this may be it. I left Stan a big quote for an expansion project. I'm hoping to get that project more than I can ever explain. You know, this is a new job for me too, so I'm very anxious to get a sale and to gain some recognition."

"I'll keep my fingers crossed. If you get the project, there may be some work in that for me too," Bill said.

"Yes, there certainly will be. You would be able to oversee that all the parts arrived here in time with good quality. It would help to have another set of eyes check in project parts as they can sometimes disappear quickly," Francine said.

Bill and Francine went to wash their hands from the dirty parts they were touching and entered Stan's office. He directed them to sit down in the two chairs in front of his desk. He was holding the quote package that Francine provided him the prior week. Francine could see three other quote proposals on his desk.

Stan put down the quote and stared at Francine while he said, "Francine, I have one question for you, and I would appreciate an honest answer."

Francine could feel an instant heat flush on her back. She wished she had taken off her jacket before she sat down.

"Yes, Stan. What is it?" she replied.

"I have four quotes in front of me. Three of them are from people that I have done business with for years. One of the three is a friend of mine, and we're fishing buddies as well," Stan said. "All three of the other quotes are from people I respect, and those three have quotes that are very similar and, in my opinion, are fair.

"Now, we get to your quote. I don't know you from Adam, and you are not a local who I've done business with before. Your quote is far, and let me say it again, *far* lower than the other three. Frankly, I don't believe it is correct. I don't know how it can be. Do you have an answer for the difference, Francine?"

Francine nodded as she gathered her thoughts and words. "Can I ask you a couple of questions before I answer your question?"

"Go ahead," said Stan.

"Do the companies that provided the three quotes have a business with a building, workers, company vehicles, and so on?" Francine said as she motioned her hand toward the various fixtures in Stan's office.

"Yes, I suppose they do," offered Stan.

Francine straightened in her chair and slightly leaned forward. She said, "My quote is correct. I checked every entry, and the quote can be pivoted to show your quote list cross-reference to my quote or vice-versa. The difference in price is that I am just me, except for Bill, on a part-time basis. I don't have a fancy office. I drive my own personal car, I don't employ a staff. I don't have any overhead. The quote I gave you is the best price from the resources that I have, mainly Standard Product Distribution, the company that employs me, and some from my old employer, Magnacraft, where I went directly to my contacts to get you the best price."

Stan didn't answer immediately. He just stared at Francine as if she weren't real.

Stan said, "Well, I just don't know what to say. These people are my friends. Like I said before, even my fishing buddy. They are locals. They expect to get the job. But your quote is so much less. I guess I never really thought about their added costs." He stopped talking and looked blankly at the wall. Billy, not knowing what to do or say, looked at Francine helplessly.

"Stan, I am all about the sales relationship. No, I might not be your fishing partner, but I am the best salesperson you could ever deal with. I left Magnacraft as a top sales representative, and I didn't get to that point by disappointing my customers or my company," Francine said. Quickly she added, "I want you to know that my intention is to build a strong trust between the network of companies that I am going to be doing business with. Sales relationships are an art. In my opinion, it is getting to be a lost art. I got you the best prices through my relationship with the people that represent the brands offered in this quote. My quote is based on their quote to me plus my commission, not a penny more. And I would like to add, since I have a strong relationship and credibility with those brands included in the quote, if there is anything defective with any item, I will get that item replaced. You shouldn't have to lift a finger to try to rectify an issue." Francine ended her explanation.

Bill looked at her again and raised his eyebrows as way of compliment. Francine smiled at him and returned her gaze to Stan. Stan shook his head as way of accepting Francine's explanation. Then he picked up the other quotes and reviewed the Total page at the end of each quote.

Stan stood up, and Francine and Bill took his lead as an invitation to leave. They stood up, and Francine bent down to pick up her briefcase.

"What are you doing?" asked Stan.

"Nothing, I thought you wanted us to leave," answered Francine.

"No, I was just standing up to come over and shake the hands of my new project representative," Stan answered. He smiled and walked around the table to shake Francine's and Bill's hands.

"Congratulations. You got the job. I will have the approval signatures done today. Can you stop back about four o'clock to pick up the contract?" Stan asked.

"Absolutely. I will see you at four o'clock. Thank you, Stan." Francine said. She wanted to say something to the effect that he won't be sorry for giving her the contract, but she thought it was a cheesy, overused line.

Francine and Billy walked out to the parking lot. The rain had stopped, but Francine hadn't noticed. She was shaking. She briefly wondered if she would get sick and vomit in Best's parking lot. *Wouldn't that be great*, Francine thought. Soon the nauseous feeling was substituted for a state of euphoria as she remembered the commission she would receive on this project. She wasn't going to fail.

"You were really something to watch in there. I couldn't believe it when you started giving your answer to Stan. Really something to see," Billy said before getting into his truck. "I can't wait to start."

Francine thanked Billy for coming with her today and told him that she was impressed with how he presented himself. Billy smiled. He said he couldn't wait to tell his wife about the day.

Francine drove to an abandoned parking lot and parked her car. She had to settle down and relax. She felt so exhilarated and relieved.

"I got the job," she said to herself as she sank into her car seat and clapped.

Since she was working on straight commission, except for the six-month starter salary she negotiated from SPD, her commission share was 15 percent. Her share of the $160,000 project would be approximately $22,000. She wouldn't receive it until the products were received, but she estimated that it would be paid in full by January. Her $8,000 bank balance would suffice until then.

She promptly returned to Best Manufacturing at 4:00 p.m. and picked up the signed contract. She then called Sam Jr. at Standard Product Distribution to tell him the good news. Her next call was to her sister-in-law, Chrissy, to congratulate her on doing such a great job on the quote package.

Francine stopped to eat at the diner and was hoping to see Mary. But Mary had the day off. Francine hoped that the family was having a good evening celebrating Bill's new opportunity. As she sat at the diner thinking about the Hanson family, her thoughts drifted to her own family. She hadn't called her parents since she left Chicago. It was time to call them.

"Hi, Mom, it's Francine! How are you and Dad?" Francine asked.

"We have been worried sick about you. It's bad enough that you lived in Chicago, but now we never know where you are," her mother said.

"I know. I've been busy with my new territory. I'm in Louisiana right now, but I will be leaving for Florida in a couple of days," Francine answered.

"How is your new territory? Are there any women that you can travel with?" her mom asked.

"No, I'm strictly on my own. But I've made some friends, and business is good," Francine commented.

"We all saw your new cowboy friends. And you! Why were you wearing that cowgirl outfit? Are you dating any of those guys in the picture? Do they come from a good family? Francine, I'm worried about you," Gertrude Pacque said.

"They are not my boyfriends. But I did have a very good time attending a rodeo event. They were clients of one of the customers. We all went to the rodeo as a company fun event," Francine lied.

She felt bad about the lie, but she wanted to avoid more conversation about the pictures. Francine and her mom spent several more minutes talking about the family and catching up on news. When they hung up the phone, Francine said to herself, "Well, that's it. Now I'm going to go to hell. I can't even tell my mother the truth."

Francine may have felt bad initially, until she realized that her family believed she still worked for Magnacraft.

"She bought it! All I have to do is tell them what they want to hear, and everyone will stay off my back," Francine said aloud.

Francine smiled and thought about other scenarios she could tell them to avoid telling them the truth.

The rest of the week was spent on finishing up details in Louisiana. Bill was trained and agreed to work one to two hours per day on inventory in the plants and up to four hours per day when the stock for Best Manufacturing started to arrive.

Francine worked with Bill to set him up officially as a contract employee. She decided that she would have to set herself up as her own company as well so she could pay her employees.

"I better come up with a name and also get some business cards," Francine said. "I have my SPD business cards, but I'll also be my own company."

She started to think up some business names, but Francine Pacque Ltd., LLC was going to be her first choice. She made a note to talk to one of her Chicago attorney friends to find out how to go about getting a limited liability company (LLC).

CHAPTER 10

Florida

Francine checked out of the motel on Saturday morning. She stopped at the diner for a quick breakfast before leaving for South Florida. The ride would be a thousand-mile drive, and Francine planned to do it in two days. She was very interested in the small cities she would be driving through en route as those cities could be included in future territories. Francine's plan was to travel directly to Naples, Florida, to develop that area as zone 2. She planned to stay in Southwest Florida until December and return to Monroe, Louisiana area prior to returning to Chicago for the Christmas holidays. After the holidays, Francine would return to the South and concentrate on the Southern areas of Mississippi, Alabama, and Georgia to develop more zones prior to returning to Florida, where she hoped to stay for the balance of the winter.

Francine's self-made territory, from Louisiana and stretching to Southwest Florida, was large. She carefully planned an itinerary so that she could travel to each zone for one week within a six-week window. That meant that she wanted six total zones, with each zone consisting of a network of companies within a two-hundred-mile radius. It was an aggressive plan for one person to handle, but she had to start with some plan.

114

Francine left her motel in Delhi, Louisiana, and traveled south to Interstate 20. She would take the interstate until she reached Montgomery, Alabama. She knew that Montgomery was within the territory of another SPD sales rep, so Francine headed toward Georgia, taking smaller highways until she reached Albany. Francine made a mental note that Albany, Georgia, could be the center of another of her zones. She rode around the area to survey the small companies in that area. She found many companies that could be potential clients, including pump, power, containerization, irrigation, and tooling businesses.

Francine decided to drive a little farther toward the Georgia-Florida state boundary before finding a hotel. There were many choices along Interstate 75. Francine pulled into one lot and quickly pulled out her smartphone to look up prices. She couldn't waste any money frivolously on a high-priced hotel.

The ride into Florida the next day was exciting for Francine. She opened the sunroof on her Audi and turned off the radio to take in the Florida air. She was surprised that the northern Florida terrain had trees similar to those where she grew up, but as she traveled toward the Ocala area, Francine started to see yet a different terrain of rolling fields with edges of trees. She smiled every time she passed a horse ranch on the ride and thought about how lucky those horses were to live in such a beautiful location. Francine pulled off the highway and into one of the Ocala exits. She took a break to stretch her legs and purchase lunch. She knew that SPD did not have a sales rep for Ocala but did have one for the Tampa area, which wasn't so far away. She made a mental note to pursue Ocala as a possible center for another zone.

Francine continued driving south on Interstate 75 with her final destination of Naples, Florida, in her mind. The next four hours of driving were so much fun for her. The ease of driving down a flat highway, without the potholes made by snow and ice in the North, was wonderful. She drove past Highway 4, the highway that would find Tampa to the west and Orlando to the east, and continued her path south.

Soon she was traveling past the exits for Sarasota, another possible zone in Florida. Francine made a mental note. After three hours of driving, Francine pulled off the highway in Fort Myers. She knew she only had another half hour or so to reach Naples, but she was thirsty, needed gas, and especially needed to stretch her legs again. Her automobile was very comfortable, but hours upon hours of driving were starting to cramp her legs. A much-needed break was appreciated.

The temperature in Fort Myers showed eighty-three degrees on her car dashboard. *Perfect,* Francine thought as she peered down the street and saw nothing but palm trees and dazzling foliage. "I can't believe all the flowers that bloom on the bushes," Francine said to herself. After her break, she sat into her car and sighed.

"Well, this is it, girlfriend," Francine said to herself. "I'm almost in Naples. This is going to be the start of my new life."

She looked on her smartphone for a hotel app that showed locations for hotels in the Naples area. She enlarged the map and studied it briefly.

"I have to be careful about where I decide to stay in Naples. I need to have a hotel that is cheap, that I can stay for a month, but I still need to look successful," Francine said.

She scanned the various hotel names, and slowly a smile appeared on her face.

"Maybe this will work?" she said questioningly.

Francine found the cheapest hotel in the area close to the highway for her primary hotel, and she wrote down several ritzy hotel names in case she wanted to impress someone. Francine started her car and turned back onto the highway. Approximately forty minutes later, she turned into the hotel chain posting the cheapest rate.

Although the hotel looked fine, Francine only booked a two-night stay. She wanted to look around Naples before booking for a longer period. She removed two suitcases, her laptop, and her briefcase out of her car. She hoped that she would be removing her clothes bags with her fancy clothes from the trunk soon.

"I should be able to wear some of those clothes here in Naples," Francine said confidently. "In fact, I think I may pick up a newspaper tomorrow and see what kind of society or charity events are coming up in Naples. Yes, I'm sure I'll find somewhere to wear those clothes." With that thought in mind, she quietly entered the hotel, ordered a pizza to be delivered, and enjoyed her first night in South Florida alone.

Francine slept late on Sunday, and when she arose, she felt like a new woman. She had a leisurely breakfast compliments of the hotel and then decided to take a tour of Naples. She changed out of her jeans and T-shirt and put on a pair of white linen pants coupled with a beige sleeveless knit top. Francine removed a small jewelry case from her suitcase and found a long turquoise necklace that would complement her outfit. She also found a comfortable pair of sandals to wear while driving, but she took along a pair of heeled beige sandals as well. She decided to take the heels for when she went to lunch or walk through some fancier hotels. She knew that she needed to look the part for the adventure she was planning.

The day in Naples was gloriously sunny, and Francine passed many gated communities with high fences. She could slightly see the large rooflines of multimillion-dollar properties peeking out over the fence tops. The trees, flowers, and bushes were lushly planted with blooming flowers of all colors. Francine maneuvered her car toward the marina area and past Tin City, a local favorite shopping and eating location. She followed a Mercedes northbound in the center of town and noticed the largest and most beautiful banks and investment buildings that she ever saw. She drove briefly north to take in the various shops and businesses, but her destination was South Fifth Avenue, where she wanted to walk on the old streets of Naples and take advantage of the numerous eateries and shops. Her GPS guided her back to South Fifth Avenue, the center of old Naples, where she was lucky enough to find a car pulling out of a street parking spot. Francine parked her car, changed into her high heels, and reapplied some bright-orange lipstick.

The avenue was not as busy as Francine imagined this late Sunday morning. It was early November, not the high season time of January through April, so the people walking on the avenue were either full-time residents or travelers taking advantage of lower rates prior to the winter. Some people were extremely dressed up among others that were jogging in sports clothes or casually attired. Francine imagined that some of the families walking down the avenue had come directly from church services and were looking for a light breakfast or lunch. She heard different languages spoken and different English dialects between the walkers. But one thing was for certain, the town oozed money. Her verification was when she glanced at the ring fingers of the women walking by her. Francine never imagined diamonds so large. Even one of the joggers, running alongside her husband pushing a stroller, was wearing a ring so large that it looked unreal. *Was it unreal?* Francine asked herself. No, this was a place unlike the cities she was used to. Even Chicago, with its Magnificent Mile, did not have the concentration of money that Naples had.

After a wonderful Italian lunch at Vergina Restaurant on Fifth Avenue, Francine was interested to drive to another area she read about called Vanderbilt Beach. She drove northbound on Gulf Shore Boulevard and wandered through beautifully named streets, such as Mooring, Banyan, and Turtle Hatch. Many of the communities were gated, but Francine still was able to enjoy true Floridian home structures. The architecture was so different than the type of housing in her native Wisconsin or Illinois. She immediately loved the neighborhood.

When she arrived at the Vanderbilt Beach area, she was disappointed to find all gated communities. But she noticed a sign for Ritz-Carlton Hotel among the shrubbery. She immediately drove into the entrance.

Francine knew in her heart that what she was about to do was wrong. She planned to invent a lifestyle in Naples so that she could be part of the community. She knew her communication skills could get her access to some of the places she hoped to visit, and she wanted access to some of the local residents who may be able to help her professionally. Her problem was money. Since she didn't have any, she decided to act like she did, or to at least act like she belonged within this community. Francine took a big sigh, closed her eyes while she put her mind in character.

"Well, here it goes," Francine said to herself as she got out of the car.

The Ritz-Carlton Hotel was a high-dollar hotel and a place where Francine could say she was staying. Francine gave her car keys to the valet and walked into the hotel while playing with her phone, trying to look somewhat bored. She glanced at the concierge and purposefully looked away from him toward the front desk.

"Welcome to the Ritz-Carlton, miss. What can I help you with today?" a young woman clerk asked.

Without saying hello, Francine replied, "I may be interested in a room here, preferably a suite, on my next visit to the area. What are your accommodations?"

The young woman quickly pulled out a brochure that showed several views of different types of rooms and suites. Francine studied the brochure and spotted one of the suites with a central sitting room and a beautiful view of the water.

"May I see this room?" Francine asked while pointing to a suite picture.

The woman typed on her computer, possibly seeing if one of the suites was available for viewing.

"When were you interested in booking?" she asked Francine.

Francine continued to type into her phone, as if something were very important. She looked up and smiled while she responded, "I'm not sure when I'll be back in this area, but I want to be sure to get a room I would enjoy. Do you have one to show me? I would also be interested in a quick tour of this hotel."

"Yes, we have several suites available, but once the holiday season begins, suites and rooms book quickly, so I urge you to make your reservation as soon as you can. I will ask one of our managers to escort you through the hotel. May I have your name?"

Francine nodded and removed one of the various business cards that she had printed prior to leaving Monroe. Francine thought, *Thank goodness for priority mail or I wouldn't have received these cards on time.* She handed the clerk a shiny white card with black script handwriting. The card had a floral design on the corner. The card simply read, Francine Pacque Ltd., LLC. It had a website, francine-pacque.com, as well as Francine's personal telephone number printed on the lower right-hand corner. The front desk clerk took the card and read it.

"Thank you, Ms. Pacque. One of our personal assistants will be with you shortly. Please have a seat and some lemon water while you wait," the front desk clerk suggested.

Francine thanked her and paced the lobby slowly while she waited. The hotel had a unique ambiance that made clients comfortable within the rich appointments. Francine surveyed the various exits from the lobby, noting where the concierge desk, the dining and bar area, rooms, and pool areas were located. Soon, another young woman appeared and introduced herself as Francine's escort around the hotel. After brief introductions, including verifying the areas that Francine wanted to view, the two of them walked to the elevators. They would start the tour at the suite.

They went to the third floor and down the richly appointed hallway to a terrace suite. The escort opened the door and walked into the room skillfully, turning on the first light switch to illuminate the suite. The escort continued to the French door and slid the translucent curtains open to gain a complete view before opening the doors to the private terrace balcony.

Francine was impressed with the beauty of the room. She slowly walked around the circumference of the room, nodding her head in approval. She was controlled enough to not show any emotion, as if staying in a suite were natural to her. Francine walked onto the balcony and looked at the amenities below. As she stood there, she thought about Brian Sherman. She wished he would be standing here with her now, but she blew it. Somehow she turned him off, and now he wouldn't even return her phone calls.

"Would you like to see the bedroom?" the hotel escort asked.

"Yes, of course," Francine answered as she turned around to reenter the inside suite.

The bedroom and en suite were lush and beautiful. Francine slowly walked around the room.

"May I take a couple of pictures? I would like to have a few future reference pictures if I decide to reserve the suite," Francine asked.

"Of course. Take as many pictures as you like," replied the escort.

Francine took three pictures, one of the main suite, one of the outside balcony view, and one of the bedroom.

"What is this room number again?" Francine asked.

The hotel escort provided the room number.

"Do you have others similar to this one, and do you have others with two bedrooms if I decide to return with my uncle?" Francine asked.

The hotel escort answered that the hotel had several two-bedroom suite options. Francine made a note on her smartphone of the club, royal, and presidential suite names.

"Thank you. I'm satisfied with this room. Can we now look at the amenities the hotel features? I may be staying here for an extended amount of time, so I definitely need to look at your spa, fitness room, restaurants, and the like," Francine said coldly.

The hotel escort and Francine spent the next hour reviewing the hotel amenities. Francine wanted to take more pictures, but she controlled herself to only listen and look at the items. After the tour was complete, Francine thanked the woman and handed her a gratuity while shaking her hand. The twenty-dollar bill disappeared from Francine's hand.

Francine proceeded to the front door, and the valet quickly asked her for her valet ticket. Shortly thereafter, her car was driven onto the main drive, and the valet held the door open for Francine to get in her car. She thanked the valet and shook his hand. The ten-dollar bill disappeared from Francine's hand quickly. *Boy, this could get expensive*, Francine thought to herself as she drove off.

Francine stopped at McDonald's on her way back to the hotel and grabbed a burger, fries, and a Diet Coke. She ate her dinner in her small hotel room near the interstate while thinking of the Ritz-Carlton. Francine checked her e-mails while she ate. She had some minor questions from Billy Hanson and several e-mails on pricing specials from Standard Product Distribution but nothing important. Her attention focused on the pictures she took today. She posted the three pictures on Facebook with only one description—Naples, Florida.

Her plan was to stay in Naples, or its vicinity, for the winter months. Francine knew she could generate sales within a network of companies in the area to make another zone. The Naples zone would be the second one of the six she planned to make. Monroe was the first zone. The other four would be from the areas in between the thousand-mile distance from Monroe to Naples. Her thoughts drifted to her money situation preventing the lifestyle she wanted. She didn't have the money or the connections to live in Naples. Francine made a pouting expression as she reflected on her situation.

Naples, Florida, is a city of approximately twenty thousand full-time residents. The population grows by another twelve thousand snowbirds, when northerners escape the cold weather and snow to reside for three to six months in southern Florida. Naples has neighborhoods that boast some of the highest home values in the United States, such as Port Royal and Aqualane Shores, because of their beautiful white-sand beaches on the Gulf of Mexico or deep-water access for yachting.

CHAPTER 11

Zone 2—Naples

Francine thought about the possibility of gaining access to some of the well-to-do residents. She picked up a copy of the *Naples Daily News* and started to read up on upcoming activities. She had a plan. Although it wasn't the high season, there was bound to be some local society fund-raiser occurring in November. Francine was correct. She spotted an event fund-raiser for Children's Hospital in Fort Myers scheduled on November 10.

"That's next week Saturday. I'm in luck!" Francine exclaimed.

She read the event details and noted the contact person's name and number. *Hmmm, $200 per person plus a raffle. I guess I'll have to buy a ticket and put in for the raffle another $100 or so, $300 total to hopefully meet some of the Naples notoriety. It's cheap, I'll have a good time, and can wear some of my fancy clothes.*

Francine wasted no time calling the event contact person the following day. She was delighted to hear that the event was a formal attire event. Francine's hunch to take her evening attire along with her on this trip was correct. She gave her full name and credit card number to the coordinator, but when she was asked for her address, Francine quickly became nervous.

"I would prefer to pick up my ticket rather than have it mailed," she quickly told the event contact.

"Well, that's fine, but we do like to have our client's address on file for future mailings," the woman explained.

Francine thought about receiving multiple pleas for additional funds in the future, but she would deal with that later.

"I can give you my home address in Chicago, but please don't mail the ticket there," Francine replied and then continued to give her townhouse address to the woman.

"And may I ask where you are residing while you are in the Naples area?" asked the woman.

"Well, at the Ritz Carlton, of course. But I still prefer to pick up my ticket," Francine lied.

She was proud of herself and the little ruse she was creating. She went out to her car and opened the trunk. At the bottom of the truck was a thick orange garment bag. Francine picked up the bag and another satchel within the trunk.

"It's time to get out my party clothes," Francine exclaimed.

She returned to her room and hung the unopened bag onto the shower rod. She carefully unzipped the bag and glided several garments out of the bag. A long emerald-green dress with ornate beading was the first item to be removed.

"I remember when I bought this one at the annual Saks sale. I went there with Sara Johnston. We both bought designer gowns for future unknown use. This is probably what I'll wear next Saturday night, but I want to see what else I brought here," Francine said as she gently slid her hand down the folds of the chiffon dress.

The bag contained three other garments, including a black cocktail dress, a splendid organza floral dress and jacket, and a fitted pink silken dress. All were designer dresses. All were expensive outfits. All were perfect for whatever Naples adventure Francine might undertake.

She placed the satchel onto her bed. The satchel was a long black fabric bag that could be hung by its hanger onto a rod. But Francine kept it on the bed and unzipped it carefully. Inside the bag were eight smaller fabric boxes that Francine purchased online. They were shoe bags. Francine carefully removed each bag and unlatched the front clear panel. She carefully withdrew one shoe from each bag. The shoes were special to Francine. She bought high-end shoes from Jimmy Choo, Prada, Manolo Blahnik, and others. Each shoe was either fabulously high, bright, or embellished. Francine carefully brought each shoe over to the emerald green dress to see how it looked with the dress. After careful consideration, Francine returned all the shoe boxes back into the satchel except for one box. That box contained a pair of bright-red ankle strap high heels by Jimmy Choo.

"Fabulous!" Francine exclaimed.

She took the shoe box to the closet and deposited them into the small closet safe.

"I don't want these babies to walk away," she said as she locked the safe.

Francine put the remaining shoe beauties back in the black satchel and zipped the bag tightly. She returned the satchel and locked it back into her car along with the garment bag containing all her expensive dresses. Then she walked into the hotel lobby and extended her reservation for an additional two weeks, making sure that she asked for an extended stay discount.

Monday morning came, and Francine knew it was time to hit the pavement and find clients for her Naples zone. Her criteria for a zone remained the same, a minimum of ten companies within a two-hundred-mile radius. She would solicit for more companies each time she visited the area.

To her delight, there were an ample number of companies in the outskirts of Naples, including some in the construction fabrication industry, plumbing, chemical, injection molding, and custom fabrication. It was definitely a smaller number of industries than she was used to in the Chicago area, but there was a market for her.

It was a hot and windy day in Naples, and Francine chose to wear a pencil skirt with a silken print sleeveless blouse. *No need for a jacket today*, Francine thought, but then she changed her mind and brought along a light sweater. She wore simple jewelry and low heels as she didn't know the types of factory environments she might be entering.

By ten o'clock she was on the road, armed with a map full of dots for the companies she wished to visit and footnotes for each dot outlining whatever business detail she could find on the Internet. Francine struck out at the first four companies she visited. They were small companies and didn't seem to understand the critical equipment inventory implications. Most were family-owned and didn't want to share any information with her. But Francine was determined to press on until she found her first client.

She drove until she spotted a local area parking lot with several trees bordering the lot. Carefully pulling into the one spot that had shade, Francine took a Diet Coke out of her personal cooler and opened the drink. She also removed an apple she was able to take that morning from her hotel's breakfast bar. It wasn't the Naples experience that she dreamed about, but she had some time to regain her energy before the afternoon sales visits.

Francine struck gold on her next visit to the custom manufacturer. She had asked for the CFO when she arrived at the factory, and after some explanation to the receptionist, a woman in her midforties came into the lobby and greeting her.

"Hello, I'm Angie Fratilo, the CFO of Creative Fabrication. What can I do for you?" the woman asked.

Francine introduced herself and went on to explain that she was new in the Naples area, but she had successfully started a network of companies in another area that shared their critical equipment inventory rather than each purchasing and holding every item in their own warehouse. Francine continued to say that the distributor that she worked for had also agreed to carry and hold some strategic items in their warehouse without any charge to the network.

Angie's eyebrows raised. "Come on inside. I would like to hear more."

The two women discussed Francine's plan for a network, and Angie agreed that it would be a win-win for her company. There was no investment, no upkeep, and someone willing to expedite any critical equipment required. There was an immediate friendship vibe between Angie and Francine, and soon, the conversation shifted to talk about their personal biographies. Francine related her personal information: no husband, no kids, no relationship, and she shared her educational and work background.

Angie was ten years older than Francine, divorced, no children, and just started a relationship with someone she met several months ago. She lived in the southwestern Florida area her entire life and was a relative of the principals of this company. Angie worked at Creative Fabrication for fifteen years and was the CFO for the past nine years.

Angie poured some coffee for Francine and herself and sat down on the side chair next to Francine. She reached across her desk and pulled a stack of papers toward her.

"Francine, your visit here has been more than an opportunity for you to break into this territory. Frankly, I've been struggling with managing the purchase orders for material needed for the factory. I had a person who handled POs, but she recently left our company to become a realtor.

"I listened to your presentation, and it is quite extraordinary that you are able to provide such good prices and terms. I'm inclined to offer you our business for manufacturing and sundry supplies. How do you think your company would stack up to others in price?" Angie asked.

Francine's eyes widened. This would be the first blanket sales order for SPD products. A blanket order covers most of a company's incoming inventory for a defined time period. It also would mean that commission would be paid to Francine on the inventory purchased each month.

"My prices with SPD are the lowest you could find. I would be inclined to suggest to you to pick a handful of your high-volume part numbers and do a comparison price check," Francine answered.

She continued to explain how her low overhead costs contributed to lowest prices.

Angie agreed to take twenty high-volume parts and get quotes from her current distributors, with Francine quoting on the same part numbers. They agreed to complete their comparison in the next couple of days. Angie was anxious to get her distributor locked in with a signed contract before the end of November and to begin the contract on the first of January. Francine knew it would be a slam dunk, and several days later, they compared the quotes, and

127

Francine's bid won. An annual contract was drawn up and signed by the end of the week.

"Francine, I was so tired of the bullshit that salesmen gave me to get my business. Your explanation of your products and services and your professionalism is so refreshing. I feel that our company will be in good hands with you and SPD," Angie related.

"Integrity and service is what sales is all about. There is no need for all the BS, lunches, golfing trips, etc. Although, I would be very happy to treat you anytime to any of the above if you would like," Francine said.

The two of them laughed, and Angie imitated a golf swing.

"I think an occasional lunch is nice, so I would be open to that, but really, I don't have time for all the frivolity. What I would like, though, is to invite you to dinner one evening as a friend, not a supplier. Maybe after the holidays, though, and after the end-of-the-year closings might be better for me. Accounting can't be put on the back burner for long. People have to get paid, suppliers paid, receipts inputted, taxes paid, and books balanced." Angie sighed.

"I know all about that. My parents own an accounting firm in Wisconsin. I know how many hours they work at year-end. But I would very much like to meet up with you sometime soon. Thank you for asking," Francine answered.

"Something else in common, accounting background," Angie said as she shook her head.

The women giggled and shook hands before Francine left the office.

It was two o'clock, Chicago time, when Francine called her boss, Sam Jr., general manager of Standard Products Distribution. Francine wanted to give him the news that she landed her first blanket sales order and also the first company to join her Naples network for critical parts.

"That's great news, Francine! Congratulations! How much in quarterly sales dollars do you estimate?" Sam Jr. asked.

Francine thought, *It always comes down to the money. You'd think he'd ask how I'm doing or something*. Francine gave Sam her estimate, and he was eager to add it to SPD's projected quarterly sales figures.

He remembered to thank and congratulate her on the expansion project in Monroe, Louisiana, too before he added Monroe sales dollar estimate into the same quarterly sales estimates for SPD.

"You're off to a great start, Francine. But how is your critical network strategy going?" Sam Jr. asked.

Francine felt herself tense up. Her network would generate some sales, but sales estimates would be a guess. The network was more of a way into those companies so that future business could be cultivated. Francine hoped Sam Jr. remembered this. She told him of her progress and reported the current sales revenue from the network.

Sam Jr. did know the potential of Francine's strategy, and he said some words of encouragement to her.

"The fruits of your efforts are going to pay off, Francine. I predict that next year we will be training all our sales reps on your strategy. Keep your chin up and enjoy that warm Naples weather. It's freezing rain here in Chicago."

"Ahhh, I remember those days well," Francine said.

They talked a few minutes more and ended their call. Francine felt happy and relieved.

The next day, Francine's phone rang. It was Angie Fratilo.

"Hi, Angie, what can I do for you today?" Francine asked.

"Hello, Francine. Actually, I may be able to do something for you. I was at one of our business consortiums last night, and I told the other businesses about you and your network. They were interested. So…I have a list of those people and their companies. I have seventeen potential clients for you," Angie boasted.

"Oh my goodness. That's wonderful, Angie. That was so nice of you to think about me," gushed Francine.

"I told you I had an immediate connection with you, and I love your network concept. I know you're going to help my family's business, and I want to help you. So I wanted to let you know that I'll be sending over an e-mail with all the information," Angie said.

"Angie, I don't know what to say except thank you. It certainly will be easier to go into companies with somewhat of an introduction. I know you are a very busy person, but I would sure like to take you to lunch or dinner sometime. Do you have any time for a little socialization?" Francine asked.

"Actually, I was going to ask you if you were busy this weekend. The guy I'm seeing is busy this weekend. We were going to catch a dinner, but then he has to run to meet some guys. I would love it if you could join us for dinner, and then you and I could either go for a couple of drinks or dessert afterwards," Angie suggested.

"I would love that. Call or text me with the details and I'll be there," Francine answered.

The women said their good-byes and ended the call.

During the next few days, Francine made appointments to see each of the names from the list Angie provided. The introductions proved to be very beneficial, with every company joining the network. Francine couldn't believe her luck. Meeting Angie Fratilo was a dream come true.

With the consent to start a network with eighteen clients, Francine knew she needed to start categorizing each of those businesses' critical equipment on her spreadsheet. Zone 2—Naples was created. It would take several weeks to visit each of those plants and input the necessary information.

One evening, Francine's phone rang. She saw it was Lilly Lee calling. Francine had quickly realized that her roommate, Lilly Lee, was probably the best roommate that anyone could have. Lilly updated Francine weekly on the townhouse and any neighborhood information she might have to share. She forwarded Francine's mail in the mailing envelopes that Francine had premade and called her if any mail looked important. Lilly periodically took pictures of the inside of the townhouse so that Francine knew she was keeping the apartment clean and tidy. She also deposited her half of each month's rent promptly into Francine's account so that Francine could pay their rent on time.

"Hi, Lilly, what's up?" Francine asked.

"Hello, Francine, how are you doing in Florida?" Lilly asked thoughtfully.

Lilly and Francine spent the next fifteen minutes on their personal updates before Lilly presented two conversational bombshells.

"I called you for two reasons. One is to let you know something and the other is to ask you something," Lilly related.

"Well then, let me have it," Francine urged.

"OK, well, the first thing is, your friend Brian Sherman stopped by the apartment a few minutes ago. He was hoping to find you here," Lilly said.

Francine's heart started pumping faster. *Brian Sherman! Why wouldn't he just call me?* Francine thought to herself, but she answered calmly, "Oh, that's nice. What did he say?"

"He said that he was hoping to find you here," Lilly repeated. "He looked real nervous. And he sounded very disappointed when I said you were out of town."

"What does he expect? That I would be there and greet him with open arms? He kind of dumped me, although we were never together. Heck, he didn't return my calls or my texts. I am surprised he remembered where I lived," Francine replied.

"He told me that he was hoping you were here personally so he could tell you that he was sorry. Francine, he seemed very sincere. He asked when you were coming back to Chicago, but I told him that I wasn't sure when that would be. Then he thanked me and asked how my schoolwork was coming and left," Lilly said.

"That's very interesting. I wonder why he doesn't just call me?" Francine repeated. Then she got unusually quiet while she thought about it.

"Francine, are you still there?" Lilly asked.

"Yes, I'm here. Thanks for letting me know about Brian. What was the other thing you wanted to tell me?" Francine asked.

"I'm afraid to tell you," Lilly said shyly. "Actually, I need to ask you something."

"What is it, Lilly?" asked Francine.

"My parents called me last weekend. They said they are coming to Chicago to visit me," Lilly explained.

"That's wonderful, Lilly! I would think you would be very excited about that. Aren't you?" asked Francine.

"Yes, I am excited. The problem is that they know that I am staying in this large townhouse alone, so they asked if they could stay with me," Lilly explained.

"I wouldn't have any problem with that. They can use my room while they are visiting," Francine eagerly offered.

"Yes, thank you. But that isn't the problem. The problem is that they are coming here at Christmastime for two weeks. They are coming the week before Christmas and staying until after the New Year. I know that is when you were going to be back in Chicago," Lilly said shyly.

Francine felt her pulse quicken again, but this time, not by the excitement of hearing Brian Sherman's name. Francine planned to be back in Chicago two weeks before Christmas and leave several days after New Year's Day. Lilly's parents' trip would be smack in the middle of that time. Francine wanted to relax so badly in her own bathtub and bed when she returned. Living in hotels for the past six weeks hasn't been bad, but it certainly didn't compare to her own beautiful townhouse.

There was an awkward silence between the two women, but finally, Francine answered, "Lilly, your parents are welcome at our home. We'll work it out. I would be home for about a week before your parents arrive and can unwind then. We can work out the details later, but please, invite your parents to stay with you at our home."

"Really? Oh, Francine! I was so afraid to ask you. I can sleep on the couch, and my parents can use my room, if that is OK with you," Lilly said, almost squeaking with delight.

"Sure, that sounds good. Let me give it some thought. I may change my schedule a little, but again, we will work it out," Francine repeated.

The call ended on a high note.

Francine sat down on her bed in the hotel room to think. Francine planned to think of the living arrangement options while the Lees were staying in Chicago, but her mind continually went back to Brian Sherman. Why was he going all the way uptown to her apartment? He knew she traveled and probably wouldn't be there anyway. Why didn't he call her? It was a puzzle, but one thing was for sure, she clearly was not over him and wanted to see him again.

She stared at the phone and his contact information. She knew she shouldn't be the one to call him, but after a few minutes and one can of Diet Coke, Francine pushed the Call button.

After a few rings, Brian's voice said, "Hi, Francine. It's great to hear from you."

Francine didn't want to be sarcastic, but she couldn't help herself. "Hi, Brian. I'm surprised to hear that since you didn't answer my calls or my texts a couple of months ago."

There was a short silence, and Brian responded, "I know, Francine. I'm sorry about that. I was hoping to explain to you in person. I stopped at your townhouse today, and your roommate told me you were still out of town."

"Yes, Lilly called me. That's why I'm calling," Francine said.

She was careful not to sound mad or sad when she responded, so she answered in her professional tone.

"When are you getting back into Chicago?" he asked.

"I'm planning on coming home mid-December. Until then, I'm working down here in Florida and Louisiana," said Francine.

"Wow, Florida. That sounds great about this time of year. It's getting cooler and cooler up here. I spend lots of my work time outside, and I'm not looking forward to the winter," Brian said.

Their conversation shifted from the awkward elephant in the room to talk of their jobs. Thirty minutes later, they were still talking. Francine thought about how easy it was talking to Brian. There was just such an ease about him. He was interesting to listen to and asked questions of her with great sincerity.

"Brian, I should probably get to bed. It's an hour later here in Florida, and I have a big day inventorying gears and such in non-AC factories in the morning," Francine explained.

She hoped that Brian would say that he would call her again soon.

"Ah, yeah, I should have thought about that," Brian replied. "Francine, I would really like to explain some things to you when you are back in Chicago, so would it be all right to see you sometime then?"

Francine quickly calculated the duration until she would be back in Chicago. It was another five weeks. *Another five weeks! He doesn't want to talk to me for another five weeks?* Francine thought. Her pulse quickened again, and her stomach acid problem returned.

With her hand pressing in on her churning stomach, she calmly answered, "If you want to see me when I'm in Chicago, give me a call. Good night, Brian."

Francine sat stunned on the bed. Part of her was elated that he called, and part of her was furious and confused. She decided to take a long bath with the hope that she would fall asleep quickly afterward, but she knew that sleep would not be coming this night.

Brian sat on his couch and stared at the ground. He hadn't expected Francine to call him, so he was unprepared for her sudden call. *What was I thinking?* he thought. *Of course her roommate would tell her I was at her house. I'm such a moron. She's probably more steamed at me now than before.* He knew he wasn't prepared to tell her the reason for his poor behavior. The truth was, Brian didn't know why he went to her townhouse today. *I actually was hoping that she wouldn't be there.* He wasn't ready to face her. Not yet.

The next week in Naples was busy with trying to get the critical equipment spreadsheet populated. Francine was careful to code each of the participating companies with a code number rather than a name to protect their anonymity. The spreadsheet was being managed solely by Francine, but she hoped that sometime in the future, she could release the spreadsheet so that each firm could look at a glance at other companies' inventory. She had not decided if she should ever release the file to the participants, but she wanted to be prepared. Francine had always been thoughtful about her clients. She knew that great salespersons were trustworthy, sincere, and careful to protect their clients. This network was the epitome of that philosophy, with clients trusting Francine to manage their most important spares to run their operation.

Francine knew she had a large project to get eighteen companies entered into her spreadsheet as zone 2. To complete her worksheet, she would have to meet with their maintenance or production manager and figure out what spares were critical for the company to run.

The best companies would already know this list as it was a standard operation principle for manufacturing. But some of these companies were not so mature or sophisticated, so some education would have to take place. All the inventories would have to be entered with very specific detail noting every attribute so that a replacement part number could be determined. It would be a tedious and rather dirty job, but at the end, Francine would be able to find a replacement at another company or at a distributor. Her strategy was to have the replacements identified and cross-referenced so that it could be quickly found when needed.

She decided to dress somewhat casual during the next workweek while she would be working in various stockrooms and factories. Francine was hoping to complete two companies per day so that all of her zone 2 clients' inputs would be done in the next two weeks.

The workweek started well, and Francine finished two companies on Monday. She was in another company's stockroom on Tuesday morning when her phone rang. It was an area code for West Monroe, Louisiana.

"Is this Francine Pacque?" an unknown voice asked.

"Yes, this is Francine. Who am I speaking with?" Francine requested.

"This is Andy Miller from Ultra Electric Co. in West Monroe, Louisiana. Say, we have a big problem here, and our general manager said I should call you," the voice replied.

After a brief conversation, it was determined that Ultra Electric had a small fire in part of their fabrication plant. No one was hurt, and the building could still be used, but there was substantial damage to about a quarter of their plant.

"We need replacement items here right away. We're hoping that you can help with that," Andy said.

Francine knew that this was a good chance to be responsive and help their company. She would get some sales from it. She was thinking that she needed to jump on a plane and get to Louisiana quickly.

Andy continued, "We have one of our contractors here already, and he'll deal with some of the structural replacements. What we need from you are a number of replacement tooling and fixtures.

135

This was a relatively new area in our plant, and we have the old records of what we need. I just have to review it and make some edits. But if you could get these items to us quickly, we can get up and running again."

Francine explained that she was currently in South Florida but would be willing to catch the next plane to be in West Monroe in person. In the meantime, she would contact her local person, Bill Hanson, to get over to the plant.

"I don't think you'll have to come up here. I'm going to send you the list, and I need you to tell me when you can get the replacement parts down here. We'll need them as soon as possible," Andy explained.

Francine called Bill Hanson immediately after the call. Bill was available and would go directly to the plant.

"Bill, this is going to be an emotional time for them. No one was hurt, but having a fire is an emotional event. Their plant is damaged, and part of their business is down. Please try to help them in any way. I'll pay you for whatever hours you can work.

"I'm on it. I'll be there in a couple of minutes. I just need to change my clothes and take our son to his grandmother's house," Billy said gleefully.

Francine knew he would be a terrific help for Ultra Electric. Francine also knew that Bill was very happy to get a chance to work and earn some money.

Francine's next call was to her sister-in-law, Chrissy. She hoped Chrissy might want to do some work finding the parts that would be on the Ultra Electric replacement list, and if she was open to the job, Francine could stay focused on entering part descriptions for her new clients.

"Hi, Chrissy, I have another job for you if you are interested. I don't have the list yet, so I can't even tell you how large it is. But one of the companies in Louisiana had a fire, and they need some equipment ASAP to get back in production," Francine explained.

"I have some sports dinner to go to tonight with Gerry," Chrissy explained, "but I would be able to work on it after I get home, if that would be all right."

"I think that would be fine, but please know each of those parts would need to be expedited quickly. Would you have time to make out the order online with my SPD access code and to talk with the SPD inside rep to make sure the order could be expedited quickly? I would need you to know what items would be coming, on what type of truck, train, or so on, and the time. Then arrange pickup with my man in Louisiana. His name is Bill Hanson. He works for me," Francine said. She hesitated at her last sentence. *He works for me.*

How funny that someone would be working for me, Francine thought.

"Man, Francine, I can try, but this sounds like a big job. I don't know if I can do it," Chrissy explained.

"Oh, come on. You are the most multitalented person I know. It is an important job, but the rep I will be introducing you to at SPD is experienced. He will help a lot," Francine added.

"I'll try. I'm actually kind of excited. It'll be the first business accomplishment that I've ever done," Chrissy announced.

"And this time, I'll be paying you. Just keep track of the hours you work. Then you'll have some spending money for yourself that Gerry can't get his fingers on," Francine added.

She knew her brother got a lot of freebies in his athletic job, but he was quite stingy on giving money out to his wife. There was always money available for things that their children needed, but Chrissy was second-string. It would make Francine very happy to get some money to her sister-in-law without going through "Pack It In" Gerry.

Shortly after the phone call with Chrissy, Francine received an e-mail with an attachment listing all the items that Ultra Electronic needed expedited. It was a long list with some of the entries crossed out. *Those must not have been destroyed,* Francine thought. She reviewed the list and realized that some of those items were items already on her zone 1 critical equipment spreadsheet.

"What good luck!" Francine exclaimed.

She quickly called Bill Hanson and told him that he needed to pick up some parts within the zone before he went to Ultra Electric.

137

She explained that she would call the plants that had spares and let them know the situation.

Francine sprang into action and contacted four companies that had replacements available. She explained the urgency of a quick pickup on those parts due to a fire at another factory. They were all aware of the fire and were glad to help. Francine also explained that she would get replacements to them as quickly as possible and would notify them of the delivery.

Francine then called SPD to make them aware of the criticality of this order. She was given a rep's name to provide Chrissy when the list was completed. The SPD representative would be responsible for expediting the order to Louisiana but would be able to provide Chrissy the information to pass on to Francine and Bill.

Her final step was to edit the list and e-mail it to Chrissy. By morning, she should have the information ready for SPD to expedite parts. Francine knew she would have to cross-check to ensure that everyone got their parts replaced and that the correct charges between plants would occur. The details were a bit confusing, even to herself, but she knew she would get the paperwork reconciled properly.

About two hours later, Francine answered a call from Chrissy.

"It's all done," she said gleefully. "I just passed the list on to the guy from SPD. He's filling the order and will get it expedited."

"You mean you got the entire list complete?" Francine asked.

"Yep! I told Gerry that I didn't really want to go to his dinner tonight. It wasn't a big deal. I think he was just as happy that I didn't go so he could sit and jaw about sports with the other guys. So I was able to do the list. The SPD guy said he should have everything done in a couple of hours," Chrissy said.

Francine was elated. If the shipment would go out today, it could be picked up at the FedEx or UPS terminal tonight. The plant could possibly have their replacement parts at their plant by night.

It turned out that Francine's prediction was almost spot-on. The shipment was on a plane by 3:00 p.m., with an estimated terminal pickup at 7:00 p.m. Bill Hanson and another Ultra Electric Company truck went to the terminal to pick up the large order. The two trucks were able to get the entire load onto their trucks. The trucks were back at the factory by 9:00 p.m., and installation began immediately. With luck, the assembly area would be ready to run in the morning.

To say that the owners of Ultra Electric Company were impressed with the quick part replacement was an understatement. They had thought that they would have to lay their employees off for the balance of the week, at a minimum. The parts that Francine's company provided quickly allowed them to reconstruct their assembly area the very next morning, and they were back in full production before the day's end.

Francine e-mailed her bill for the parts and expediting fees the same day as the parts arrived. She thought that the extra charges for expediting would be more readily received knowing that they were back into production so quickly. Her hunch was right. She received a thank-you letter drafted by the owner of the company with an acknowledgment that her check was in the mail. The owner also mentioned in the letter that they planned to give Francine and the company she represented, Standard Product Distribution, more business in the future in appreciation.

Francine read the e-mail and smiled at the accomplishment. She wrote a thank-you reply back to the owner and stated that she would be back in the Louisiana area early in January. She also sent a copy to her boss at SPD. Next, she wrote a thank-you e-mail to Bill Hanson for his extra effort in picking up the parts at the airport and delivering them quickly to Ultra Electric Co. She also said that she would be giving him a special bonus of $100. She knew that Bill and his family would be happy to hear that news. Finally, she wrote her sister-in-law, Chrissy Pacque, to tell her that the shipments arrived safely and were installed immediately, letting the company start production by the next morning. She thanked Chrissy and said she would be giving her a little something special in her check.

Word of her responsiveness reached other companies in the Monroe zone, and Francine received several texts of acknowledgment from those companies. She also received one e-mail with an attachment for a quote on providing regular inventory parts from her. She immediately researched the inventory list and was able to provide a strong quote the following day. The quote was almost immediately acknowledged by an acceptance letter and contract. Francine's reputation was growing, and additional, repeatable business was coming her way.

By Saturday, Francine was exhausted and dirty. She had worked as planned, inputting spare parts inventory for two companies per day. Francine slept late on Saturday and then left the hotel in search of a nail salon. It was time to get her polished replaced so she looked good for going to dinner with Angie Fratilo that evening. They were going to eat at one of the restaurants along Fifth Avenue in Old Naples. Angie's boyfriend was going to eat with them before he had to leave for another engagement. Francine and Angie would decide what to do later, but it probably would involve a few cocktails.

Francine was excited to get to know Angie a little better. Besides being one tough financial officer for her uncle's business, Angie was an accomplished musician. She had studied music in college before deciding on the safer, more-longevity field of accounting. Angie was married to a man she met in college, but their marriage fell apart after ten years. Angie didn't want to discuss those years and referred to them as her lost years. She recently met a Naples businessman through a mutual acquaintance, and they had been exclusively dating for about six months.

Francine agreed to meet Angie at her workplace, and the two women would share one car for the ride into Naples. Francine wore a flowy light-pink skirt paired with a light-pink chemise. She wore clunky jewelry to bring in some color to her ensemble. She admired herself in the mirror. She looked fashionably chic. Her hair was loosely draping her shoulders. *I wonder if I should get my brown hair colored with some streaks of sunlight blond or cut into a sleeker style?* Francine thought. She may get a better idea of what the young women of Naples were doing with their hair tonight. She was excited for a fun night out with a friend.

Angie and Francine met at six o'clock in the parking lot. Angie looked radiant with a bright-orange floral top with black netting on the shoulders. Her blouse was quite low-cut and revealed an amble bosom covered with several long gold necklaces. She also wore tight black ankle pants with black ultrahigh heels. Angie looked like an entirely different person from the bland, highly professional woman she portrayed at work. She was gorgeous, with her shiny straight black hair cut in a bob style and bright lipstick matching the orange in her blouse.

"Wow, Angie. You clean up well!" Francine announced. "I mean, you always look great at work, but you're a force to be reckoned with tonight. I feel like I should go home to change clothes."

"You look great, but thank you. I'm not getting any younger, so I might as well wear these types of fun clothes while I still can," Angie replied.

Francine agreed, but inside, Francine felt like she always did back in her high school days when she went somewhere with her sister, Genevieve. Everyone always stared at Viv, and no one knew she was even there. Francine knew that tonight would be one of those nights.

The women drove to one of the restaurants on Fifth Avenue. It was a good choice because they could walk to other venues after dinner. Angie's boyfriend, Ben Vukas, was very nice. He worked in one of the large investment firms that lined Highway 41 in Naples. His profession required a certain way of dressing: suit, white shirt, and tie. Shoes always buffed to a high gloss. He arrived at the restaurant wearing one of his suits but wore a brighter melon-colored shirt. Angie mentioned that he called her to ask how to dress, and she suggested he wear his melon shirt.

Ben was clearly enthralled with Angie. He listened to every word and adoringly looked at her when she spoke. Francine was impressed with Ben. *He's a keeper,* Francine thought.

Francine answered honestly any questions that were asked by Angie or Ben. She was guarded about any explanation about Magnacraft and the reason she left that company but open about other topics. The conversation included Francine's family, schooling, her past relationship, sales experiences, and how it had been during the past six weeks of travel. Ben had visited Chicago numerous times, so much of the conversation revolved on Chicago's sights and sports venues.

Dinner was exceptional, and the three of them dined slowly and enjoyed their dinner and wine. When Francine left the table to visit the ladies' room, Ben said, "Baby, I like this woman. I'm glad you made friends with her."

"Yes," Angie said. "I wish she would have a boyfriend here so we could double date."

"She just got here! She'll find someone. A girl like her won't be alone long," Ben answered.

Unaware of the compliments she was receiving from Angie and Ben, Francine stood at the mirror in the ladies' room and thought, *Why am I always alone? Why can't I meet someone nice like Ben? They must think I'm a loser, traveling all the time with no husband or boyfriend, no one to go home to.* Francine's opinion of herself continued to be low.

The dinner ended, and Ben left to meet some of his buddies to watch a Saturday night football game. Angie and Francine decided to stay at the restaurant and have an after-dinner drink in the bar. Two women sat down at the bar and introduced themselves as Eileen and Barbara. They were 100 percent Irish cousins that worked in a nearby shop. The four women laughed and joked with one another while the band played live music. It was a wonderful time, and Francine knew that she now had four local friends in Naples. After the four women exchanged phone information, they promised to meet up again before Francine left for the holidays and returned to Chicago.

It was the latest night that Francine had since she started her new territory. Sunday was dedicated to doing laundry at her hotel and mapping out her workweek. She had a lot to accomplish and planned to inventory two facilities per day until Friday. On Friday, she wanted to get her hair cut, colored, and nails redone. Next Saturday was the charity event that Francine was attending.

CHAPTER 12

The Charity Event

The week went well, but Francine didn't quite meet her work goal. Francine calmed herself knowing that she had the entire next week to finish up all plants. On Tuesday, Francine decided to drive to a local address to pick up her $200 charity event ticket for Children's Hospital. She had called ahead and received the address of where to pick up her ticket. When she entered the address into her GPS, she was happy to see that the address was in a residential neighborhood.

"I hope it is some fabulous residence. I'd like to see a multimillion dollar home here," Francine muttered to herself.

Francine wasn't disappointed. The home was on a beautiful drive with bay water access. She parked her car in the circular driveway and walked to the front door. The door was nine foot tall with intricate glass etchings in it and two matching side panels. It was a stunning entrance. She rang the bell, and in a short while, a woman as stunning as the home answered the door.

"Hello, I'm Francine Pacque. I called you earlier about picking up my ticket to the charity event," Francine said.

"Hello, I'm Noel Noirty. Please come in," the stunning woman answered.

Francine was mesmerized by Noel. She clearly had a European background and, to Francine, seemed like royalty. Noel glided across the room in her golden slippers peeking out from a black-and-gold caftan. The woman was about forty with long blond ringlets surrounding her perfect face. As they walked through the foyer, Francine noticed the grandeur of the home. It was elegantly appointed in rich satins of beige and orange among oversize French country decor. There were paintings and sculptures around the sitting room. Francine knew it wasn't the discount variety that she had on display in her townhouse.

Knowing that most people liked to talk about themselves, Francine started a conversation by asking, "How did you get involved in this charity event?"

"Oh, my husband and I have been involved in different charity fund-raisers for years. My friends and I take turns doing various duties for all of the events. This time was my turn, and I agreed to do ticket sales since I have lots of contacts who attend these types of functions," Noel shared.

"That's very admirable. I'm sure there are many people who only attend the events but never participate in organizing it," Francine added.

Noel nodded. "I have your ticket somewhere around here. Would you like some tea or something while I get it?"

Francine jumped at the opportunity. She hated tea but thought she'd choke it down to have a chance to mingle with the wealthy for a little while.

Noel motioned for Francine to follow her and headed to the outside entertainment area. The area overlooked an infinity pool and a private boat dock on the bay. Noel picked up a carafe of tea and two glasses with ice from a wet bar area and brought them to an elegant outside dining table.

"So, Francine, where are you from?" Noel asked.

Francine answered that she lived in Chicago and was originally from southern Wisconsin. Noel looked unimpressed. Francine could feel Noel's gaze on her as if she were doing an evaluation.

"And what are you doing in Naples? Vacationing?" Noel asked.

Francine was prepared for the question. She planned on going incognito at the society function and needed an appropriate background.

"I'm here at my uncle's request. He is planning to purchase a home and a yacht in the area and sent me to do some prework for him," Francine answered.

"Hasn't he visited this area for himself? Naples isn't a large town, so it is easy to decide on what area you want. You just have to know how much money you want to spend," Noel responded casually.

Francine shifted in her chair, hoping that Noel wouldn't ask about her *fake* uncle's budget. She took a sip of the tea and choked. *Yuck, I hate tea,* she thought. She repositioned herself in her chair to appear at ease. Noel expected Francine to respond to her remark, and the absence of any comeback startled her.

"What type of property is your uncle interested in?" she asked.

Francine responded, "I think his taste is similar to your beautiful home. He would want a stunning house with a big view of the water and a dock for his yacht."

"Oh, I thought you said he wanted to purchase a yacht. Does he already own one?" Noel said furrowing her brow.

"That's correct. He wants to buy a new yacht but would prefer to buy an existing home," Francine said.

"What broker are you working with?" Noel asked.

Francine shifted in her chair again, saying, "I haven't met with any brokers yet. Can you refer one to me?"

"Well, yes. I can introduce you to a broker friend at the event on Saturday. My friend only represents the most discriminating clients, but it sounds like a fit for your uncle," Noel said offhandedly.

Francine thought, *Oh brother, now I'm in for it. A high-dollar broker...I can't believe it.*

Francine said, "Wonderful. I can't believe my luck meeting you."

She felt the tea churning in her stomach. She hoped she would make it out to her car before vomiting in the plastic bag she carried for just-in-case instances.

"What line of work is your uncle in?" Noel asked.

What's with all the questions? I have to make it out of here fast, Francine thought. He heart was pounding faster and faster. *Think quick, Francine, think!*

"He owns a capital management company out of Chicago," Francine lied.

Francine had uncles, but they were middle-class working men. Francine's thoughts were crying out, *Please don't ask for his name.*

"And what is your uncle's name?" Noel asked, as if she had a direct conduit into Francine's mind.

Francine knew it was time to stop this. She was aware of a man's name who was owner of a capital management company, but she didn't know him personally and didn't want to fraudulently say she was representing someone when she was not.

Francine stood up as she set her glass down on the patio dining table. She casually picked up her purse and put it on her shoulder.

"When the time is right, I will present my uncle's name. Thank you, Noel. It was lovely meeting you, and thank you for the tea," Francine said as she reached out to gently shake the woman's hand.

Francine walked as casually as she could to her car and waved to Noel, who was standing in the doorway. She started the car and slowly drove onto the street. When she was out of Noel's sight, she pulled her car over and reached for her emergency plastic barf bag.

Noel, on the other hand, stood for a moment, looking out the door as the back of Francine's Audi pulled out of her driveway. *Hmmm, she sure told me in a roundabout way that it is none of my business. She'll fit in with my group just fine. I can't wait to tell Dave that I may have found a new customer for him,* she thought. She walked back into her home and wiped her already immaculate outdoor dining table. She walked into the kitchen to retrieve her cell phone and called her friend Mitzi.

"Hi, Mitzi. Say, I just met a young woman who is coming to the charity event this Saturday. She's looking for a home for her uncle in the Bay or Port Royal area. Big bucks! She isn't represented yet, so I told her that I would introduce her to a broker for elite clients."

The week leading up to the charity event had several surprises for Francine. Billy Hanson called her on Wednesday to say that one of the zone 1 companies asked him about expanding his role to include doing inventory on many of their common fasteners, such as screws, bolts, and hinges. Francine explained to Billy that many companies had an outside vendor inventory and resupply sundry items. The service was called vendor-managed inventory. Francine was hoping that at some point she could expand business to include vendor-managed inventory because it provided a steady stream of income. Francine thanked Billy for calling her immediately and told him that she would contact the plant for a contract. She told Billy that she would be stopping in Monroe before heading back to Chicago next month, and they could set up the system at that time.

A second surprise was that another company in zone 1 had a critical part failure, and the plant was totally down. When Francine looked up the part on her spreadsheet, she was happy to find an exact replacement at another zone 1 company. She was able to arrange for Bill to pick up that part and deliver it to the compromised plant. The plant was up and running within three hours, and the leadership of that plant was ecstatic. The CFO stated that he was able to justify his decision of joining Francine's network of companies.

Finally, Saturday arrived. Francine had made an appointment at one of the premier hair salons to have her hair highlighted and cut. She was excited for a makeover and was standing at the doorway when the owner unlocked the door for business at 9:00 a.m.

The hairstylist took one look at Francine's long brown locks and frowned. Francine's hair was pretty but without style. She showed her a picture from a hair catalog and proposed a complete change. Francine thought, *What the heck. I don't have anything to lose.* She agreed to the style but was adamant that she still have shoulder-length hair. The stylist agreed to her demand.

Two and a half hours later, Francine's color, cut, and style was complete. The stylist rotated the chair toward the mirror so Francine could finally see herself.

"Where am I?" Francine asked while turning her head from side to side.

The woman's image in the mirror wasn't the mousy brown-haired girl that Francine knew for her thirty-four years. This woman was glowing. She stared at herself and saw golden hair with a hint of brown on lower layers. She had bangs for the first time in her life. The bangs were bluntly cut in an arch, showing off her eyebrows, but gliding longer at the side. Her long locks were gone, and her hair barely touched her shoulders. There were several layered cuts in her hairdo to provide some lift and body. It was magnificent, in Francine's opinion.

She left the salon and headed to her nail salon to have bright-red nails painted. The bright red would match the Jimmy Choo sandal heels she would be wearing that night.

The charity event started at 6:00 p.m. for cocktails, with a dinner at 7:00 p.m., followed by the auction. Live music would be provided for those who cared to dance or just enjoy music. Francine calculated that it would take twenty minutes to drive to the country club where the event was taking place. She didn't want to arrive too early, so she decided to leave the hotel at 6:15 p.m. She carefully put on her beautiful emerald-green gown, her red sandals, and a pair of oversize fake-emerald earrings. She wore no other jewelry and, in fact, had no other fine pieces of jewelry to wear.

Francine stared at herself in the small mirror over the hotel desk and in the bathroom mirror. She couldn't quite see her entire self, but she knew she looked good. The gown with her new hairdo looked amazing.

"I wish I had someone to go with and someone to tell me I looked pretty tonight." Francine sighed.

She grabbed her dressy clutch and event ticket and headed to her car. She never felt so glamorous.

The country club was lit up against the darkened November skies. There were many cars already parked in the parking lot. Francine didn't know where to park before she noticed that there were some valets standing at the entrance. She drove up under the canopy of the club.

One of the valets quickly ran over to the door to park her car. When the door opened and he saw that it was a woman, he took her arm and helped glide her out the door. He handed Francine the valet slip as she walked around the back of her car to the entrance. On her way to the door, she overheard the valets talking to one another.

"Wow, what a babe," said one of the valets.

"Yeah, I wonder who she is?" said another.

Francine smiled as she walked. *This must be how Viv always feels to be fussed over. It feels good,* she thought. She was ready for her entrance.

The massive lobby in the clubhouse had intricate wooden panel walls and oversize plush couches and chairs. A table was set up by the side wall for participant check-in. Francine expected to see the woman who sold her the ticket at the table, Noel Noirty, but instead, there was a young couple behind the table. Several people were waiting for check-in, so Francine took her time to look for her ticket in her clutch purse. She was excited to be a part of the event but unsure of how to proceed with her identity ruse.

When the crowd lessened at the registration table, Francine carefully and slowly walked up to the table, making sure that her posture was straight and regal. She handed her ticket to the couple and soon received a silken cloth packet containing several items, including an informational packet about the Children's Hospital charity event, a list of all the raffle items, which would be on display tables in the dining room, and a card with her name and table number.

Francine took a deep breath and walked in the dining room. She estimated that there were approximately two hundred people attending the event. Francine wanted to find her table number and then get a much-needed cocktail to calm her nerves. *Table seven,* Francine read on the card. She slowly walked through the tables, looking for her table. She was surprised to see it was in the second row of tables, directly behind the center front table. *Not bad!* Francine thought.

She slowly placed her silken packet by the name tag with her name written in script. *Hold it together, girlfriend,* Francine thought. *This could be the start of a wonderful time in Naples. Just play it cool and pretend you belong here.*

A group of five women were talking with one another in the middle of the room. They were obviously good friends and laughed, giggled, and touched one another's arms as they conversed. One of the women was suddenly distracted by something, and the others stopped their conversation and focused their attention on the woman.

"What's the matter, Shauna?" one of the women asked.

"Who is that young woman in the green gown? Does anyone know her?" Shauna asked.

"No, but she is stunning. I wonder if she is here with anyone. Who did she walk in with?" another woman asked.

The women shook their heads and shrugged as no one had seen the stunning woman in green with fabulous blond hair in a severe shoulder-length bob.

"Well, if she didn't come in with someone, she'll be walking out with one of the guys," another woman joked.

"Wait a minute," a member of the group said. The woman was in a beige chiffon Grecian gown with a large diamond and ruby necklace with matching earrings. "I think I know that woman. I have to see her face. I'm going over there."

Noel Noirty grabbed a second glass of champagne from a waiter passing by with a champagne tray and walked toward the woman. As Noel walked toward Francine, Francine happened to turn in her direction.

"Francine, I didn't recognize you. You look absolutely amazing! I love your hair blond and in that style. Stunning, Francine, absolutely stunning," Noel said as she looked Francine over and handed her a glass of champagne.

"Thank you, Noel. You look beautiful too," Francine said as she raised her glass to toast with Noel. "This is a beautiful venue to have your event. You've done a beautiful job arranging the table settings."

"Oh, I didn't do anything except handle the tickets. We take turns doing different jobs when we prepare for one of these things. Naples is actually quite a small town, and it usually is the same people arranging events," Noel explained. "Come with me, Francine. I would like to introduce you to my friends. One of them is Mitzi Vanderlooth, the realtor that I wanted to introduce you to. I have you sitting at her table."

Francine quickly realized why she was so lucky to be seated at a prime table. It was her new acquaintance, Noel, who knew everyone in Naples, who was her benefactor.

"I would love to meet your friends," Francine replied.

They walked to the group of women. While they walked, Noel stopped at every guest and greeted them by name. Hugs and kisses on the cheek were exchanged with each guest. Francine wondered how Noel's makeup would hold up by the end of the night. Finally, they reached the small group of women.

"I'd like to introduce you to my friend Francine Pacque. This is Mitzi Vanderlooth, Shauna Delgado, Pepper Franklin, and Babs Simmons," Noel said as she pointed to each of her friends as she introduced them.

Francine was amused at the nicknames some of the women had. They sounded like TV stars or porn stars. She laughed silently as she thought she should reintroduce herself as Fanny Pack. Francine instead shook each one of the woman's hand and said a genuine hello.

"Mitzi, this is the woman I was telling you about. She is looking for a water-access house for her uncle. Maybe you can refer her to some properties. Actually, I was thinking about the house down the street from me. I believe it is still on the market," Noel said.

"Yes, the house is on the market. The owners are from Europe and decided to buy a home on the French Riviera, which would be closer to their business in France," Mitzi acknowledged. She turned to Francine and said, "I have several distinguished estate homes on water that I can show you."

Francine felt her stomach knotting up quickly, but she continued as if all were natural.

"That would be wonderful. I need to get the feel of the house before I can recommend one to my uncle. My uncle was recently divorced, and he may be biting off more than he can chew with a large home. Maybe a condo would be better for him," Francine replied. Inside her head, she was thinking, *More is less, more is less, keep your mouth shut, Francine, before someone finds you out.*

"A condo? I thought he wanted to buy a yacht and have it moored on his own pier," Noel added.

Francine nodded in agreement. "Well, yes, he does want that."

"Then why don't you two make arrangements to meet each other tomorrow?" Noel added. "Houses can go fast, so why put it off? You are here to look at houses, aren't you, Francine?"

"Tomorrow will be fine with me," Francine said. She added, "As long as we don't have too bad of a hangover tomorrow."

The six women giggled and toasted their glasses before sipping the champagne. Francine thought, *So this is how deals happen. One minute it is a drink, and the next you're looking at real estate. I may be a good saleswoman, but I don't have anything over on these women.*

The women immediately embraced Francine as one of their own, and they gossiped about some of the people in the room. Francine learned quite a bit about the people she would never be a part of, including who was married to whom, who was divorced from whom and remarried, who was cheating on their wives, and in a few instances, who was cheating on their husbands. Francine was having a wonderful time, giggling and drinking with the women. Several times people would come up to the group to say hello, and Francine was always introduced. It made her feel important. A photographer also took several pictures of the group to the delight of Francine.

Finally, a distinguished-looking man stepped to the podium and asked for everyone's attention. The man announced that dinner would be served in twenty minutes and that guests were urged to bid on the raffle items up until dinner. After dinner, there would be another thirty minutes before the raffle closed. The charity event keynote speaker, Dr. Flanerty, would be next on the agenda, presenting information regarding Children's Hospital and the hospital's needs. Pledge cards would be handed out to all guests with follow-up calls to each guest in the next two weeks. Then the raffle winners would be announced. The final hours would be dedicated to music, dancing, and mingling.

"Pledge cards!" Francine gasped to herself.

Shauna Delgado grabbed Francine's arm as she asked, "Are you all right, Francine?"

"Yes, I'm sorry. I must have choked as I was about to say that pledge cards is a good idea," Francine answered.

She was pleased at her quick comeback. Francine was not prepared for another cost besides the hundred-dollar raffle tickets she purchased in the lobby. She quickly decided to concentrate on the moment. Her plan for the raffle was to wait until shortly before the end of the raffle and casually look at all the items but really look to see what canister had the fewest raffle tickets inside, and place her tickets in that canister. She desperately wanted to have her name announced as a winner of a raffle prize.

Suddenly, a voice announced on a loud speaker that it was time for dinner. The women dispersed and went to their respective tables. Mitzi grabbed Francine's arm and led her to their table. Francine was glad to have someone to eat with rather than all strangers. Mitzi was married to an older gentleman named Paul. Introductions were made between all eight people at their table before a generous dinner of salmon or beef tips was served. Dinner was uneventful except for several people at the table commenting on Francine's beautiful dress. Paul Vanderlooth added that Francine was beautiful, period. Francine thought that this was one of her best days ever. She was so happy that she came to the event.

Of course, as dinner conversations go among unfamiliar people, the subject of what Francine did for a living came up. There was no need to lie as Francine could have chosen to say she was here on business and also representing her uncle. But Francine was afraid to compromise her "uncle's rep" explanation for being in Naples. Francine answered that she worked in management for a large distributor in the Chicago area. She was vague with her profession title. Then she casually added that her visit here was to scout homes and yachts for her uncle.

The comment about her uncle opened up another can of worms. Successful, rich businessmen liked to hear about other successful, rich businessmen. Francine wondered if it was truly interest or to determine who had the most money. Francine gave the same answer she gave a week ago to Noel, when she said that her uncle owned a capital management company in Chicago. She added that he didn't want his name disclosed at this time. One of the men at her table reinforced her answer.

"Capital management, hey? That's a rich businessman's game. I can understand why he wouldn't want everyone knowing his name and contacting him for this or that," the man said.

The man's wife added, "Good for you. I hope you find your uncle a wonderful home in the area."

"Oh, I'm sure she will," the realtor Mitzi Vanderlooth added.

When dinner was completed, Francine made her way to the raffle tables. Most of the people had already deposited their tickets, so there were only a few women looking at the items. Francine walked down the line of banquet tables and reviewed the raffle gifts. There were many fabulous gifts, including large liquor baskets, fishing trips, dining certificates, etc., but Francine's eyes were searching for the booby prizes, as she referred to them. These were the prizes in less demand. One of the items was a bucket of cleaning supplies.

Who in this room does their own cleaning? Francine questioned. There were only a couple of tickets in that raffle container, so Francine put ten tickets inside. *I hope I didn't waste fifty dollars*, Francine thought.

The remaining ten tickets, another fifty dollar's worth of raffle tickets, she deposited in a raffle container for a fast-food restaurant. There were some tickets in that container, but Francine thought she would still have a good chance to win with her ten-ticket deposit. *I could use this prize*, she thought.

She decided to go to the ladies' room to freshen up her lipstick. As she walked in the lobby, Noel softly yelled to her, "Francine, come her a minute, my dear."

Noel was holding the arm of her husband. Francine noticed him at the front and center dining table next to Noel. She walked over to the couple and smiled.

"This must be your charming husband," Francine said while extending her hand to the man.

"Yes, this is my charming husband, Dave Noirty. Darling, this is Francine Pacque, the woman I was telling you about," Noel said.

"Hello, my, you are very beautiful. It's nice to meet you, Francine," Dave Noirty said as he gently shook Francine's hand.

"Now my work is done," Noel said. "You two have finally met. I know you will have a lot to talk about."

"Oh?" Francine shyly asked.

"Yes, my husband is a yacht dealer," Noel stated.

Francine's blood pressure hit the moon, and Francine felt her face and body flush with despair.

"Very good," Francine answered. "Dave, it is nice to meet you, and we should talk later. Now, if you will please excuse me, I need to use the ladies' room."

Francine hurried into the bathroom. There were several women primping in the mirror in the dressing area of the room. Francine moved quickly into one of the stalls and just stood there.

"What am I getting myself into...a yacht dealer? Oh my god. What were the chances of that?" Francine muttered softly.

She spent a few minutes getting herself together and letting her blood pressure return to normal before she went out of the stall. Surprisingly, Noel was waiting for her in the dressing room.

"Francine, are you OK? You got so flushed!" Noel exclaimed.

"I'm fine. I think the champagne has gotten to my head on an empty stomach. I should be all right in a few minutes since we just ate," Francine replied.

"Good. I was worried about you," Noel replied. "Let's get back to our seats. The speaker should be starting soon, and I don't want to be late."

The keynote speaker, Dr. Flanerty, gave a poignant speech about the work that Children's Hospital did for the community. He talked about the various programs that the hospital provided and gave some tear-jerking examples of some patients' recovery successes due to past donations from past fund-raisers.

Then he paused and said, "Now I want to tell you the programs that we cannot cover because of lack of equipment or support and the types of sicknesses that cannot be addressed due to the lack of equipment."

It was a very effective line, and the audience was glued to the next examples of precise equipment needs. Dr. Flanerty was so precise that he even had the projector list the equipment and each of their costs. He went on to say that without today's support from the participants at this event, child patients would have to be turned away and travel far from their families to get the care they needed. He prioritized the list of equipment with a running tally to show what the cumulative efforts of this charity event could accomplish. When he completed his speech, Dr. Flanerty received a standing ovation and thunderous clapping from the participants.

There was a short intermission before the raffle winner announcements. A number of people quickly used the restroom or went to get another drink at the bar until an announcement was made for everyone to return to their tables.

The raffle committee moved to the raffle tables with a portable microphone and started at the far end of the tables, having one of the committee members reach into a container and remove one winning raffle ticket. The name of the first winner was announced, and a woman raced to the table as if she won the lottery. Her tablemates yelled and clapped in approval. The woman took the dining certificate she won and held it up to the crowd. Francine wondered why all the excitement when all these people could probably buy their own restaurant.

The process continued from container to container. Soon they reached the cleaning supply prize, where Francine put half of her tickets inside.

"And the winner is…Francine Pacque," the announcer said as he read off the raffle ticket.

"That's me!" Francine said to her tablemates, and she stood up proudly.

Mitzi and the rest of people at her table clapped and yelled as Francine walked to the table to collect her prize. She walked directly but slowly as to make a statement. She heard several people ask who she was or comment on her beautiful gown. When she had the cleaning bucket prize handed to her, she proudly held up the bucket and laughed and shrugged. Everyone in the room roared as if it was very funny. It was funny to most of the people in this room, but Francine knew she could take this gift back to Louisiana and give it to the Hanson family. They would be thrilled with the variety of cleaning supplies.

She returned to her seat and knew she made an impact. She was seen, and the crowd enjoyed her winning performance. Everyone in the room heard her name. She was part of the group now.

Raffle winners were continued to be announced until the last prize was gone. Francine did not win the other raffle she entered for the fast-food tickets, but she was happy that she had won one prize.

Shortly after the raffle, the music and dancing began. Francine was used to past gatherings that she had attended where no one dances for quite a while until a few brave souls danced with everyone staring at them. This wasn't the case. Francine was surprised at the quick turnout on the dance floor by many people.

"Mitzi, I'm surprised that the dance floor filled up so quickly. Is that usual?" Francine asked.

"Oh my goodness, yes. We all know each other well and attend so many of the same functions that everyone feels at ease with each other. You'll see as you come down here to visit your uncle," Mitzi said.

Francine didn't answer her with any response, so Mitzi quickly asked, "You will be coming down here sometime to visit and maybe even do some more representation for him, won't you?"

"Sure, I'm sure I'll be coming down here sometimes," Francine responded without emotion.

"While we are sitting here, what else can you tell me about the residence your uncle is looking for? I will be showing you the property close to Noel's house tomorrow, but I would like to line up some additional properties as well," Mitzi asked. "Deep-water access, a dock, a pool, an estate-sized home, but what else?"

Francine answered, "My uncle goes by feel a lot in his line of work. If something appeals to him, he'll want it. I will know when I see the houses if it has the right feel for him and let him know."

"Are you his authorized agent? Are you authorized to buy the home for him? And what's his limit?" Mitzi asked.

Francine felt confident in her answer, "People like him are not bound by a limit. If it feels right, he'd buy it. But remember that he recently got divorced, and I don't think he needs or wants a huge mansion to roam in all by himself. So don't show me anything so large to scare me off."

Francine could see the furl in Mitzi's brow as she thought about available properties.

"I think I know what you mean. You and I will have some fun tomorrow. Do you want to meet for brunch and a mojito before we look at the homes? We may as well enjoy the weekend too," Mitzi said.

"You have a date," Francine answered and touched Mitzi's glass with hers.

The two of them discussed details of where to meet on Sunday. Suddenly, a large hand touched Francine's shoulder lightly. It was Noel's husband, Dave.

"May I share a dance with you?" Dave Noirty asked Francine.

"I would love that. Thank you for asking," Francine answered quickly.

"Why wouldn't I want to dance with a beautiful woman? Every man's eyes were on you tonight, my dear," Dave answered.

"I have nothing over your gorgeous wife," Francine added.

Dave nodded lovingly at his wife with approval.

Shortly thereafter, they were dancing among the society of Naples. Francine was as happy as she ever felt. The song finished, but they continued to stay on the dance floor. Noel, Dave's wife, waved to them as she danced with another man. The band played a wide variety of music, and Francine thought the band may have been the best dance band she had ever heard.

The rest of the evening went well, with Francine mingling with her newfound friends. They danced, drank, and shared stories. It was a glorious evening. Francine was careful to stop drinking liquor early in the evening so she could drive home. She was happy to see some treats come out on the buffet table at 10:00 p.m., so she could get some more food in her to soak up the champagne. She felt fine at midnight when the event ended.

The valets were fetching cars, while Francine, Noel, and Dave Noirty and several other people talked. Shortly thereafter, Francine's Audi was driven up, and she drove away.

As she turned onto the street, Dave frowned and said to Noel, "Maybe we shouldn't have let her drive home."

"Why?" Noel asked.

"Well, didn't you say she was staying at the Ritz-Carlton?" Dave asked.

"Yes, she is," replied Noel.

"Well, she just turned the opposite way on the street," Dave answered.

"Hmmm, maybe we should check to make sure she got home safely?" Noel suggested.

"It's late. Mitzi is going to see her in the morning. Maybe we should leave her alone tonight," Dave added.

Francine never knew how close she just was to being found out. Although, in the long run, maybe Francine would have preferred to be found out tonight.

A gentle rain was falling as Francine woke up on Sunday morning. She lay in bed and thought about the glorious evening she had at the charity event. She was told she looked beautiful by several people last night, which was a term infrequently used to describe her in the past. She met some interesting people from the society of Naples' elite. She had a fabulous meal, had drinks, and danced the night away with a number of gentlemen. This was the life Francine had always wanted. If only she could brag about it with her family.

"I should have taken some pictures so I could post something. Then, maybe my family would think better of me," she said disappointedly. She added, "Heck, what would have been better was if I had someone to share the experience with. Almost everyone there had a spouse or significant other. Why not me?"

As often when Francine thought these negative thoughts, her mood changed to depression. She longed to be back in her old life, with her old job and old friends. She wondered what Brian Sherman was doing now and if he had a new girlfriend, job, and life. She picked up her phone and looked through her pictures until she found one that Brian and she took the first night they went for pizza after they met at the employment agency. She noticed how happy they looked together, toasting with beers in hands.

CHAPTER 13

Real Estate

She noticed the time on her phone and jumped out of bed.

"Mitzi," she gasped.

She only had an hour before her meeting with Mitzi Vanderlooth to look at some real estate. Francine took a quick shower without getting her hair wet. Her hair still looked great from the styling that she had done earlier yesterday. Forty minutes later, Francine was in her car, heading to a restaurant location at Tin City, where Mitzi and she planned to eat before going to the houses.

Both women arrived at the restaurant at the same time. Both women were dressed up, unlike most of the casual tourists who visited the Tin City shops and restaurants. They gave each other a hug and talked about the past evening over mojitos and breakfast. By noon, the women were ready to look at real estate.

"I have two homes and one condo to look at today. I know your uncle was interested in houses only, but this condo comes with a deep-water dock, so let's not dismiss it for now. The first home is the one near Noel and Dave's home. It is only one home south of theirs. The home is in an exceptional location, where only the distinguished elite live. It has four bedrooms, six bathrooms, an outside entertainment area, pool, and deep-water dock," Mitzi said.

Francine was trying to keep interested and calm, but she already felt her breakfast churning inside. She nodded her head approvingly but said nothing.

"The home has been vacant for most of the year, and the owners have only recently put it on the market as a pocket sale listed through myself. It is an exceptional home listed at considerably below market to the right buyer," Mitzi added. "You are going to love it," she added.

"I'm sure I will," Francine responded. "What is the asking price?"

"It's a steal at 3.49 million," Mitzi cheerfully replied.

The breakfast started to come up on Francine. She choked and put her hand up to her mouth.

"Are you OK?" Mitzi asked.

Francine nodded her head and waved for them to continue walking to Mitzi's car as she continued choking.

Shortly thereafter, the two women arrived at the magnificent home. It was a beautiful one-story home with a curved driveway and lush landscaping around the beige stucco home and attached three-car garage. Mitzi walked to the door and unlocked the nine-foot double doors. Francine noticed that the layout was quite similar to the Noirtys' home and made a comment about that to Mitzi. Mitzi explained that both homes were custom homes built by the same builder but assured Francine of the uniqueness in cabinets and finishes. Francine agreed as she gazed into the rooms.

Francine and Mitzi toured all the rooms as Mitzi explained various features. The pair then headed outside to a lavishly appointed bar and outside kitchen. Beyond the outside entertainment room was a long infinity pool. A large screen engulfed both areas. Although the outside furniture were gone due to the long absence of the owners, all the inside furnishings were still intact and available for sale.

The dock appeared to be in excellent shape and had features for docking and lifting a boat. Mitzi was not knowledgeable about the dock, which was a blessing for Francine as she was feeling very inadequate among such grandeur.

"Well, what do you think, Francine?" Mitzi asked after the tour concluded.

"I think it is a beautiful home. I'm just not sure if it is comfortable for one person to live here," Francine lied, referring to her fake uncle who would be living here alone.

"Oh, many people live alone in big homes around here. It isn't as if he would be doing the cleaning," Mitzi said while laughing.

"Yes, I know that, but I don't know if it has the right "feel." That's what I mean," Francine responded.

Mitzi frowned and said, "Well, I'll have to think about that for a minute."

The next property the women looked at was a larger home near the marina. It was spectacular and more money. Francine had a suspicion that Mitzi brought her to that particular home to reinforce that the first home was a better fit for Francine's uncle. They then went to another area in Naples called Park Shore. They looked at a condominium residence in the backwater from the Gulf. It was in a beautiful location near the beach, shopping, and major highway. The condo itself was much smaller than the homes seen earlier, with private docks and a community pool. Francine wished she could buy a place in this area. But playing the uncle's rep role, she quickly told Mitzi that this condo would not be suited for her uncle.

Mitzi drove Francine back to her car and asked for feedback on each residence.

"Am I on the right track?" Mitzi asked, referring to the list of requirements for Francine's uncle.

"Yes, Mitzi. You took me to a variety of different features. I think the first home would fit his needs the best," Francine replied.

"Are you authorized to make an offer? That home won't last long on the market, even if it is a pocket listing and off the MLS," Mitzi added.

Francine had to think carefully and quickly as to why she couldn't buy the home now.

"I am authorized, but I would want to talk to my uncle first and show him pictures. But I'm stuck on the fit aspect. There may be a lot of single people in Naples that live in big homes alone, but my uncle is not used to being alone. He was married for a long time. I don't know if having a home as big as that one is prudent for him. I may suggest to him to wait for a while before purchasing something," Francine said.

She was happy with her response and thought Mitzi would back down from her sales pitch. But she was surprised when Mitzi suddenly pulled her car over and said, "Francine, hold off on that for a moment. I need to make a phone call. Do you mind waiting in the car?"

Francine responded favorably, but when Mitzi got out of the car, Francine could not imagine why. *Why did she pull over so suddenly, and why did she have to leave the car?* Francine wondered. She watched Mitzi as Mitzi walked in a circle, talking to someone over the phone and gesturing with her arms.

After several minutes, Mitzi returned to the car. She turned seriously toward Francine and said, "Francine, I have an idea and had to get approval before I suggested it to you."

Francine softly asked, "OK?"

"I just spoke to the owners of the first home. They are personal friends of mine and wonderful people. I told them that you are seriously considering purchasing their home for your uncle but that you are concerned about the feel of such a big home for a single person. Anyway, after discussing my idea, my friends agreed to it," Mitzi said.

Francine looked quizzically at Mitzi and said, "I'm listening."

"I'm suggesting that you check out of the Ritz-Carlton and stay as a guest in their home. Then you could get the feel of the home and send pictures or videos at will to your uncle. How long were you staying in Naples?" Mitzi asked.

Francine was astonished. It was a dream come true. She could stay in an estate home for a while. Her body became flush with excitement, and she knew she needed to stay cool in her response to Mitzi.

"I was staying here through Thanksgiving. Then I need to leave to conduct some personal business in Louisiana," Francine answered.

She felt her heart racing and folded her arms while answering.

"That sounds perfect! Then you'll have about two weeks to try it out. Don't you think that is a wonderful idea?" Mitzi asked.

Francine smiled broadly and said, "I think it sounds like a great idea. What would be the logistics as far as cost, cleaning, or other responsibilities?"

Mitzi said, "Nothing! Just move right in. The owners already pay for cleaning, which is really only dusting right now. When you're there, the cleaning company will finally earn their money," Mitzi said. "If there is any extra cleaning or laundry needed when you leave, I'll pick it up out of my real estate budget."

"Then I would love to try out the house," Francine answered.

"Great! Why don't we go right now to the Ritz-Carlton and you can check out. I can help with getting your luggage into the house and give you the keys," Mitzi suggested.

"Hmmm, no, I would rather come tomorrow. I have a guest stopping to see me tonight at the Ritz," Francine lied.

"A guest! Francine! It sounds like a booty call night to me. Good for you," Mitzi responded.

"Mitzi! No! It's just an old friend I used to work with and his wife. Nothing as much fun," Francine replied.

That answer satisfied Mitzi.

She said, "How about meeting me tomorrow morning, say about ten?"

Francine knew that tomorrow was a workday. "How about later in the day? There are some things I need to do tomorrow during the day," Francine suggested.

"That would be fine. Six then?" Mitzi asked.

"Six o'clock sounds fine. I'll be there," Francine said.

Mitzi stopped her car next to where Francine was parked at Tin City. As Francine got out, she overwhelmingly thanked Mitzi for showing her homes in Naples.

Mitzi answered, "You're welcome, Francine, but I still think you have a booty call tonight and are expecting a late morning or afternoon tomorrow."

Francine laughed and shrugged her shoulders. "Only I know for sure," Francine responded.

The two of them hugged and gave a short kiss on the cheek to each other. A very proud Francine got out of Mitzi's car and got into her own car.

"I can't believe this! Oh my god! I'm going to live in that house! *Ahhhh!*" Francine screamed with glee.

Francine returned to her hotel, the cheapest in Naples, and told the desk clerk that she would be checking out in the morning. She went to her room, removed her professional clothes for wearing to her clients tomorrow, and packed the remaining clothes in her suitcases.

CHAPTER 14

Overload

Monday came, and Francine anxiously checked out of the hotel. She dressed in her work clothes because she had a full day of work prior to going to her new lodging. Most of her work clothes were presentable enough to wear to any occasion, and she was glad she took advantage of all the wonderful sales in Chicago while she was working in the Windy City.

Her first stop was at Creative Fabrications Company, the company where Angie Fratilo was the chief financial officer. She was anxious to see Angie because she genuinely liked her company, plus Angie was the person responsible for getting the other seventeen companies to sign on for the zone 2 network. Francine checked inventory in the stockroom before going to the office complex to say hello to Angie. As she walked into the complex, Angie waved her into her office while she was completing a phone call.

The phone conversation finished, and Angie said, "I didn't know you were going to the Children's Hospital charity event."

Francine was caught off guard. She didn't know what to say in response. *How would Angie know I was at the charity event?* Francine thought.

Waiting for an answer but not receiving one, Angie moved the newspaper across her desk toward Francine. There in the society section was a picture of the five women Francine talked with before dinner at the charity event. Francine's picture was in the middle. She vaguely remembered a photographer taking their picture.

"You look beautiful! Did you know the other ladies or did you just meet them at the event?" Angie asked.

Francine read the caption and smiled.

"I didn't know about the picture. I never was photographed before and put in the newspaper," Francine babbled.

She was thrilled about the picture, and she was pleased at how good she looked.

"I love your new hairdo. I hardly recognized you when I first saw the picture, but then I read the caption, and it listed your name. You looked great," Angie responded.

"Thanks. I saw an advertisement for the event and thought, 'Why not?'" Francine said.

"Very nice. Did you have a good time?" asked Angie.

Francine explained how she won a raffle prize of a bucket of cleaning supplies, and both women laughed. They spoke a few more minutes about the event before going over a summary of the inventory replacements that Francine would be ordering for the company.

As Francine left, a queasy feeling filled Angie. Something didn't seem right to her. Something in the way Francine talked about the event seemed forced.

"Hmmm, I'll have to ask Noel about it when I see her," Angie said to herself.

Finally, the workday ended, and Francine met Mitzi at the home on Rum Row. Francine was still dressed in her casual work clothes, but Mitzi didn't seem to notice, or at least she didn't say anything about it. Mitzi showed Francine to a guest room with an en suite rather than taking her to the master bedroom. She explained that the owners were open to Francine trying out their home but not open to her using their personal bedroom and bath. Francine said she understood perfectly.

As soon as Mitzi left the house, Francine opened several suitcases and removed most of her clothes. She wanted to wash and dry everything as using hotel laundries for the last several months left her clothes dingy and hard. She changed into a comfortable pair of lounging pants and a tank top and headed to the kitchen. She was happy that she brought a little bit of groceries, soda, and wine with her.

"I deserve a nice glass of wine by the pool, I think," Francine said.

She poured the wine, grabbed a local newspaper purchased earlier in the day, and sunk into one of the cozy lounge chairs by the pool. She opened the paper to the picture of her at the charity event. "Naples Comes Together to Support Children's Hospital" read the headline. A brief paragraph followed that explained the event, location, keynote speaker, and committee chairpersons. Below the paragraph were several pictures. The prominent picture was the one where she stood in the middle of five other women. The caption read, "Charity participants included Noel Noirty, Mitzi Vanderlooth, Francine Pacque, Shauna Delgado, Pepper Franklin, and Babs Simmons."

Francine put down her glass and picked up her cell phone. She took a picture of the newspaper photograph and caption. She then took a selfie of herself seated at the pool. Soon, both were posted on her Facebook page.

"I hope someone will notice these!" Francine said.

She settled back in her lounge chair and took a brief nap.

A faint buzzer sounded that awakened Francine. She quickly identified it as her laundry buzzer. She got up and attended to her clothes. Then she took a long, leisurely tour through the magnificent home, taking some pictures to post online.

Each bedroom was outfitted with large closets and private en suites. She walked through the three similar bedrooms before entering the master bedroom suite. Two large walk-in closets flanked the hallway to the massive bathroom. A luxurious large soaking tub sat under an etched glass window. There were two showers. One was a walk-in shower with jets and a rain showerhead. The other was located through a small outside door that led to a private walled patio with an outdoor shower.

"I may not be able to use the master bedroom, but I am definitely trying out this baby," Francine said to herself. She quickly went to her suite and retrieved her toiletries and a bathrobe. Within a few minutes, Francine was stripping down outside to enjoy this private outside shower oasis. She felt like she was in heaven.

The next day was business as usual, and Francine went to the next set of companies to check inventories. She knew that having these eighteen companies was a good start but hardly enough to keep her finances afloat after the New Year. She needed to cultivate another territory or get additional business soon. At midday, her phone rang.

"Hello, Francine. How was your night?" a voice asked.

Francine hadn't looked at the phone number when she answered, but she immediately recognized Mitzi's voice.

"It was very nice," Francine replied.

She didn't want to lay it on too thick.

"I enjoyed it," Francine added.

"Good to hear. I think you will find that your uncle would have the lifestyle he is requiring," Mitzi said before saying, "Where are you now?"

Francine had to think quickly. She was working, but she was not sharing that information for fear that Mitzi could become suspicious.

"Why, is there a problem?" Francine asked.

"No, no problem. I stopped at the house to check on you and saw you were gone. That's all," Mitzi said.

"Oh, I'm not one to sit around too much. I like to drive around and check out things," Francine said.

"I'd like to stop by one day this week to talk a bit about the property. What day would work for you?" Mitzi asked.

"Any day you want to stop will be good for me. Just let me know when," Francine responded.

"OK, great. How about Wednesday? Then maybe you and I can go to lunch with Noel. How does that sound?" Mitzi said.

"That would be fine," Francine answered.

"Good. I know you just checked out of the Ritz-Carlton, but I would love to go there for lunch. I know that Noel likes to lunch at the poolside restaurant. So let's go there, OK? You'll probably enjoy seeing them again anyway, because I know the Ritz makes a point of knowing all their guests. I'm sure that anyone staying in the suites, like you were, will be missed," Mitzi stated.

Francine groaned to herself as she thought, *How am I going to pull this off? The Ritz-Carlton won't know me from Adam.*

Francine pulled herself together and answered, "Yes, they are wonderful there. It's a wonderful idea. Let me know what time and where to meet."

"Let's say noon and I'll pick you and Noel up. If that doesn't work with Noel, I'll let you know," Mitzi responded.

Francine sat in the stockroom at the company she was working at and stared at the phone.

"How am I going to pull this one off?" she asked aloud. As she worked through the day, a plan emerged.

Instead of heading back to the house on Rum Row, Francine headed to the Ritz-Carlton Hotel. She thought she better have another look around so the hotel would be familiar to her. She drove into the entrance of the lushly landscaped grounds and looked for a parking lot. There wasn't one. Finally, she drove up to the entrance, where there were three valets on duty. One valet pranced to the car.

"Welcome to the Ritz-Carlton. Are you a guest here?" he asked.

"No, but I would like to go to the restaurant," Francine answered.

He opened the car door and helped Francine out of the car. When she exited, he handed her a ticket and drove her car down the driveway to a hidden location. Francine entered the building.

Francine was used to beautiful hotels and frequented many of them through past work travels, work dinners, or conventions. She lived in Chicago and visited many of those beautiful hotels, such as the Hilton and Intercontinental on Michigan Avenue. All of them had luxurious large lobbies and allowed people to walk freely around to the restaurants, bars, and pool area. But this hotel, the Ritz-Carlton, had strict policies to protect their distinguished guests.

Upon walking into the beautiful lobby with curved windows and columns and a grand staircase, she was met by two women strategically placed in the center of the lobby. Both women were armed with a clipboard. One of the women immediately walked toward Francine and asked if she could help her.

Francine answered that she was interested in seeing the poolside restaurant.

"Are you dining there alone? Are you a guest?" the woman asked while looking at her clipboard.

Francine answered that she was alone and that she was planning to dine there. In actuality, Francine did not plan to dine, but it may give her the opportunity to plan for Wednesday's lunch. The woman walked with Francine to the appropriate doorway that would lead Francine to the poolside restaurant.

As Francine walked to the restaurant, it occurred to her that the women with the clipboards may have pictures of the hotel guests. She noticed that the other woman called one of the guests by name when they walked by. Francine never saw such service in her past hotel days. Now she understood why Mitzi made that comment about the hotel being happy to see Francine again and that Francine would want to see the hotel staff again too.

The restaurant hostess seated Francine at a table near the pool. The hotel had a marvelous outside dining and pool area, and Francine noticed guests lounging and frolicking in the pool. When Francine's waiter came to the table, he introduced himself and welcomed her to the restaurant. He also asked if Francine was a guest. She responded that she was not a guest at this time. She looked at the menu and ordered an appetizer and a glass of wine.

Francine noticed that the hostess called guests by name as they arrived at the restaurant. She noticed that the wait staff also referred to their table guests by name. *I'm screwed* was all Francine could think of. As her waiter returned with her wine, Francine decided to bear out her problem to him.

"Can I ask you something?" she asked Tom, her waiter.

"Of course," Tom responded.

"I'm in a pickle. I don't know how to say this and not sound bad, but here it goes...I met some women, wonderful women, at an event in Naples. I was too embarrassed to let them know I was only a poor, working woman, not from society, like them. So I told them I was a guest here at the Ritz-Carlton."

Tom smiled and nodded.

"Now, they want to come to lunch here on Wednesday. I actually came here to get familiar with the hotel and this restaurant. But now, I can see the personal service that guests get when they come here. I don't know what to do," she confided to Tom.

"You could check into the hotel," Tom answered and smiled.

"Thanks, but I can't afford it here, and I already have a place where I'm staying. Well, thanks, now you know that I'm a fraud. It's not your problem. Sorry to have said anything," Francine shyly added.

Tom left and attended to the other guests in his station. A few minutes later, he returned with Francine's appetizer. She was too embarrassed to look up at him but soon realized that he hadn't moved. She looked up at him, expecting him to ask if there was anything else she required.

"You aren't the first person to fake that they are staying at the hotel. People do it all the time," Tom said.

Francine's mouth gaped open. "Really?"

"Uh-huh. When were you coming for lunch?" he asked.

"Wednesday about twelve thirty or one o'clock," she answered.

"Good. I'm working that day. Just ask for Tom's section. I will put down a reservation under your name," Tom said as he gave Francine a pen and a piece of paper.

"Write down your name and the number of guests. I'll enter it in the reservation log," he continued.

Francine wrote down her name and pronounced her last name for him. Tom nodded.

"I'll take care of it. Us little guys have to look out for each other. They do," he added, referring to wealthy society helping one another.

"Thank you so much, Tom," Francine said before adding, "I wish there was some way I could help you someday."

"Well, if you ever know of a job that would get me out of this place," Tom whispered.

"Don't get me wrong, the Ritz is a great place to work. But I have a degree in business, and I'm working as a waiter!" he added.

Francine smiled. "Well, Tom, I may be able to help you with that. Why don't you write down your full name and number. I may have a job you might be interested in doing," Francine said.

Tom look astonished. "Really?"

She nodded and raised her eyebrows. "Yes, I do. Let me call you tonight if you're available and give you some insight."

"Great! I get off work at seven," Tom said.

"OK. Expect a call around eight," Francine replied.

Tom left her table, and Francine ate her delicious treat and finished her wine. Francine thought about her work needs in Naples. She needed someone to work her inventory when she left the Naples area to develop the next zone. She thought that the Fort Myers area would be a great zone 3. If Tom wanted to take on zone 2 maintenance with an upcoming zone 3 in a few months, he might work into a permanent full-time position. Francine smiled as she handed her ticket and five dollars to the valet as she left. She may have solved more than her Wednesday lunch dilemma.

That evening, she called Tom Bender, the waiter at the Ritz-Carlton, and explained the position she had for him. It initially would be a part-time position of about ten hours per week. He could pick and choose the time, as long as he realized that the companies in Naples work primarily day-shift hours Monday through Friday, so his hours would have to be within those constraints. Tom said that he could shift his Friday hours at the Ritz-Carlton to Sunday and have every Friday available. He also would have more time to work during the week, but it would be dependent on his weekly Ritz-Carlton schedule.

Francine told him her vision of moving from only critical inventory parts to a vendor-managed stock program. Tom was familiar with the term from his manufacturing class at college. He was eager to gain some experience in the business field and to get some more hours of wages.

They discussed the possibility of the job growing into a full-time position as Francine added the Fort Myers area as zone 3. Tom could potentially be the agent for the area if he and the customers worked well together. The conversation finished with a discussion of the hourly wage. If a part needed pickup and delivery, an additional wage would be given. Francine gave the same wage structure she gave to Bill Hanson in Monroe, Louisiana.

Tom thanked her numerous times. Francine and Tom set up a formal appointment time to visit a couple of companies so she could demonstrate the needs. It was set. Francine had some help after she left the area.

Francine felt like a chameleon living two lives. She devised a plan to leave the Rum Row house for work between 8:30 and 9:00 a.m. every weekday. She decided it was best to turn onto the street in the opposite direction from the Noirty family's home to avoid any questions as to why she left the house every day. She also decided to wear a sunhat in the car so it appeared as if she might be going to the beach.

Work was going well for Francine, and she continued to pick up sales other than her critical equipment network. The companies in the Naples area were not used to all the personal attention, and they continually asked her to give prices on items they needed to purchase. She was also able to install sundry supplies as a vendor-managed item in most of the companies. Sales in these small companies was not large, but it provided continual commission, and the sales added up each month.

Francine's success in the Monroe, Louisiana, area called zone 1 was growing exponentially after the articles in their local newspaper credited Specialty Products Distribution, the company that Francine represented, as paramount in the quick start-up after the fire at Ultra Electric Co. It appeared, as Francine had predicted, that the Southern companies placed loyalty to suppliers who personally helped them. In the few weeks that Francine had left Louisiana, sales had quadrupled. Bill Hanson was working up to forty hours a week, plus doing his part-time construction job.

Francine talked to Bill Hanson frequently on the phone. Bill was also setting up vendor-managed areas in some of the plants. He told Francine that he had leads on new companies to include in the zone 1 network. Francine was very pleased at the progress that Bill had made and in the improvements to the computer files for the networks. The network file was now professionally designed with lookup tables for products, features, and company information. Francine knew that she owed Bill more than the wage per hour that he was currently getting. It was a difficult discussion when Francine called him on Tuesday morning.

"Hi, Bill, it's Francine. How are you doing?" Francine asked.

"I'm fine. Say, when are you getting back here to Louisiana? I have some people asking about joining our network," asked Bill.

"I'm planning on driving up the weekend after Thanksgiving. I would be there on Monday. OK?" Francine replied.

"Sure. I just wanted to make sure I told these guys the right info. So you would be seeing some of these potential customers during that week?" Bill asked.

"Yes. If you would like to make appointments with them for us to visit them, that would be great," she said.

"You want me there too?" Bill asked.

He wasn't able to hide his excitement.

"Yes, Bill, you too. Actually, that is why I called you this morning. I wanted to discuss something with you," Francine said.

"Our zone 1 network is working well, and we are adding vendor-managed sales and other company supply sales. That was what I expected for the zone, and I know we will continue to grow this zone both in size and in sales dollars. What I don't know yet is what to expect on a monthly basis, as what I will call core sales. Core sales would be normal or average monthly sales dollars. Do you understand so far?" Francine asked.

"Yes, ma'am. I get it," he replied.

"Good. You have done a great job so far. I couldn't be happier with your performance and the urgency and personal attention that you are giving our customers," Francine said.

"Thank you. I really like what I'm doing," Bill replied.

"So this is what I've been thinking, I would like to be able to offer you a full-time position soon, if you would be interested. If not, then I would put on a second part-time person," she said.

"Wow! Wait until I tell Mary!" Bill exclaimed.

"I'm glad you are excited, but I can't quite offer you full-time yet. I need to establish that normal core sales income so we can both make some money. I'll be talking to my dad during Christmas about setting up a real company. Remember, right now I'm just paying you by personal check. If we pursue this, I have to pay taxes, workers' compensation, and so on," she said. "My thought is to continue to pay you an hourly wage but a higher one."

"Would I get benefits?" Bill asked.

"See, this is what I have to talk to my dad about. He and my mom own an accounting firm, and they handle many small companies. He will be able to mentor me on owning my own firm but contracting to support SPD's products. My thought is yes, you should get vacation benefits and I'm thinking a special monthly payment to cover you and your family's personal insurance," Francine said.

She kept quiet, waiting for his response.

"Thank you, Francine. I can't wait to tell Mary. She's always worried about our next check in the construction industry. This would be a real job and a real opportunity for me. Thank you so much, Francine," Bill said.

His voice shook slightly as he finished his response.

"That's wonderful. Talk it over with Mary, and like I said, I should be able to tell you more when I return from Chicago in early January. So remember that for now, this is what I'm thinking, and I think it only fair to let you know my strategy, but it will be confirmed in January. That's my plan," Francine said.

They continued talking about particular sales issues that arose in the past couple of weeks. All of them were handled quickly through either the contact at SPD or through Chrissy Pacque. Bill had called Chrissy several times for help with expediting items. He said that the SPD contact was always helpful but had other items to expedite too. Calling Chrissy and having her arrange the details was much faster and less stressful for him.

Francine was surprised to find that her sister-in-law had been helping Bill so frequently. She hadn't heard anything from Chrissy about it. She made a mental note to call Chrissy but decided to call her directly after she hung up from Bill.

"Chrissy! How are you doing? How are the kids?" Francine asked as soon as she heard her sister-in-law's voice on the phone.

She didn't ask how her brother was because she tried to keep him out of all her conversations. She was proud of her brother but knew that he rode on his athletic achievement's coattails too long. He transitioned directly into the athletic department of Northwestern after college and didn't really know how real life and real people had to work. He was a blowhard, in Francine's opinion, who bullied her most of her life.

"We're all fine. How are you?" Chrissy asked.

Francine heard a quick gasp followed by Chrissy saying, "Francine! Oh my god! We've been looking at your Facebook page. Oh my, you look great! I love your new hair, and that dress you wore to the charity ball was fantastic. Tell me everything!"

Francine knew she posted those pictures but didn't think she would be getting such a grand review. Francine shared some of the details of the charity event but didn't get too far before Chrissy asked her about the pool picture.

"What's with that mansion you are lounging by in the picture by the pool? And the other pictures of some of the rooms. Wow, is that where you are staying?" Chrissy asked.

Francine hated lying to her sister-in-law, but she didn't see another way around it.

"Yes, one of my connections here offered me a chance to stay at the house. She knows the owner. I'm paying a little fee, but it was well worth it," Francine lied.

She felt her stomach harden as she chose to lie.

"So you actually get to live in the house? Francine, that's wonderful. You sure are doing well at your job," she replied.

Francine's stomach tightened further as she remembered that she hadn't told her family about her job loss at Magnacraft. Chrissy deserved to know. She wanted to tell her sister-in-law but decided to hold off until she got back to Chicago in mid-December.

"I hear that you have been helping Bill Hanson quite a bit with looking up items and expediting supplies," Francine stated.

"Yes, I've been helping him once in a while. He'll call me or text me from time to time, and most of the time I am able to help," Chrissy said.

"I hope you have been tracking your hours. I only first heard about it before I called you," Francine asked.

177

"I hope you aren't mad? Are you?" Chrissy asked.

"No. Of course I'm not mad. I just want to make sure that you get compensated for your time. That's all," answered Francine.

"Well, I actually haven't logged in any hours. I just wanted to help. You know, it makes me feel useful in a non-Mom kind of way," she answered.

"Chris, I know you want to help out, and I'm really appreciative. So does Bill. But this is a business, and you need to get compensated. Try to make out some kind of log. Maybe you can backtrack, looking at your past texts or phone calls to Bill. I need to pay my favorite sister-in-law. OK?" Francine asked.

"OK. I can do that. I keep notes on the issues that I worked on, so it won't be difficult," Chrissy said.

"Good, then send me your log or at least text me the hours," Francine suggested.

They continued to talk about the family, including Gerry, and about Thanksgiving prep. Chrissy said everyone was going to her house for Thanksgiving. Francine was quiet, as she would have loved to be there with them. Working on the road was lonesome, even in a grand house, and Francine was missing her friends and family.

"Chrissy, is Gerry going to be doing any traveling in December?" Francine coyly asked.

"Absolutely. Right through Christmas is a big time for football. Gerry will be on the road most of the month, looking for recruits and eyeing up college games. For me, it makes it easy to decorate the Christmas tree and make cookies and such. I try to involve the kids as much as possible so I don't go nuts," Chrissy explained before adding, "Why are you asking?"

"Well, I have a problem. Remember the young student that is staying at my townhouse? Lilly Lee? She's actually a graduate student from Northwestern," Francine explained.

"Yes. I remember that someone is staying at your place while you're gone. Is she working out?" Chrissy asked.

"She's completely wonderful. I can't believe my luck in finding someone so great. But I have a problem that I'm slightly afraid to ask you," Francine said.

"What is it?" Chris asked.

Francine continued, "Lilly is from Japan, and her parents are coming to visit her. She asked if they could stay at the townhouse, which I think is great. But part of the time, I will also be in town. I was looking forward to relaxing at home, but I don't want to be there when Lilly's parents are visiting. Is there a chance that I could stay by you when Gerry is gone? I could stay at Mom and Dad's on Christmas Eve and Christmas night to give you some privacy," Francine asked.

"Yes, yes! That would be awesome! I'd actually have someone to talk to and eat cookies with who isn't under ten years old," Chrissy answered in delight.

"Excellent! Then it's a deal. We can discuss details closer to when I get back, and don't be afraid to tell me the nights you want to be alone. I love my brother, but I really don't want to be around him 24-7," Francine confided.

"I know. He can be so mean to you. Calling you that nickname and making fun of everything you do. I've spoken to him so many times about it. I'm sorry that he teases you so much," Chrissy answered.

"As long as he doesn't talk to you and the kids like that, I can handle it. He just thinks he's being funny," Francine said.

"You know, he's been real quiet about you lately. I showed him your Facebook page, and he just stared at it. He said to me that you have really made something of yourself. I'm not kidding. He just stared and stared. I think he even said something like, 'My sister has really grown up. Look at her now,'" Chrissy said.

"Really? That makes me feel good. I can't remember one time where he complimented me. Thanks for sharing, but I'm not betting that he'll be so nice to me at Christmas. We'll see, but my guess is that he'll call me Fanny Pack as soon as he sees me. We'll see," Francine said before the sister-in-laws said their good-byes.

Francine barely hung up when she received another call. It was Angie Fratilo.

"Hi, Francine, are you busy?" she asked.

Francine remembered that she hadn't done any inventory work yet this morning. All she had been doing was talking on the phone.

"No, Angie, what can I do for you today?" she replied.

"I have another colleague that is going to be starting a business. It is an import business on a grand scale. He's going to be looking for everything to start up his warehouse. Are you interested?" Angie asked.

"Yes, I am. Thank you for the referral. Do you have his contact info so I can get a hold of him?" Francine asked.

"I do, but he is a very elusive person. He's wealthy and used to more of a personal approach than you giving him a cold call. He's from the old country. European. He has expensive taste and expensive items. He's the kind of person that has to be swayed, cultivated, until he trusts you. Then, you are a friend for life, you're family," Angie explained.

"How do you know him, Angie?" Francine asked.

"He's a relative, kind of. As I said, once you know him and he accepts you, you're family. He and my parents were friends before my parents came over to America. He has so many beautiful artifacts that my family convinced him to start a business some years ago. He became richer and started collecting more. Now he wants to start an import business in Naples," Angie explained.

"So how do you suggest I get acquainted with him?" Francine asked.

"Dinner at my place. He'll be in town Wednesday night. Would that work for you?" Angie asked.

Francine remembered that she was having a lunch date with Mitzi and Noel on Wednesday, but their lunch and visit should be over in time for dinner.

"That would work out well for me," Francine answered her. "What can I bring? How about several bottles of Italian wine?"

"Perfect. I'll text you a couple of suggestions and my address. How about seven o'clock at my house?" Angie asked.

"Sounds like a plan. Angie, you've been such a good friend to me. Thank you from the bottom of my heart," Francine said.

After the call, Angie sat back in her desk chair and smiled. She was so happy to find a new friend and colleague. She longed for a friend she could trust, and Francine filled that gap so well. Angie picked up the phone and called her uncle and her boyfriend, Ben, to firm up the date and time.

Francine was tired by the end of Tuesday, and she had substantial paperwork to do. She took a quick shower when she got to the house and put on some comfortable shorts and top. She went to the dining room and spread her paperwork out on the massive dining room table to sort companies and deliverables. She was almost done sorting when a melodic tone sounded. It took her a few seconds before she realized it was the doorbell. Peeking out the edge of the dining room window, she saw Noel and her husband, Dave, standing outside.

"Oh shit," she whispered. She quickly picked up each sorted pile and made one huge pile. Then she picked up the paperwork and whisked it into a cabinet in the dining room. She went to the door to greet her visitors.

"Hi, Noel. Hi, Dave, excuse my looks. I was just settling down after a shower," Francine said.

"I tried to have Noel call you before we came over, but she wouldn't do it," Dave replied.

"You don't have to tell her everything, you big oaf. I wanted to surprise her. Can we come in?" Noel asked. "We brought wine," she added.

"Of course, come on in," Francine dutifully answered. She longed for a quiet night, and tomorrow was the day she was going to see Noel for lunch.

The couple came in and walked directly to the outside lanai area. It was apparent that they had been inside this residence before. Noel sat down, while Dave went directly to the outside bar to open the wine and fill three glasses.

"We are here on official business," Noel said and continued, "unless you have someone here that you are entertaining. Mitzi suspects you are having a little monkey business with someone."

Noel raised her eyebrows at Francine.

"I had a friend I wanted to see the other evening. That's all. Mitzi has quite the imagination," Francine answered.

"We all do. That's what we do. And if there isn't anything interesting going on, we shake it up a bit," Noel said.

Dave added, "Or they go shopping."

"That goes without saying. We always go shopping. You want us to look good, don't you?" Noel said to Dave.

He gave his wife a peck on the cheek as he quickly pinched her bottom. "You always turn me on, baby," he said.

Francine giggled, and they had a toast to the evening. Soon the conversation turned to business. First the couple asked about the house and if Francine thought it would be a fit for her uncle. Francine had been practicing her excuses for not purchasing the house, so she was ready for them.

"I spoke to my uncle today, and we discussed the house. He's on the fence about it because frankly, I'm not sure it is right for him. It's beautiful, but I'm stuck on the size of it. Heck, I've hardly walked more than three rooms so far in my stay here," Francine said.

"That's why we are here, Francine. It's not about a house. It's about a lifestyle. We pride ourselves in this community of being a family. We have dinners with each other, volunteer with each other, party, golf, and boat with each other. You uncle would not be alone. He would have a whole community," Noel said before adding, "We came here for two reasons. One, we would like to invite you for Thanksgiving dinner at our house. There'll be several people from the charity event there that you will know. Second, Dave wants to talk yachts with you.

"Oh!" Francine exclaimed.

Her mind raced as to how to get out of this mess.

"Noel, I didn't know you cooked," Francine said.

"I do, but I won't. It's being catered. I'll make something, like appetizers, but I want to enjoy everyone's company too. If you cook, that's all you do, you know," Noel answered.

"Let's just cut to the chase. Francine, you are coming to dinner next Thursday, period. Now to the important part—yachts. Your uncle wants to live the lifestyle, and nothing helps that more than a beautiful new yacht to cruise in the Gulf," Dave said. "I have the finest yachts in the area."

Francine said, "I've noticed your yacht at your dock. It's beautiful."

Dave and Noel looked at each other and laughed.

"That's not our yacht. That's just a small pleasure craft that I take to work. Our yacht is parked at the marina," Dave said.

Francine thought, *I'm screwed.* She picked up her glass to avoid attention to her shaking hands. *This is so wrong.*

"Does your uncle have a yacht now?" Dave asked.

"He has a boat at the Chicago marina. But it is about the size of the boat you call a pleasure craft. I don't know much about yachting," Francine added.

"Well, it is about time you learn, young lady, so you can steer your uncle my way. Does he drive his boat himself or does he have a crew?" he asked.

A crew! I'm so out of my league, Francine thought.

"He drives it himself, but most of the time, it is docked. He'll party or stay on board, but that's about it. You know, he is busy with his company during the week," Francine answered.

"Is he planning to move down here or just come on holiday?" Dave asked.

"Oh no, he still will be running his business. He would come for vacations and probably some extended stays. But he wouldn't be living here. That would be some years down the line," Francine said.

"Enough with the secrecy, Francine. We are all friends. We love you! But talking about your uncle as your uncle rather than a name is getting old. Who is he?" Noel asked.

Francine shifted in her seat. She didn't have a good answer and didn't want to appear rude.

Finally, she looked up and said, "I'm sorry, but I promised him that I would have his back. When he is ready to divulge his name, then I'll do it, but not now."

"Leave her alone, Noel. You can be quite a badger. Francine, how about coming to my marina on Thursday or Friday so we can talk boats? I'm sure I have a selection of crafts that your uncle would like to order," Dave stated. "What day works for you, Francine?"

Francine needed to work, and she already was going to miss tomorrow's workday. She answered, "Friday is fine. Can I be there around three? There's some business I need to attend to earlier."

"See, Dave. She's got someone here," Noel answered as she threw the last of the wine in her mouth.

Dave smiled but continued talking to Francine, "I will need to know what your uncle is planning to spend on his yacht. Please call him so we have an idea before your visit on Friday."

"Yes, I can do that. I suppose we're talking several hundred thousand, right?" Francine asked.

Dave looked at her sternly and said, "Don't even waste my time if that's what your uncle wants. Our new yachts average three to five million."

Francine almost choked on her wine but maintained a steady gaze at Dave.

The three of them finished their wines, and Dave and Noel left the house, walking a short distance to their home. Francine went back into the dining room. It was too late to start sorting paperwork. She sat down on one of the upholstered chairs and laid her head onto the table. She started sobbing.

"What am I going to do? I guess I have to play it along until I finally tell them that my uncle decided to purchase something out West. That'll work," she told herself before heading to bed.

Francine woke up early on Wednesday morning refreshed and ready for her day. She left for one of the companies earlier than usual because she had to stop work at about eleven o'clock to get to the Ritz-Carlton to have lunch with Mitzi and Noel. Shortly before eleven, Francine stepped into the company's office women's room with a small suitcase. She emerged several minutes later wearing a melon gauze dress with a multicolored wide belt. She wore a large necklace with matching earrings and a pair of divine Michael Kors flat shoes.

Francine headed to the Ritz-Carlton aware that she needed to arrive there prior to her guests so that the valet would have her car already parked. Traffic was light, so she arrived in plenty of time. She drove up the driveway and told the valet that she would be several hours while she dined with friends.

When she entered the hotel, she immediately went up to the two women who stood guard over the lobby and explained that she was waiting for her friends for lunch. One of the women asked which restaurant she would be dining at and if she had a reservation. Francine advised her, and the women scurried off to check if the reservation was true. Francine sat on one of the couches and waited. She remembered to leave her purse in the car and only took a small leather mirror holder, which she conveniently used to hide her credit card inside. Mitzi and Noel arrived early, and Francine got up and hugged them as they walked into the center lobby. Then the three ladies headed to the poolside restaurant.

As Francine walked, she noticed the hostess looking at the group, her reservation log, and the seating chart. Thankfully, Tom, the waiter that Francine befriended, walked up to the hostess and told her that these were the guests he was expecting.

"Good morning, Ms. Pacque," the hostess said to Francine. "Your table is ready. This way, ladies."

The three women followed the hostess to a fabulous vantage point table. Tom was already waiting there with a chair pulled out for Francine.

"Hello, Ms. Pacque. How are you this afternoon?" Tom asked as he pushed in her chair.

He quickly moved to Mitzi and then Noel to assist them with their chairs.

"I'm fine, Tom. How are you today?" she asked the waiter.

He was carefully giving each woman a menu. When he reached Francine, she slyly slid her leather holder carrying her credit card to him. He discretely put the card into his pocket.

It was a glorious lunch. The women had several appetizers with their wine before lunching on a specialty salad entrée. At the end of the lunch, Francine asked for a dessert menu, but her friends graciously declined the offer. Tom approached the table and handed Francine her receipt.

"Oh, Francine. You didn't need to buy lunch for us," Noel stated.

Noel and Mitzi argued for a short while that they didn't want Francine to pay. Francine answered that it had been her privilege to get to know both of them, and they had been very gracious to her while in Naples. Francine insisted on paying. The bill was over one hundred dollars…for lunch and wine.

As Noel and Mitzi left, Francine gave them hugs and said she needed to talk to the clerk. The women left as Francine strategically watched them out the window. The desk clerk asked what he could help her with. Francine asked him about rates at several times in the future while she kept an eye on her friends. Finally, Mitzi's car appeared, and she and Noel drove away. Francine thanked the clerk for his help and slowly walked out of the hotel, handing her valet ticket to the valet.

"I got away with it," she told herself and smiled.

It was one thirty when Francine left the hotel, and she still had a dinner function at seven this evening, so Francine decided to take the day off. She stopped at a liquor store to purchase a couple of bottles of wine to take to Angie's home tonight and continued home.

"I haven't been in the pool yet. I think that I deserve a quick swim," Francine told herself.

She changed into her bathing suit and swam laps until her arms tired. Then she lay on one of the lounge chairs under a canopy and fell asleep.

Francine slept for about forty minutes and woke up refreshed and alert. She decided to get the paperwork out of the dining cabinet where she had jammed it when Dave and Noel unexpectedly visited. She smoothed out the paperwork and checked her files against her deliveries and billing sheets. The paperwork was reconciled quickly, and Francine felt relief that she checked her orders. She prided that her work was correct for her clients and for her company, SPD.

Evening came quickly, and Francine arrived at her friend and customer Angie Fratilo's house shortly before seven. Angie lived in an immaculately manicured gated community. Francine had to give her name to a guard at the gate entrance. He checked his list, and the gate opened for her to enter. The guard gave her instructions to get to the correct street within the community.

Angie Fratilo's home was more grand than Francine expected. She didn't exactly know what to expect, but Angie was only slightly older than Francine and divorced, so Francine imagined her to have a small condo somewhere in Naples.

"CFOs make good money, I guess," Francine commented to herself.

There were several cars in the driveway already, so Francine guessed that Ben, Angie's boyfriend, and her uncle had already arrived. Ben answered the door and gave Francine a quick kiss on the cheek. Ben was dressed more casually than the other time Francine met him, but he had an air of sophistication in the way he put himself together. He was wearing light-blue pants with a blue-and-yellow striped shirt. Ben had expensive light-gray loafers with no socks.

Angie got herself a good catch, Francine thought to herself.

Ben led Francine into the dining room, where Angie was standing next to a distinguished older man.

"Hello, Francine. I'm so happy you could join us," Angie said while whisking over to Francine to give her a hug.

"Come here, my friend. I want to introduce you to my uncle, Dominic Pepino. Uncle Dom, this is Francine Pacque, the woman I wanted you to meet to help with your import start-up," Angie said.

Uncle Dominic took a while to stand up and extended his hand to Francine.

"It is my pleasure to meet you. Please sit down next to me," he said to Francine.

"Thank you, but it is my honor to meet you," Francine said.

Uncle Dominic held Francine's hand while she sat, and they exchanged friendly conversation until dinner was served. Angie made traditional spaghetti for her uncle accompanied by some juicy large steaks.

"Ben is a meat and potato kind of guy, so I had to make both." Angie laughed.

Francine helped her with serving the entrées, while Ben poured the wine. The food was exceptional and the company even better.

Angie mentioned to Francine that it would be impolite to talk business at the dinner, and Francine obliged. At 9:00 p.m., Uncle Dominic announced that he needed to get home because his advanced years were catching up to him.

Angie, Ben, and Francine all gave him a kiss before he left.

As he was walking down the stairs, he turned around and said, "Angie, make an appointment to talk business with Francine. Tomorrow would be good for me."

Angie nodded and turned around to find Francine standing right behind her.

"See, that's how it is done in the old country. Friends first, then business," Angie said.

"I see that," Francine replied.

They made a verbal appointment for Thursday morning to meet in Angie's office with Dominic.

Angie, Ben, and Francine walked back into the house and decided it was way too early to call it a night. Francine was exhausted from her two outings, but she was energized by her new friends to stay a few more hours. The three of them lounged in the deep sofa in Angie's family room and talked about nothing of importance. They spent most of the time arguing about the reality of reality TV. Francine left for home at eleven. She smiled and giggled while reminiscing about the evening.

Morning came fast, and Francine hurried to get properly dressed for a professional meeting with Dominic and Angie. She put on one of her favorite summer dress suits in black and white. It was another beauty by Antonio Melani. She put on her black high heels and looked at herself in the mirror. She still did not recognize the girl in the mirror. She didn't look like her dumpy self. Naples changed her. She liked her new sleek hairdo and blond hair color. She never would be the skinny fashion-model body type, but she was slender and curvy. Satisfied with her appearance, she left the house and drove to Angie's office.

Uncle Dominic was already seated with a large coffee mug in hand when Francine entered the office. Angie quickly handed her another mug and said, "Let's get to business, shall we?"

They cozied up to Angie's desk, where Dominic had pictures of his import stock. It was a massive lot.

"When I do something, I do it big," Dominic said. He continued, "I had many of these items stored in my hometown in Italy for years. My hobby became my obsession, and now, I have many items to display."

"And sell," Angie added.

"Well, yes. And sell," he said. "This is the warehouse I purchased. It has a storefront that I want to remodel to display some of my items. I want to display them as if they are in a real room. You know, with furniture staged and my imports being an integral part of the room. But...my real desire is to have most of my items categorized and displayed in glass cabinets or glass lockers so that people can walk down the aisles of the warehouse and view all the items."

"That sounds like an exquisite idea but an expensive one to have all those items in glass cases," Francine replied. "I'm good at analyzing inventory space, and you would be tying up most of your warehouse."

"I don't care! This is my life! My passion," Dominic cried out-,."Angie told me something similar, but I don't care."

"That's fine, Dominic. I just wanted to make sure you realized the expense and space. Your idea is very inventive. Do you know any other importers who do something similar?" Francine asked.

"No. They all have a big display room with items everywhere. I don't want that, and I don't want anyone walking off with small items in their pockets either," Dominic boomed.

"I think you have a very good idea and will have a store that everyone will want to visit. I have some ideas of cabinets, almost like small lockers, that come with glass doors. White cabinets would not distract from your items. Do you want me to give you a price for a set of them with locks on the doors?" Francine asked.

"Yes, Francine. That is what I want you to do. I have my items here already, in boxes. I want to have this warehouse and showroom done by the end of the year in time for season," Dominic stated.

Francine's eyes got like saucers. She didn't think she could have the cabinets here in a month, plus she was returning to Chicago soon.

"The cabinets are available but not a stock item, so they will need to be ordered. I will get an estimate of how many you will need, the cost, and the estimated delivery. But, Dominic, the end of the year will not be enough time. Hopefully we'll start getting the cabinets here by end of year, and we can start categorizing and filling them. Plan on opening your store February first. Your remodel will take time too to get your storefront done," Francine said.

Dominic looked at her and smiled. After a short pause, he said, "Francine, I like you. You have a good head on your shoulders. I want you to oversee the entire build and categorization. I will pay you accordingly. You are part of the family now."

Angie smiled at Francine and raised her eyebrows in happiness when Francine glanced her way. She was happy that her uncle had faith in her friend, and she was happy that Francine would be spending more time in the area.

"Thank you, Dominic. I want your business to be a showplace. Fantastic! But I will need to do my regular job as well, so if I am going to oversee your project, I don't think February first is feasible. I'm going home soon to see my family and am planning on returning in January. But I also have other customers in Louisiana and in Naples to service," Francine admitted.

"You are the man for the job. Even if you are a woman," Dominic said, and they all laughed. I would rather the job get done right by you with a slower timeline than have someone I don't know handle the job," he said.

Angie added, "March is the highest season month down here. I think we need the shop open by then."

"Let's shoot for getting it done in February and maybe plan an extravaganza gala for early March. We could make this a special event," Francine suggested.

Dominic and Angie looked at each other and whispered something to each other. Soon Angie sat upright in her chair and said, "Francine, you got the job. Will ten thousand a month cover your cost?"

Francine was dumbfounded. She expected a thousand to cover the entire job.

Angie looked questionably at her. "Francine, isn't ten thousand a month for probably three months enough?"

Francine nodded her head agreeably but in disbelief.

Angie said, "We value family. And you are now family."

She got up from her chair and went around her desk to give Francine a big hug.

"Thank you, Dominic. Thank you, Angie. Should I write up a contract?" Francine asked.

"No, we'll shake on it. I want you to know that I'm returning to Italy for business, so please correspond with Angie. The files and pictures we looked at are copies for you to estimate our needs, so take those with you. Here is the address to my warehouse, and here is a key. Security already is aware that you have total access at any time," Dominic explained. "Now, I have to leave. I have several other appointments today. Angie, keep me informed. I know you will. Good-bye, Francine."

He stood up and steadied himself before he took a step toward Francine. Suddenly, he bent down and kissed her cheek.

"Good luck, my pretty lady. Make me a masterpiece," Dominic said.

"I will. I can't believe my good fortune meeting Angie and then being introduced to you. I can't wait to get started," Francine answered.

"Good. That's what I wanted to hear. Here is the card to my contractor who will be remodeling the storefront. He has a plan that I have approved. But I'm sure you will need lights, supports, etc., for the cabinets. Use him for these items. He has a blanket order contract, so use him," added Dominic.

With that, Dominic walked out of the room. The whole discussion took twenty minutes.

"Oh my god, Angie. I didn't imagine everything would be settled today," Francine said.

Angie giggled and said, "I think we will be seeing a lot of each other in the next few months, my friend."

"Yes, and that is so great for me," Francine replied and then added, "I have to run. I have so much to do for my normal business.

Good-bye and thanks again. Oh! And thank you for such a great evening with you and Ben. I had a great time."

Francine drove away and couldn't believe her good fortune.

"Thirty thousand dollars!" she muttered to herself. "That will sure help get me out of the red and make sure I can pay Tom."

Francine worked hard and late trying to get her work done at every company in zone 2. Her spreadsheet of critical inventory was working well, but there were a few breakdowns that required her immediate attention. She met with Tom Bender at one of the zone 2 companies and showed him what his new job would entail. She also showed him a vendor-managed area that was starting to be adopted by the companies Tom would support. He was exceptionally bright and understood his duties quickly. He accepted the job, and Francine and Tom went over wage details. Tom said he could easily get Fridays off as that was one of the prime weekend tip days. So they planned a schedule of Tom working at least four hours each Friday and another four to six hours sometime during the other weekdays.

Thursday and Friday morning passed quickly and Francine knew the dreaded time of Friday afternoon's meeting with Dave Noirty was fast approaching. She quit work at noon and headed home to change into some clean casual clothes.

"Ha-ha!" Francine muttered to herself. "Casual clothes befitting a three-million-dollar yacht. That's crazy."

She purposely wore high platform sandals for riding on a boat. Her blue gauze pants and top looked appropriate for the venue. Francine picked up her purse and headed for Dave's marina.

As Francine drove to the marina, she was aware of her stomach knotting up. Bile was mounting in her stomach.

"Oh, great. I suppose I'll upchuck as soon as I get onto the boat," she muttered.

She took two anti-acid pills from her purse and quickly chewed them.

When Francine got to the marina area, she noticed several boat dealers. She quickly located the store owned by Dave Noirty, parked her car, and strode into the dealership. She was surprised at how many people worked in the store. *How many people can afford yachts around here?* she thought.

"Good afternoon, may I help you?" a receptionist asked.

"Hello there. I have an appointment with Dave Noirty. My name is Francine Pacque."

The receptionist looked impressed and said, "Dave is expecting you, Ms. Pacque. Please follow me."

She led Francine to the back of the dealership but to an office overlooking the dock. It was beautifully appointed. Francine knew that Dave's wife had a hand in the decorations.

"Francine, you're here. Come on in and sit down," Dave said and quickly added, "So did you talk with your uncle? How much is he planning on spending?"

Oh no, Francine realized, *I completely forgot about that. Now what do I say?*

"Yes," Francine said casually. "He thinks he'll go as high as a million. No crew. He wants something he can handle himself."

"Hmmm, that's not what I thought. Our line averages more like three to five million. Those are crew ships. Do you have a letter of funds to present to me?" Dave said. He looked sad to Francine.

"No, I don't. My uncle wants me to test out the boats and see which one rides smoothly and looks great," Francine said.

"I see. Well, the yacht business doesn't work quite like that. I would think your uncle would know that from having a power boat in Chicago," Dave said. "Yachts are a wealthy man's sport, and fortunately, there are plenty of them around here. But we have to have proof of funds and even a contract for a new yacht before we go one on a sea trial. If we didn't have strict rules such as that, we would be taking every Tom, Dick, and Harry out on boats all the time."

"Oh, no. He didn't explain anything like that to me. He just said to look at the boats and find out the specs on one I liked. He actually didn't say that I would be going on a boat ride. I added that. Excuse my ignorance," Francine replied.

Dave sat back in his chair and looked pensively at a list on his desk. "Well, Francine, I can show you some boats, not really yachts, in that price category in dry dock. That's the best I can do for you.

You need to have your uncle come down here and talk personally to me."

"I get it. Yes, if I could see a few options, maybe I can recommend something to him. I'm sure he'll be coming down here soon and he could see you personally," Francine replied.

Dave nodded, but Francine could see the tension in his face. He wasn't happy. Neither was Francine's stomach.

"I'm going to introduce you to one of my salesmen. He can show you some boats and suggest appropriate motors. Now, if you will excuse me, I have some other business to attend to. Someone will come and get you in a moment. Bye, Francine. Maybe next time will be more fruitful," Dave stated.

He walked out of his office. *I think he's mad*, Francine thought. *I can't imagine what other work was so pressing that he is having someone else show me around. I wonder what he'll say to Noel.*

Francine desperately wanted to get out of the store. She was out of her league, and she didn't know what to do or what to say. *If only I would have done some homework on this yacht thing, I wouldn't have sounded so stupid*, she thought to herself.

Several minutes passed, and a salesman, Joel, came into the office. "I'm here to show you a few boats," he said. "My name is Joel."

"That would be wonderful. Thank you. I'm afraid I am a novice at boating, so excuse my ignorance," Francine replied.

"No problem. That's what I'm here for," Joel said.

Francine and Joel headed to the marina storage area. There was a large canopied area that held a number of large boats and one megaboat that Francine imagined was one of the three-million-dollar yachts.

"What is that boat?" Francine asked while pointing to the large one.

"Ahh, that's our premiere line. All custom. Is that what you're interested in seeing?" he anxiously asked.

"See, yes, but I can't buy that one," Francine answered.

"You're a friend of Dave's, so I don't know why you can't see it. Let me get the cabin key," Joel said and ran across the area into the office.

Soon he was back, key in hand. They climbed a portable ladder to gain entrance to the docked yacht. Joel opened the cabin door.

"This way to elegance," Joel said as he gestured Francine to enter.

She walked into the cabin and gasped. The cabin was huge and lush. There were neutral-colored built-in couches on both sides of the cabin with a mahogany coffee table secured to the floor. Behind the couch area was a wet bar and a dining room table.

"This boat has a dining room table!" Francine exclaimed.

"Actually, it has two. This one is the smaller, more intimate dining table. There is an outdoor one that is larger for entertaining," Joel answered.

They walked through the galley kitchen, which was set up to be either personal or professionally managed. Then they walked down a staircase to a crew cabin area and a large master suite. There were two additional bedrooms and a bathroom for guests.

"Oh my goodness. Some people actually own yachts like this?" Francine asked.

"Yes, they do. Quite a few of them too," Joel answered.

They continued walking through the entire yacht, but Francine couldn't concentrate on the words Joel was saying. As they went back through the lounge area, Francine asked if she could have her picture taken.

"Sure, give me your camera. Do you want another picture in the master bedroom?" Joel asked while Francine struck a pose.

"That would be awesome," Francine answered. "I can't wait to post these on Facebook!"

After the grand yacht tour, Joel took Francine to look at some smaller pleasure crafts. She couldn't believe the cost of the yacht didn't include the motors. Joel did some quick math to come up with several scenarios for one million dollars. The boats were incredibly beautiful, but next to the large yacht, the million-dollar boat seemed inferior.

CHAPTER 15

New Love

Francine left the marina with several pieces of literature to give to her "uncle." She felt bad deceiving Joel, who was so nice to her. She also felt bad deceiving Dave and Noel Noirty. Instead of driving home, Francine went to one of the dockside bars and asked for a wine. It was happy hour, and the waitress brought two.

What the hell, Francine thought. *I guess two wines will go down well today.*

As Francine sat at a bench dockside, anxiety and regret filled her emotions. She started to cry. She tried to keep her emotions in check, but the tears rolled down her cheeks. She didn't want to hurt anyone with her deception, but keeping up her false identity was getting difficult. Francine started to think about the amount of work she needed to do. She couldn't afford the time to keep living the lifestyle of Naples elite, and of course, she couldn't afford it financially either.

She removed her phone from her bag and phoned Mitzi.

"Hello, Mitzi, this is Francine," said she.

"Francine! How lovely that you called. Do you have any good news for me? Are you submitting an offer to purchase?" Mitzi asked.

Francine paused for a moment to get her wits together before saying, "Mitzi, I haven't made a decision on the property, but I'm tending to think it may not be right for my uncle. That isn't why I called. I have to leave Naples earlier than expected, so I will be leaving the house after tonight."

"Really? Before Thanksgiving? Did something happen at home?" Mitzi quizzed.

"I have some urgent business, and I'm very sorry, but I need to leave tomorrow," Francine said.

She fully intended to stay in Naples but back at the cheap hotel so she could concentrate on her work.

"We are all going to be so sorry to have you go. Will you be coming back soon?" Mitzi asked. "We were just talking about inviting you to some of the Christmas galas next month. I hope you will be able to come back by then?"

Francine could honestly answer that she wouldn't be in Naples until after the New Year, but she didn't want to tell anyone when she would return. She knew she couldn't keep up the charade, even as appealing as it was for her.

She answered, "I'm not certain when I'll be back in town. You know that I'm a working girl and have to make a living. I'm not rich like my uncle."

"Well, then, I hope to see you again soon. And hopefully your uncle will come down here. You will give him my information, won't you? He still will need a broker," Mitzi said.

"Yes, of course. I will give him the house information as well as the other properties you showed me. And I will recommend that he contact you. You were amazing, Mitzi. I thank you so much," Francine answered.

"OK. I'll let the owners of the house know that you'll be leaving. They have been pestering me about an offer. I better let them down easily. Good luck to you, Francine. Are you going to talk to Noel before you leave?" Mitzi asked.

Noel. I owe Noel a good-bye, Francine realized.

She dreaded contacting her, but she answered, "Yes, I will call or see Noel. Thank you again, Mitzi. It was a pleasure to meet you and your friends."

"You talk like we'll never see you again. You'll be back before you know it," Mitzi said before disconnecting the call.

197

Francine sat there and quietly said to herself, "No, I'll never see you again. Good-bye, my dear friends. Forgive me."

She started her second glass of wine amid tears dripping down her face. She shouldn't have gone to the boat dealership. The house ruse was enough of a sham. She thought about how the house availability happened and at least took some solace that it wasn't her intention to stay in the house but was Mitzi's idea. She stared blankly at her glass.

A hand gently touched her shoulder and startled her. She looked up and saw an unknown handsome young man.

"Are you all right?" he asked.

"Yes, thank you. I didn't think anyone noticed me sobbing away like a little girl," Francine answered.

"I saw you at the marina with Dave, and you looked so happy. Did something happen there to you?" he asked.

The marina! Francine thought. *This man was at the marina? OMG, now what?*

She felt her stomach churn and answered, "Oh, everything was fine at the marina. I saw some beautiful boats and one spectacular yacht."

"I know. I'm the captain of the marina. I work for Dave," he said.

Francine turned her stool toward the man. She looked up, and chills went up her spine. Not chills from being scared or embarrassed. It was more like chills from seeing a man talk to you who was way out of your league. The man was about Francine's age, had dark hair, a dark tan, and was absolutely handsome.

"You're the captain of the marina? Wow. How does someone get that position?" she asked.

The man laughed and said, "Well, I was born into it. My uncle is a yacht builder, and he is very particular about who drives his boats. My name is Peter Manuchi, but everyone calls me Captain Pete."

Francine quickly ran through the scenario that she was at the dealership because of a fake uncle, but here was this gorgeous man who really had a rich yachting uncle.

"And I am Francine Pacque. I'm happy to meet you, Peter," she said.

"Pack? What nationality is Pack?" Peter asked.

"My parents' parents where French. My last name is P-A-C-Q-U-E," Francine answered.

"Hmmm, so we are both from Europe. I'm Italian, of course, with a last name of Manuchi. Do you mind if I sit and have a drink with you?" Peter asked.

"No! Please join me!" Francine said while gesturing to the stool next to her.

Her heart was beating way too fast, and she thought, *Wow, this is the best Naples present. A handsome young man, who I think is single, asking to sit with me. A yacht captain as well. My nightmare day may end up being my best day here in Naples.*

Small talk gradually got to how Francine knew Dave Noirty.

Francine didn't have a good answer, so she continued her lie. "I got to know Dave through his wife, Noel. I met Noel shortly before a charity event in Naples."

"Do you live here now?" Peter asked.

She replied, "No, I actually live in Chicago."

"How come you were at the dealership?" he asked.

"I was looking for a boat for my uncle who may move down here soon. He asked me to look at some homes and a boat while I was here," she answered.

"The marina has very good boats. I'm partial, but it is true. Did you find one?" he asked.

"Not really," she answered. "I didn't know anything about boats or yachts or motors. I thought I could just ask for a test ride and try them out."

Peter laughed while shaking his head. "That won't work. You have to come with a big check before you get a sea trial."

"I found that out the hard way. It's my fault. I should have done some investigating before I saw Dave. He's probably mad at me now for wasting his time," Francine admitted.

"Nah, Dave's not like that. And you are a friend of his wife," Peter said. "I tell you what. I have a boat. Would you like to go on a ride with me?"

Francine's heart skipped a beat while she thought, *Is he asking me out?*

"I would love to go on a ride on your boat," she said demurely.

"Then, it's a date. I have to do an errand. Can I meet you back at the marina about five o'clock this evening?" Peter asked.

"I'll be there. Can I bring anything?" she asked.

"You just supply your beautiful self. I'll provide the drinks," he said while smiling and displaying a set of the most beautiful white teeth Francine had ever seen.

He got up and gave her a small kiss on the cheek.

"See you at five," he said and left the bar.

Francine's tears were gone and replaced with a new excitement.

"This cannot be!" she told herself. "I'm just getting out of a jam, and now I'm getting sucked right back in."

Quickly she justified herself by saying, "What the heck. I've been Fanny Pack way to long. It's about time that I have some fun."

She took out her cell phone and looked at the two pictures of her on the yacht. She quickly posted them on Facebook.

"Eat your heart out, everyone. Francine's on her way," she quietly said.

She went to her car and quickly drove home. She had a couple of hours before her five o'clock date. Francine slowly walked around the house and packed up her personal belongings. She washed and dried the dishes in the sink and straightened up her room. She removed the bedsheets and left them on the floor for the cleaning personnel to wash and remake in their professional way.

Francine loved this house. She wished she had a rich uncle to recommend for it. Every room was beautiful and homey even though the house was so large. She walked outside by the pool, dock, and outside entertainment area, taking more pictures of all the rooms and outside areas.

"I'll miss you, house. At least I got to stay in a house like this for a week. Most people wouldn't ever have an opportunity," she said.

She walked by the couches and bar and touched them affectionately. Then she spun around and quickly returned to the house, locking the sliding door behind her.

Francine had told Mitzi that she would leave her house key on the dining room table, and Mitzi would pick it up on Saturday using the garage entry code to enter the house. Francine sat down on one of the dining room chairs. She opened her purse and removed a thank-you card that she purchased on her way to the house. She took out her pen and wrote a message on the card:

> *Mitzi, thank you for the kindness you shared when showing me around Naples and, most importantly, for arranging for me to stay in this magnificent home. I will always cherish my memories of the time we spent together at the charity event, looking for property, and having lunch at RC. I have enclosed two items. One is a thank-you gift card for your trouble. The second is a check made out to the owners of this home. I researched online and found that off-season rates are $10K per month for similar homes. I enclosed $2,500 for the week I stayed here. Please pass the check on to the owners with my thank-you.*
>
> *Your friend,*
> *Francine Pacque*

"This won't make up for the wrong I've done, but it is the right thing to do," she said.

Francine put the check and gift card in the card and wrote Mitzi's name on the sealed envelope. She put the keys on top of the envelope and walked to the door. Her suitcases and garment bags were already packed in the car. She picked up her computer bag and looked backward into the house one last time.

Francine drove to the marina. She waited in her car for a while, waiting for Pete to show up. She finally got out of her car and walked on the dock. A man waved to her. It was Pete, and he was already in his boat.

The boat was probably a yacht. Francine didn't know the difference. Pete's boat wasn't as long as the one on display, but it was still longer than the other boats passing by in the marina. Business must be good for Pete's uncle.

Pete helped her get on board and guided her into the cabin. Francine was a little apprehensive, but not enough to say no. She giddily went inside like she was a teenager. Pete surprised her by having a wine bottle and two glasses on his small dining table along with some cheese slices. Next to the cheese was a bag with two submarine sandwiches inside.

"I didn't have time to eat and didn't know if you ate, so I bought us a sandwich. I know, it's not gourmet, but it's food," Pete said, smiling at her.

"This is good for me. I was busy too and didn't eat. Actually, I didn't eat because I was afraid I may get seasick," Francine admitted.

"It happens to the best of us. If you do, don't be upset. The head is here. Use it if you feel ill," he said as he pointed to the boat's bathroom.

Francine couldn't believe how attentive, thoughtful, and handsome her date was. She was swooning. Francine wasn't one to get hit hard with immediate emotions toward a man. It happened for her with Brian Sherman and now with Peter Manuchi.

They ate their sandwiches and drank some wine, but suddenly, Pete got up and said, "We have to shove off now or we'll miss the sunset."

"The sunset? We're going to see the sunset?" Francine babbled.

"Of course. Being on the water is the best way to see it, and tonight is clear," Pete said. "Why don't you come up on deck while I take this boat out?"

She took her wine and went up onto the deck. Pete guided her to a captain-style chair next to the controls.

When Pete sat on his captain chair, Francine cried out, "Captain Pete! Captain Pete! Let's get this tin can out of here."

Pete looked at her peculiarly and laughed. "Hold on, my friend. Here we go!"

He guided the boat without a wake until the boat got to open water, then he pulled the throttle, and the boat quickly responded.

Francine was flung backward into the back of her chair, spilling a little wine on her.

Pete laughed and said, "You asked for it."

"I had no idea that this was a race boat," she said.

"This boat is hardly a race boat. It's fast, but a race boat would have thrown your ass overboard," he answered.

They laughed and quickly focused on the sea before them. The waves were not high, but Francine was not used to hitting waves. She felt a bit queasy, and Peter recognized the signs.

He slowed down the boat and said, "This is good. We can watch the sunset here."

Francine realized that the boat was drifting, because the landmarks on the coast kept changing. She found the gentle rolls of the waves while drifting were intoxicating for her, or maybe it was the wine she drank earlier. She felt warm and happy inside. Pete and Francine sat in their chairs and watched the sun fade toward the horizon. When the sun reached the horizon, it was so large that Francine thought it was a mirage. She was mesmerized.

After sunset, Pete started the engine and drove slowly along the coastline so Francine could see the many beautiful homes and protected wildlife areas as the skies darkened. They finally arrived back at the marina.

"This was a wonderful evening. I really liked your boat and your company," Francine confided to him.

"I had a good time too. I was wondering if you are free tomorrow night. There's going to be a small get-together at Dave and Noel's house. I would like to take you as my guest."

Francine's internal alarms were going off in her head. She should stay away. She already left the property on Rum Row and told everyone that she had to return to Chicago. But her emotions got the best of her.

"I would love to go with you," she replied.

He smiled and shook his head in approval.

"Good. I was hoping to see you again," he said.

"Should I pick you up at the house you're staying at down the road from them?" Pete asked.

What am I going to do now? Francine thought. *I already gave up my key.*

"Yes, pick me up there," she answered while secretly thinking that she would like to see his shoes under her bed.

"OK, I'll pick you up at seven. We could probably walk over to their house," Pete said.

Suddenly, several people at the marina came over to Peter to ask him some work-related questions. Francine waited for a while and then thought she should leave. She had something important to do quickly. She found Pete and told him that she was going to leave and that she'd see him tomorrow. Pete nodded and raised his hand to signal his coworkers that he needed a minute. He lightly grabbed Francine's hand and pulled her toward him. He kissed her passionately on her lips and said his good-night to her.

Francine couldn't remember how she got to her car after that kiss. She sat in the car to get her wits about her before she dialed Mitzi Vanderlooth's private cell number.

"Hi, Mitzi. It's Francine. Say, I don't have to leave until Sunday. I already left the key inside the house, so can I get the garage code and stay until Sunday morning?" Francine asked.

"Sure, Francine. The owners think you are staying another week. Yes, here is the lock number," Mitzi answered.

Francine jotted the number down and headed back to Rum Row.

"Enough for my honesty," Francine muttered to herself.

She dismissed her guilt and started to daydream about Pete Manuchi.

Going back to the house was the biggest mistake that Francine made.

Francine got back into the home easily and went into her guest room. She quickly put the sheets back onto the bed from where they were lying on the floor. She hung her clothes in the closet and opened her garment bags to look for what she should wear tomorrow to Noel's party. She wanted to look desirable to Captain Pete.

Saturday morning came fast, and Francine jumped out of bed. She wanted to get a manicure and pedicure early before all the working women started visiting the salons. Francine called a salon exactly as it opened, and they said that she could go right in for her mani/pedi. She put on a pair of shorts and a simple tank top and hurried out the door.

After the salon, Francine headed to Fifth Avenue South to do a little shopping. It was bad enough that her dwindling checking account was going to be down twenty-seven hundred dollars after writing the check for the house owners and giving a gift card to Mitzi. Francine was going to have a balance of three thousand dollars after the check cleared. But having a fabulous outfit for her date with Pete was more important to her.

Francine went into several stores and was delighted when she ran into the women she met several weeks ago when she first went to dinner with Angie and her boyfriend, Ben. The cousins worked on Fifth Avenue and were excited to help Francine find a perfect outfit.

Francine selected a mosaic sundress that fit her figure perfectly. The dress was classy but not too fancy, and Francine thought her choice would be good for the venue. She also liked how the dress hugged her curves, which she hoped would be enjoyed by her date. Francine knew she had a pair of Prada heels to wear that were the same shade as the dress. She was overjoyed.

At seven thirty sharp, the doorbell rang. Francine almost floated to the door to let Pete inside.

Pete was not a stranger to high-dollar homes, so he took a cursory look around and said, "Nice place."

"Thank you. I wish it was mine, but I'm only trying it out for my uncle. Tonight's my last night here," Francine said.

"Then let's make it a memorable one," Pete said, raising his eyebrows to see her response.

She tried to look coy, but a big smile came over her face.

"We'll see" was her only answer.

Francine went to the dining room to retrieve her purse. She noticed the envelope on the table for Mitzi and decided to take it along to the party. If Mitzi wasn't at the party, she could give it to Noel.

Francine and Pete walked only several hundred yards to get to the Noirtys' driveway. There were already a number of cars, mostly exotic, in the driveway.

"Dave and Noel throw a good party. There will be a lot of people there from the marina, so if I ignore you once in a while, I'll be talking work," Pete informed her.

"So is your work really *work*? It seems like you have it made, Captain Pete," Francine added.

"Yachting is in my blood. I love it…the freedom…feeling the wind in your face…being part of the sea…you name it. I guess I am lucky because I do love my work," he informed her.

He took her hand as they headed up the driveway. Francine quickly became a little nervous because Noel hadn't invited her to the party but, instead, invited her for Thanksgiving dinner that coming Thursday.

"I hope Noel and Dave aren't upset that I'm coming here tonight. They must have planned this party for some time, and they hadn't invited me," Francine commented to Pete.

"No problem. They know I'm bringing you. I mentioned it to Dave, and he was so happy that he texted Noel while I was there. They love you, and I'm almost family to them. They probably didn't invite you because, as I said, this is pretty much a work party for Dave. Lots of yachting customers and such," Pete said.

"That's good to hear," Francine said.

He squeezed her hand, and they walked up to the door.

"Francine! Peter! I'm so glad you could make it," Noel said a she let them inside. "You look beautiful, Francine." Pete nodded in agreement.

The couple walked inside, and instantly, several men pulled Pete away to ask him some yachting question. He looked at Francine and mouthed "Told you" to her. She nodded and smiled. Francine headed to the bar area to get a cocktail. She noticed several familiar faces from the charity event but not anyone she was introduced to. She stood at the bar and exchanged some pleasantries with a couple standing next to her.

Several minutes passed before Noel came up to Francine and grabbed her hand.

"There you are, girlfriend. Most of these people are business or marina people that I don't know very well, but I did invite my cousin. I told her all about you, and she's excited to meet you," Noel excitedly said.

"That's great to hear, and I would love to meet her. Say, is Mitzi here tonight? I have something to give her, and I don't want to forget it," Francine asked.

"No, this is mostly a party of Dave's friends and business partners. But I see Mitzi all the time. I can give her whatever it is," Noel stated.

Francine opened her purse and took out the envelope with Mitzi's name written. She handed it to Noel, who promptly placed it on a small desk near the door.

"Come on, Francine," Noel said as she pulled Francine along and looked for her cousin. As they walked, Noel was continually stopped by her guests, and they exchanged small talk. Francine loved being with Noel because Noel always made her feel important. Finally, they arrived at Noel's large circular couch in the outdoor entertaining area.

"There she is," as she pulled Francine along.

Francine's smile turned into despair as she was dragged over to Noel's cousin, Angie Fratilo.

"Angie, here's my friend I wanted you to meet! Francine, this is Angie. Angie, this is Francine," Noel said with delight.

Angie's face turned bright red, and her date, Ben, grabbed her hand. Francine knew her own face had to be the same shade. Angie stared at Francine speechless, and Noel immediately knew something was wrong.

"Hi, Angie. Hi, Ben. It's nice to see you tonight," Francine nervously said.

Angie did not respond and looked downward at her lap.

Ben knew that Angie was shocked, so he said, "Hi, Francine. Fancy seeing you here tonight. I had no idea that you knew Noel."

"Oh! So you already know each other?" Noel said inquisitively. She stared at her cousin, who continued to look downward.

"Hmmm, I didn't expect this reaction," Noel confided.

Francine knew she was caught red-handed.

"Yes, we know each other. I'm doing some work for Angie's company while I'm down here," Francine revealed.

Several yachting wives noticed Noel standing and quickly came up to her to talk. Noel took advantage of the awkward situation by leaving with the women. Francine took a small chair and pulled it across from Angie. She sat down and tears started flowing down her face.

"How could you?" Angie sharply said. "I trusted you. I helped you get more customers. I suggested you run my uncle's remodel. And I know that Noel trusted you too. She told me all about your uncle and how she hoped he would buy the house by her and a yacht from her husband. She told me she hoped you would move down here too because she liked you so much. She just never said your name."

Francine nodded her head in agreement and said, "I know, Angie, I know."

Ben didn't understand the reason for the initial response given by Angie until he heard his girlfriend rant to Francine. He put his arm around Angie to give her support.

"Everything I did for you. Everything Noel did for you. It's all a fraud. You're a fraud. And Angie Fratilo does not do business with frauds. I'm done with you," Angie said abruptly.

Francine sat there speechless. She had nothing to say. Angie was right. Francine never imagined that her work life and fake personal life would intersect. She was caught.

"I'm sorry, Angie, I never meant to hurt anyone," Francine said slowly, with tears rolling down her cheeks.

Angie was crying too. She was so happy to have a good friend that was more business oriented than socially oriented. She loved her cousin and her other socialite friends but was never completely comfortable with them. Francine was different. She was smart and innovative, and she gave business solutions to Angie that Angie was unaware of previously. She didn't want the relationship to end, but she knew it must.

"No, I don't accept your apology. Maybe Noel will, but not me. Please leave me alone," she said as she buried her head on Ben's shoulder.

Ben was quiet, but he did wink at Francine while he gestured with his head that she should leave them.

Francine got up and found the nearest bathroom. She had a good cry and sobbed as she fixed her makeup ruined by the tears. She stayed in the bathroom for quite a long time and was aware that other people were trying to get in by the frequent jiggling of the doorknob.

When she opened the door, she quickly went to the area where Pete was talking. He waved her over and introduced her as his date to several young couples. Francine was quickly swooped up into new conversations, which calmed her down. The couples, including Pete and Francine, walked as a group to the kitchen area to get some food. Francine looked toward the couch where she talked to Angie but didn't see her. She was relieved and enjoyed another hour or so with the group.

There were about thirty people at the party, so there were groups gathered around the residence, enjoying the food, music, and conversation. Francine was nervous about seeing Angie again, and she glanced nervously around the groups throughout the night. As she walked to another group of people with Pete, she noticed Angie and Ben sitting with Noel in the living room. She could tell it was a serious talk.

"Noel, I need to talk to you and Dave about something serious," Angie quietly said to Noel.

"Sure. I know something happened between you and Francine. Can it wait? Dave's busy with his guys right now," asked Noel.

"I would have to say no. Dave needs to hear this too," Angie said.

Noel went to find Dave, and in a few minutes, they met Angie and Ben in the living room.

"What's up, Angie?" Dave asked.

"I need to tell you something that is very troubling. It's about Francine Pacque, I'm afraid," Angie answered.

The four of them sat down in a small alcove of the living room as Angie started her story.

"When Noel told me about her new friend, she didn't say her name. I was anxious to meet her as Noel thought we would all get along so well. She told me that this woman was from Chicago, which is true, and that she was sent here by her divorced uncle who asked her to be his representative to find him a residence and a yacht," Angie said.

"Yes, that is right," Noel said.

"And how did you meet her again?" Angie asked.

"I met here when she picked up a ticket at my home for the Children's Hospital charity event several weeks ago," Angie explained.

"I see. Did she pay for her ticket to the event?" Angie asked.

"Yes, she did. And she bought a number of lottery tickets at the event too. In fact, she won something there. I don't remember what she won," said Noel.

"So when did she tell you about her uncle?" asked Angie.

"Hmmm, let me think. Oh yes, we were sitting here at my house when she picked up her ticket. I asked what brought her to Naples. That's when she told me. Why? What's the matter?" Noel said.

"Yeah, Angie, I have a household of people here. Many are prospective clients, so I would like to get back to them," said an anxious Dave Noirty.

"Then I'll get to the point. Francine Pacque is a fraud. She isn't anyone's representative. She's a salesperson for a company in Chicago. I hired her and recommended her to a lot of other businesses, that's what is the problem. She's taking you for a ride," Angie said.

"Oh, so she doesn't have an uncle who is looking for a place in Naples?" Noel asked.

"I'm sure she does not. She's a simple girl who is taking advantage of people I care about. And I don't do business with users," Angie said. "I had to tell you. So what did she get from you with her lies?"

"Nothing from me. I just introduced her to some other people. Mitzi Vanderlooth got her permission to stay in the Blumbergs' home. She won't be too happy about this," Noel answered.

"She came to the marina at my urging," Dave said. "You know, I was trying to work a sale. But she wasn't herself at the marina. Didn't know what questions to ask or even what type of boat her uncle wanted. I just passed her onto one of my salesmen. I don't usually get too involved in transactions anyway. Now I get it. She was very uncomfortable when she got there. Well, now we know why." He paused and continued, "I have to get back to my party guests."

Dave rose from the chair and hurried back into the party.

"I feel bad about all of this, and I'll have to call Mitzi tomorrow morning. Francine was staying a second week at the home, but she told Mitzi that she had to go back to Chicago on business. I think she may be out of the house tomorrow," Noel stated.

"Well," Angie said, "she's working at our company next week as well as other companies. And I suggested to my uncle Dominic that she oversee his import warehouse construction. I'll have to call him in Italy now. I can't work with her anymore, and I'm sure that Dominic won't want to either."

"That's too bad that she did this. I really like her and was hoping to be good friends," said Noel. "But I doubt if she'll be staying in this area long after word of this gets out. It's really too bad. I was already missing her when she was originally supposed to leave after Thanksgiving," Noel added.

"I'm sorry to have to tell you, but you needed to know the truth. I don't like liars or users," added Angie.

Noel nodded before getting up to join the party. Angie and Ben remained seated.

"You're awfully quiet," Angie commented to Ben.

"I just don't know what the big deal is," Ben said. "So she told a little lie. It's hard to be accepted here by the insiders. I don't know if she intended to hurt anyone."

"What? You're justifying her lie!" Angie cried out.

"No, but think about it...men tell stories all the time. We lie about our golf score, our money, our fish stories, and so on. It's part of being a man. Salesmen are the worse. So here is this young woman from Chicago who is here all alone. She has a chance to fit in with the 'Naples Housewives.' I don't think she did anything so terrible, and certainly nothing to you," Ben explained.

Angie flushed with anger. "I can't believe you would say that! What she did was wrong, and tomorrow I'm going to write a letter to her boss and all the businesses I referred her to as an agent."

"Angie, I think you are just hurt. You really liked her, and here she is with this secret life. She didn't do anything wrong to you. Just

211

sleep on this before you write a letter that could end her career. That's all I ask," Ben said.

"I'll do whatever I want, and now I want to leave," Angie said while jumping out of her seat and nervously picking up her purse.

"Stop being such a woman, Angie," Ben said.

"What did you say to me?" Angie angrily asked.

"I meant stop thinking like a woman businessperson. Men say bullshit all the time," Ben explained.

That was not a statement that Angie wanted to hear. She raced out the door to the car, but unfortunately, she rode in Ben's car, so she had to wait a little longer for him. It was a cold ride home, and Ben was not welcome to stay the night.

Angie Fratilo felt angry and hurt when she arrived home. She was angry at Francine for lying to her cousin and angry at Ben for not thinking Francine did anything too terrible. Angie immediately went into her study and turned on her computer. She composed a letter to send to all the seventeen clients that she recommended Francine, with a copy to Francine's boss at Specialty Products Distribution, Sam Silverman Jr.

It has come to my attention that the salesperson I recommended for your company to hire for supplying critical and vendor-managed inventory is a fraud. Francine Pacque misrepresented herself to a number of people in the Naples area as being a representative for a rich family member, thus opening doors for some valuable amenities for herself.

I am deeply sorry for my poor judge of character for Francine Pacque and for getting each of your companies involved with a deceitful person. Our company's involvement with her will cease immediately, and I urge you to consider doing the same.

If you have any questions or want further information, feel free to contact me.

Thank you and apologies,
Angela Fratilo, CFO of Creative Fabrication Inc.

Angie's instinct was to press the Send button, but Ben's words kept coming into her mind, *"Sleep on it before you send a letter that could end her career."* She didn't care if Francine's career was ended. Francine hurt her, and there should be a consequence.

It was late Saturday night, and Angie decided that the letter could wait until Sunday morning. In fact, she didn't want to ruin anyone's weekend, so she decided to send it early Monday morning. She went to bed.

Back at the party, Pete noticed Francine fidgeting with her purse while standing in the corner of the room.

"Hey, are you all right?" he asked.

"Not really. What I could use is another drink right now," Francine answered.

"OK. Two drinks coming right up," Pete said as he hurried across the room to the bar and got two more cocktails for them.

Francine took the first cocktail and gulped it down. Then she grabbed Pete's drink out of his hand and drank that one almost as quickly. Pete didn't know what was wrong, but he went to the bar and retrieved two more cocktails. Francine didn't remember the rest of the evening.

She woke up during the night in her bed. As she sat on the edge of the bed, the room was spinning. It was dark in the room, and she carefully stood up and steadied herself. She stepped on something unfamiliar, so she reached for the lamp on the bed stand to turn on the lamp. The room glowed with a dull golden tint as she looked down to see what she stepped on. It was a pair of men's shoes. She turned her head slowly toward the bed to see her date, Pete, lying next to her.

Francine jumped up. *Oh no. I don't even remember last night,* she thought. She looked down at her clothes and noticed that her bra and panties were still on.

Hmmm, I don't think we had sex, although I wanted to, she thought with a slight smile. *At least he's a gentleman. He took me home and got me safely in bed.*

She walked into the hall to the bathroom then went into the kitchen and poured a glass of water to drink. She sat there for a long while, thinking about the events of last night.

"I'm going to have to give an apology to Noel and Dave. I'll have to think about how I want to do that," she muttered to herself. "But as for Angie, oh my god. Who would have thought she would be at the party?"

She started thinking about her deception. Francine had always prided herself as being honest, dependable, responsive to her customers, and trustworthy to her employer. She always prided herself for having good values. Values she learned from her hardworking parents and reinforced through years of working.

"It's my fault. What was I thinking? Of course someone would eventually recognize me. I'm glad it's now rather than a year from now," Francine muttered. "I'm going to have to tell Pete what I did when he wakes up."

She sat there and thought how embarrassed she would be if her family and past coworkers would find out what she did. Suddenly, she thought about her friend Brian Sherman. She thought about the fun they shared when they were both broke and jobless. She thought the most about how disappointed he would be if he knew she was a liar.

He's probably met someone by now. He's such a great guy, how could he still be available? Francine thought. *He wasn't interested in me anyhow.*

Francine curled up in a big chair in the family room and slept. She didn't want to go back in the bed and be there when Pete woke up. Pete had been wonderful to her, but she wasn't part of his world. She knew that their friendship would never become a relationship, but she was so glad for the time they did spend together.

About 9:00 a.m., she woke up hearing a voice.

"Francine? Are you here?" he asked.

"Good morning, sleepyhead. I'm in the family room," Francine said. "I have coffee made if you want some."

"Yep. I may need a lot of coffee. Let me get one and I'll be right there," he said.

In a couple of minutes, Pete walked into the family room and took a seat on the couch across from Francine.

"You got pretty wasted last night. I hope you don't mind that I stayed over," he said with a smile.

Francine laughed while she said, "Well, I was a little surprised when I woke up this morning and saw you in my bed."

"Oops! I guess I could have slept in another bed, but I was pretty wasted too. Nothing happened, you know," he said.

"I pretty much figured that out. But thank you for bringing me home and taking care of me," Francine said.

She noticed that Pete was staring directly at her while he drank his coffee. Finally, Francine realized that he was expecting her to explain her unusual behavior last evening.

"Peter, I owe you an explanation, and I'm dreading it," Francine finally explained.

She took a breath and told him the whole story, from the reason why she came to Naples, how she met Noel Noirty, and how she developed this lie to fit into Naples society. Pete sat quietly and drank his coffee as she explained how she was offered usage of this house, invited to Dave's dealership, and even invited to Noel's Thanksgiving Day feast on false pretenses. She explained her business relationship with Angie Fratilo, Noel's cousin, and that last night her fraud was exposed. When she was finished, she put her head down on her lap and sobbed.

Peter sat there, speechless, as he absorbed what he heard.

Finally he said, "You know, just because someone has some money, doesn't mean that they are different than anyone else. They may have more toys, but most of them work hard to maintain their lifestyle. The Noirtys are good people, Francine. I can't be involved with anyone who openly deceived them."

"I know, Pete. And you are a good person too. I deceived you as well, and I am sorry," Francine said slowly.

"When I met you, I didn't know if you were wealthy or poor. I just liked you and asked you out. Money had nothing to do with it," Pete said. He shook his head from side to side. "I should go," he said as he stood and walked back into the kitchen with his coffee cup.

Francine followed him but stood at a distance.

"Good-bye, Peter, and thank you. I want you to know that I will apologize to Noel and Dave.

"And you should. Good-bye, Francine," Pete said without looking at her.

He walked directly out the door, and Francine knew he was permanently out of her life.

CHAPTER 16

Penance

Francine removed the sheets from the bed and put them on the floors for the housekeeper to wash. She tidied up the slightly used bathroom and kitchen. She was thankful that she already gave Noel the envelope with payment for the house and a gift for Mitzi's time before her lie was identified. At least they would know that her payment was sincere.

She felt horribly guilty for the first time in her thirty-four years. She knew that she owed Noel and Dave an explanation and apology. It was eleven o'clock on Sunday morning, so it was possible that Noel and Dave would be home. She checked to ensure all the house doors were locked and left the house through the garage door.

She drove her Audi past the Noirtys' home several times while she tried to gain confidence. Finally, she drove up the driveway and parked. She walked up to the door and rang the doorbell. The door opened, and Noel smiled at her.

"Hi, Francine. Did you have a good time last night? Where's Pete?" Noel asked jovially.

Francine was shocked at Noel's casual comment. *Did she forget my lie?* Francine thought.

"Good morning, Noel. I came to give you and Dave an apology. I owe you that," Francine said as her voice cracked.

"Come on in. You look like a wreck," she said, putting her arm around Francine as she led her to the kitchen.

Dave was sitting at the table reading the paper. He looked up and smiled as the two women walked in.

Francine sat down and Noel handed her a mug of coffee. It was definitely a late night for the Noirtys, and they were still trying to wake up. Francine explained the entire story. She told them that her intention at the charity event was to fit in. She didn't have any ulterior motives, but as the opportunities arose, she accepted everyone's generosity rather than tell them the truth.

Francine said, "Please remember to give Mitzi the envelope I gave you last night. I have something in it for Mitzi's time and a $2,500 check to the owners of the house I stayed in. I owe them that. I hope my payment will help everyone to forgive me."

"I forgot about the envelope you gave me. Yes, I put it in the hallway desk. I'm sure the Blumbergs will appreciate getting something for the time you spent in their house. That is a nice gesture," Noel said while looking at Dave.

Dave said, "Francine, forget about it. You didn't do any harm to me. I asked you to come to the dealership. In fact, I almost bullied you to come. It's no problem. I've been through a lot worse many times."

Noel smiled while her husband spoke and then looked at Francine.

"You don't owe me any apology either. I liked you, and I still like you. It's Mitzi that may be a little miffed, but then again, you gave that envelope to give her." She continued, "But as for my cousin Angie, that I'm not sure what to tell you. She was really angry, and I think she was hurt and possibly a little jealous of our friendship."

"Jealous? Jealous of me?" Francine asked.

"Not that way, but Ben told me that Angie was very excited to meet you and thought that the two of you were going to be great friends. Ben thinks Angie was jealous that you were having all this fun with me and my friends," explained Noel.

"I also thought that Angie and I had a special relationship. We had a professional friendship and a personal friendship…" she said as her words trailed off to silence.

"Well, time will tell, Francine. Are you really leaving the area today? Angie said you weren't leaving until next week," Noel asked.

"I'm staying until Friday or Saturday. Then I have to head up to Louisiana for work. I checked out of the house so I could move back into a hotel and do work for my Naples clients. I needed to finish some things before I leave. It's difficult to get my work done with all the partying that you guys do," Francine said.

"Isn't that the truth," Dave added while he continued reading the newspaper.

"Good. Then I want you to reconsider coming here on Thanksgiving for dinner just as we planned. Three p.m. I don't think you would be working on Thanksgiving, would you?" asked Noel.

"You still want me to come here? I didn't think you ever wanted to see me again," a surprised Francine asked.

"Nonsense. We're friends now, and you didn't do anything wrong to hurt Dave or me. We expect you to come here as planned," Noel said definitely.

"Will Angie be here?" Francine asked.

"She will," said Noel.

"I think I better say no then. I don't want to ruin her Thanksgiving and cause a problem for everyone," said Francine. "Thanks for the invitation. I hope I will see you two again sometime in the future."

"That's up to you, but our invite stands," Noel said while giving Francine a big hug.

Francine left the Noirtys' house feeling reasonably good. Noel and Dave were not angry at her, and she expected Mitzi to forgive her when she got the envelope. She was honest with Pete, and he was frank with her. Their fresh relationship was over, but Francine never expected a long-term romance.

Francine went back to a hotel chain near the highway and checked in for the workweek. She hauled her luggage and suitcase into an identical small room like she previously stayed. She was happy to get back into this surrounding. She took out her records and started to work on Dominic's warehouse rearrangement. By evening, Francine had renderings of a prestigious warehouse layout with white glass cabinets and locking doors. She arranged items by category and verified Dominic's vast inventory against the cabinet sizes. By midnight, she had a full list of what supplies were needed to complete the display cabinets. It was a masterpiece.

Francine did not want to run into Angie Fratilo when she dropped off the warehouse renderings and supply estimate on Monday morning. She got up and dressed very early and drove past the Creative Fabrication plant. Workers were going into the facility. Francine parked her car and walked up to the side employee entrance. A company guard stopped her at the door. She asked if he could give this package to Angie Fratilo, and he agreed. She was gone from the small plant by 6:15 a.m.

Francine went back to the hotel and put the Do Not Disturb sign on her door. She had worked most of the night, and she needed some sleep before going to the zone 2 companies a final time before leaving town. She planned to work with Tom Bender on Tuesday and Wednesday to ensure he could handle the zone while she was gone.

Back at Creative Fabrication Inc., the day started like any other Monday. The front office people arrived at the office between seven and nine in the morning, depending on the employee's position. Angie Fratilo arrived at 8:00 a.m. She walked into her office without speaking to any office personnel. The office staff noticed Angie's abnormal behavior, and they commented to one another about it.

Angie closed her door and started up her office computer. She immediately pulled up the file containing the letter about Francine that she wrote to all other zone 2 companies and Francine's boss. She pressed Send.

Angie sat at her desk, satisfied with her decision. Angie was a proud, hardworking woman, and relationships and honesty were paramount with her. She stood up and walked around her office while she considered other items on her daily agenda. Finally, she opened her office door and walked into the office to the coffee machine. She noticed that her office staff was unusually quiet and looked around the office. No one acknowledged Angie's glance. They all looked directly at their work.

Hmmm, Angie thought, *I wonder what's wrong with all of them.*

She walked toward her office when the receptionist handed her a package.

"What is this?" Angie asked.

The receptionist answered, "The night security guard handed it to me this morning. He said a woman dropped it off for you early this morning."

Angie frowned as she reflected on the package. She returned to her office, closed the door, and opened it. She withdrew the contents and spread out the professional presentation on her desk. There was a note handwritten on the top of the proposal. She opened the card:

Angie, enclosed is the proposal for your uncle's warehouse. I have reconciled the list of his inventory with the sizes of the items. The cabinets are arranged by category rather than color or size. The cabinets have a flat white background with locking glass doors. The cabinets have adjustable shelf sizes to accommodate future items with different sizes.

The cabinets are not custom but are not in stock. About a third of them would be ready for shipment by the end of the year with the remaining available in two increments within the next six weeks. The prices I have quoted cannot be matched or beat.

If you are satisfied with the proposal, you can contact me or my zone 2 contact, Tom Bender. Tom will be able to assist you in any way.

I wanted to finish this proposal for you and your uncle because of his request to have the warehouse done as soon as possible. I hope it is satisfactory, and I actually think it looks quite spectacular. I hope you and Dominic agree. Please accept this proposal at no cost. I would have done it for nothing before your uncle offered that generous wage.

Your friend and colleague,
Francine Pacque, sales representative
for Specialty Products Distribution

There was a smaller note folded inside the larger note. It read, *"Dear Angie, I'm sorry. I value your friendship beyond my job."*

Angie sat back in her chair and examined the renderings. Francine was correct. The warehouse looked spectacular. Her uncle's business would be a masterpiece with customers and spectators lining up to see his unique imports.

Angie didn't expect to hear from Francine, much less to get this fabulous proposal. She didn't know what to do. She still needed to talk to her uncle about the personal transgressions by Francine, but now she urgently wanted to please him with these renderings. She remembered the words Ben told her when he said to wait before sending the e-mails to Francine's customers and boss. She did wait an additional day but sent the e-mails a few minutes earlier.

"Should I have sent it?" she asked herself. "Yes, it was still right to send it."

She knew it was evening in Italy, but she dialed her uncle's phone number. Dominic answered his phone, and Angie told him everything.

"Angie, I think you overthink everything. I also did some things as a young businessman that may have been somewhat unethical. I think about it from time to time. It's not something that I'm proud of, but I'm not perfect. Now we know that Francine is not perfect too," Dominic told Angie in his deep accent.

"Can you scan me the proposal? I would love to see my warehouse," Dominic asked.

"Of course, Uncle Dom," Angie answered. "I'll do it right now."

A few minutes later, Dominic Pepino was looking at the renderings for his import business. He sat down and gasped in delight. The renderings not only had rows of beautiful white display cabinets but cushioned white benches between the rows so people could sit and view his imports. It was like a museum. Another rendering showed larger sculptures that would not fit in cabinets. Francine had cushioned chair settings for those areas. It was spectacular in Dominic's opinion. He knew that his warehouse of artistic and antique items would be a prestigious place for his clients to browse and purchase items.

Dominic called Angie and said, "Angie, my darling, you did good. You found someone who understood the importance and value of these items to me. The cabinets with the seating arrangements are outstanding. I would have never considered this possible."

"That's wonderful that you are happy, Uncle Dominic. I was worried," Angie admitted.

"Nonsense. You had a nose for finding someone to construct my vision. Go ahead with the work, Angie. I want it completed on the timeline we discussed," Dominic said sternly.

"Yes, Uncle Dominic," said Angie, pausing for a short while before she continued, "I would rather not work with Francine after the incident. So I'll work with her counterpart, Tom Bender."

"Nonsense! You will work with Francine. This is business, so you need to put your personal vendetta behind you. Call Francine and have her order the supplies. Good-bye, Angie, I have a dinner engagement, so I have to hang up," he said.

Angie sat there dumbfounded. She knew the proposal and renderings were great, but she just recommended that everyone in her business consortium discontinue working with Francine Pacque. *What are they going to say when they see Francine working on this project?* Angie thought.

Angie sat at her desk and pondered the incident. She knew her personal feelings were hurt. Francine didn't do anything unethical to her or her colleagues as far as her zone 2 business. But the damage was already done. She had already sent the e-mail to all of them and to Francine's boss. She shrugged her shoulders, knowing it was too late to go back and undo her e-mail. It would be up to each of the customers to decide if they wanted to continue doing business with her.

Angie felt a sense of relief and decided to e-mail Francine at the end of the day with permission to proceed with the project. She didn't want to talk to Francine right now. She imagined that Francine's boss was probably contacting her about now.

Angie's phone rang fourteen times that day as the other business consortium colleagues asked her questions about the nature of the fraud mentioned in the e-mail. She explained the misrepresentation and said that she did not know any work-related issues. Angie did explain that her uncle was retaining Francine to work on a project but that she was still ending Creative Fabrication's association with Francine. It was a tiring day of explanation, and by the end of the day, Angie called the remaining few companies who hadn't contacted her to explain.

Francine had gone back to the hotel to take a short nap since she worked late the previous evening. She was on her way to one of her customer's plant when her phone rang. It was Joe Silverman Jr., Francine's boss.

"Hi, Joe, how are you doing?" Francine asked joyfully. She was unaware of the e-mail that Angie had sent.

"Not too good right now. Francine, do you have a minute to talk?" Joe answered.

Francine instantly had a bad feeling, and she pulled her car into a local parking lot.

"Of course, Joe. I take it this isn't a social call," Francine said.

"No, it is not. I received a copy of an e-mail that was addressed to seventeen companies this morning, recommending that they cease business with SPD, and you specifically, due to fraudulent misrepresentation," Joe stated.

"Oh my god!" Francine gasped while she asked, "Was it from Angela Fratilo?"

"Yes," he answered curtly. "Francine, this is serious. What happened here?"

Francine explained the entire story and emphasized that in no way was there any fraudulent misrepresentation done to any clients.

"Well, that's good. I'm amazed at the sales you have had in these low-market areas, Francine. Everyone at SPD has been keeping a watch on your progress. Are you sure that you didn't do or say anything unethical at a customer level?" Joe asked.

"Yes, I'm 100 percent sure," Francine answered.

"Then let's see how your clients react. We'll give them a couple of weeks," Joe said.

"OK, I'll be leaving Naples on Saturday, but I'm spending two weeks in Louisiana to build the business there prior to returning to Chicago," Francine said.

"She only sent letters to anyone out of what you refer to as zone 2, so I think you are good there," Joe replied.

"Joe, I think I should personally visit each of the companies that were sent this letter to explain and apologize in person," she suggested.

"I think that would be wise. But don't expect a warm reception at them, and God help you when you talk to this Angela woman. I would expect that our business there is over," Joe stated.

"Maybe, but possibly she will accept the man I hired to oversee the stock levels for her company. We'll see. Joe, I'm so sorry for what I did. It was so unusual for me to do something like this. I also posed as a journalist for a rodeo in Louisiana. What was I thinking? My personal ethics are part of my business ethics. I'm so sorry and so embarrassed," Francine said with her voice trailing off in despair.

"Let's see how it goes this week and talk about it when you get back to Chicago in a few weeks. I'm not sure how our conversation will be, Francine, when you return. Personal ethics and business ethics should work hand in hand," Joe stated.

Francine was thankful Joe didn't fire her today.

"Of course, Joe, and I hope you have a happy Thanksgiving holiday," she said.

"You too, but I doubt it will be so happy for you. I think you are going to be in for a difficult time," Joe predicted.

Joe was correct. Francine had lots of work to do while training her hire, Tom. But she visited each CFO's or controller's office at each of the companies to explain her indiscretion. She apologized for her mistake, reassured them that she had been 100 percent honest in her dealings with their company and with all the companies in zone 2, and urged them to not leave SPD as a supplier, because they were the best in the business.

"If you prefer to deal with someone else besides me, please deal with my associate, Tom Bender," she suggested. "Here is his business card." She repeated with her apologies to each company.

At the end of Monday, Francine was exhausted and returned to her hotel room to take a nice shower and relax. She checked her e-mails at about 7:00 p.m. and was surprised to see one from Angie. She opened the e-mail, nervous for its contents. It was a brief note saying that Dominic approved Francine's proposal, and she should proceed with the order ASAP.

Francine sat there in disbelief. The order was several hundred thousands of dollars for the cabinets, benches, and chairs. Angie sent her the approval to proceed. Maybe there was some hope that she and Angie would become friends again as they worked together. She also realized that she would benefit with commission on the order, even without the fee.

Francine called Angie's cell phone to thank her and ask if she could talk to her before she left town. There was no answer. She left a message and also wrote an e-mail to her. Angie never returned the call or e-mail.

The week was busy as Francine hurried to get all her work in zone 2 complete and train Tom. She decided to avoid the Noirtys' Thanksgiving dinner party and texted Noel with regrets saying that she needed to complete some paperwork before leaving Naples. Friday was cleanup day for anything not completed in her zone 2 companies. Most of the companies were closed on Friday, but several had small crews working. Francine packed up her Audi with all her belongings and settled her bill so she could leave early on Saturday morning for Monroe, Louisiana.

Francine checked her e-mails on Saturday morning before leaving the hotel. She was thankful that she hadn't received any cancellation e-mails from her zone 2 customers yet. She drove north from Naples, happy for the good times she had in the area and already looking forward to returning sometime mid-January to start developing zone 3 in the Fort Myers area.

CHAPTER 17

Face the Music

The next two weeks were uneventful except that her hire in Louisiana, Bill Hanson, had several leads on new businesses. Francine and Bill visited those companies to give their sales pitch. The companies were interested but wanted to start business after New Year. Francine agreed to visit them on her return to the area in January. Bill was beaming as he knew his business was growing, and Francine said they would do some cold call selling in outlying areas in January. She explained to Bill that she would remain as the primary salesperson for zone 1, with him supporting the business on an ongoing basis. Bill was thrilled.

It was mid-December, and Francine anxiously returned to Chicago. It had almost been three months since she had been home. She drove through the potholed streets and realized how fortunate the streets in Florida were for not having frost and snow. The weather was cold, but there was no snow on the streets. Francine shivered as her lightweight coat wasn't much protection as she unloaded her car after parking by her townhouse.

"I'm home!" Francine called as she entered the townhouse.

Lilly ran out of her bedroom wearing pajamas and fuzzy slippers.

"You are here! I'm so happy to see you, Francine," Lilly said while the two women exchanged hugs.

"Me too. It feels good to be home," Francine said while dragging her suitcase into her own bedroom.

Lilly helped Francine get all her luggage into her room, and the girls settled down on the couch to catch up on their personal news. Lilly told her that she had been getting all As at school, and she was so thankful to have a quiet, safe place to study in the townhouse. She also said that her boyfriend, Cory, was a student at Northwestern, and he had been driving her to school and back home since the weather got cold. Francine said she was anxious to meet Cory and meet Lilly's parents when they arrive from Japan next week.

"Francine, do you have a boyfriend there?" Lilly asked.

"No, I wasn't as lucky as you to find someone," Francine answered.

"Oh, then who is that cute guy in the pictures you posted?" Lilly asked.

Francine had to think for a few seconds and remembered that she had posted several pictures of Pete from different dates, including on his boat, at her house, and at Noel's party.

"That's Pete. We did go out a few times, but it's over. He was real nice and definitely handsome, but we were from two different worlds," Francine explained.

"Too bad. You looked good together. But I bet I know someone who probably is jealous," Lilly said coyly.

"Who would that be?" Francine asked.

"Your friend Brian. He must be into you. He looked so devastated when you were not here," Lilly answered as she imitated Brian's look from the day he stopped at the townhouse.

"I wish you were right about that. He's my type, for sure," Francine said while knowing in her heart that ship had sailed.

Francine told her about Naples and showed her pictures of the charity event, the house she stayed at, and the boats. Lilly was enthralled as she never saw such fancy homes.

"You fit right in, Francine. You look fabulous with your new hairdo and blond hair. I wanted to tell you that earlier, but I was overcome with surprise when you walked in," Lilly explained.

Francine and Lilly talked for another hour about various things that transpired in the past two months. Francine listened but kept thinking about Lilly's remark when she said, "You fit in." She wished for the first time in her life that she wasn't that good at fitting in.

The next morning, Francine dressed in one of her most professional attire before driving to SPD. She knew that she would have a one-on-one with her boss, Joe Jr., about her behavior in Naples. She was dreading to discuss it all again but knew it was inevitable. Knowing that she might lose her job today, she took a preventative anti-acid before entering the office.

SPD had a large office area with cubicles for field sales personnel. Francine found her cubicle and set up her computer. She checked her e-mails and found several orders from both zones. She submitted the orders and checked backorder status. All was good with the orders, so she closed her laptop and headed to the executive office area to find the general manager, Joe Silverman Jr. He was talking on the phone when he noticed Francine and waved her into his office.

When the call was over, Joe Jr. got up from his chair and walked around the desk to sit in the unoccupied chair next to Francine. She was nervous.

"Francine, how was your ride home? Did you run into any bad weather?" Joe Jr. asked.

"No, the weather and traffic was fine. I got home last evening," Francine said.

She sat very upright and professional. She tried not to appear nervous by fidgeting.

"Glad to hear. Glad to hear," he repeated.

Joe lowered his head while gathering his thoughts before speaking.

"Let's get right to it. The Naples incident. Do you have anything more to say about it?" he asked.

"No, I don't have nothing more to add. I did visit all my customers within the week. Most just passed it off as nothing, and several were curious and asked a couple of questions. They all said that they would do business with me in the future," Francine said.

"All of them? Including this woman, what was her name again?" he said while he reached for his notes.

"Angie Fratilo," Francine said, correcting the first name.

"That's right. Did you speak with her?" he asked.

"No, but I tried. I telephoned her, left a message, and I wrote her an e-mail asking her to contact me," Francine said. "I haven't personally talked to Angie, but she did send me the authorization to proceed with a large project for her uncle. That's a good sign," Francine said.

She handed the order for Dominic's warehouse cabinets and accessories to Joe Jr. He looked at the long order list page by page. His eyebrows rose when he read the total sales dollars on the final page.

"She gave you this order? It's hard to believe," Joe Jr. said with a curious smile.

Francine explained the import business that Angie's uncle was starting in Naples. Francine showed him her renderings from a copy of the proposal. Joe shook his head in amazement.

"This is good to hear. We haven't seen any cancellations at our end either, so far. But, Francine, I'm still not happy with what you did. Your personal behavior is a reflection of you and the company you represent. If I didn't have a long-term knowledge of your work from when you were with Magnacraft, I wouldn't be so lenient on you. But that being said, I think you have been through a lot during the last several months, and your sales performance has been extraordinary. I am leaning on giving you a strong warning for this indiscretion. I would like you to document the events you told me about how you misrepresented yourself, and I'm going to put it in your file. The file will not be in the normal personnel file for everyone to see but will reside with me. If there are any more issues, then you are gone. Do you understand?" Joe Jr. said.

Francine nodded and said, "Yes, sir. I understand. Thank you so much for giving me another chance."

Francine stood up and extended her hand to Joe Jr. They shook hands before Francine left his office.

Worry and weight lifted off her shoulders. What Joe Jr. asked her to do was very fair. She didn't lose her job, and she was thankful. Francine went back to her cubicle and typed up her recollection of the lies and the opportunities she took in Naples. She also included her rodeo journalist ruse from Monroe, Louisiana. She wanted a clean slate.

CHAPTER 18

Christmas at the Pacques

Francine took the opportunity to see her old friends from Magnacraft, Sara Johnston and Jim Ruscher. It was fun to catch up with them on their lives and on the gossip from Magnacraft. Both of them were in the same jobs as when Francine left the company, so much of the conversation surrounded the success Francine was having in her two sales zones. Her friends were happy for Francine's success although they terribly missed working with her.

"How's Karen Warnette doing?" Francine curiously asked.

Karen Warnette was the woman who received the intern sales executive promotion. Karen's promotion was a shock for the entire sales team at Magnacraft and a personal shock for Francine, who expected to get the promotion.

"Oh! Didn't I tell you? She's gone! No one knows where she went, but the word is that she didn't know how to act around the customers. You know Mike Goodly, don't you? Well, Mike was included in some high-level meeting with an international customer. Karen was to make the presentation. She was awful, according to Mike. She couldn't respond to their questions about the products, wasn't up to speed on the pricing, and so on. Mike said it was embarrassing," Sara explained.

"Wow. Well, we personally know she never made a cold call or wrote any presentation on her own. So she's gone, huh? It makes me kind of happy because I feel vindicated, but I still feel sorry for her. Losing a job isn't fun," Francine said.

"We don't miss her a bit. But everyone still misses you. I wish you could come back Francine,?" Sara replied.

"Ditto on that," Jim said.

"Thanks, but you know what? I really love what I'm doing. I had a feeling that my strategy would work, and I got to implement it. It's been hard work, but I love what I'm doing. I even have a couple of people helping me now," Francine shared.

As they talked, Francine's thoughts reflected on how happy her new position at SPD has made her feel. She felt proud of herself for the first time. She refocused back to the conversation, and the three of them laughed so hard about past times that they almost cried.

Francine left her townhouse on Saturday to stay at Gerry and Chrissy's house while Lilly's parents were visiting. Chrissy was eager to have some adult girl time, as she was alone with her three children most of the time. Gerry was supposed to be out of town on football-related business, but when Francine got to their house, she was unhappy to be greeted by her obnoxious brother.

"Fanny Pack. It's good to see you, sis," Gerry said.

Francine rolled her eyes and pretended to be happy to see him. "Hi, Gerry, I thought you were out of town?"

"Yeah, I'm hitting the road in about an hour. So how have you been?" he said.

"Where are Chrissy and the kids?" she asked.

"They should get home anytime now. Chrissy went to the store, and I didn't want the kids bothering me, so she took them along," Gerry admitted.

"Doesn't she *always* have to take care of the kids? Maybe she would have liked a little privacy herself," Francine sternly said to nonlistening ears.

Gerry shrugged and walked into the kitchen.

"Come on in, Fanny Pack. Bring you stuff in here," he said without lifting a finger to help her with her luggage.

The hour before Gerry left for his trip couldn't come fast enough for Francine. Finally, Gerry's ride honked the car horn. Gerry picked up his own luggage from the hallway and turned to Francine.

"Hey, sis. I saw those pictures of you on Facebook. It looks like you're doing really well for yourself, or Magnacraft is really paying you well. Good for you. I've never been in a house like that or on a yacht. Good for you, sis."

He smiled at her and walked out the door. Francine never had a chance to respond. She was so shocked that her brother gave her a compliment. She couldn't remember him ever giving her a compliment.

When Chrissy returned home, she screamed with delight that her sister-in-law Francine had arrived. The kids jumped on Francine as she always brought small gifts for them. Francine pointed to three gift bags on the kitchen table, and the kids ran into the kitchen to get their new toys.

Chrissy hugged Francine and told her how happy she was that Francine was staying there. Francine wasn't surprised after her brother displayed his lack of help with the children. Francine, Chrissy, and the children played until it was the children's bedtime, and they all had fun.

After the kids went to bed, Chrissy made a giant bowl of popcorn and brought two Diet Cokes into the living room. They ate popcorn while they talked about family things.

When that conversation ended, Chrissy said, "I'm so happy you are here, and I'm especially happy to be able to help you with some of these orders. It uses some of my underutilized skills."

"You've been a big help to Bill Hanson. There will be more work with another man I recently hired, Tom Bender, in Naples," Francine replied.

"It works out great for me because I can still be here and work around the kids' appointments and Gerry's things. I want to thank you so much," Chrissy said. "Magnacraft has to be very happy about the new zones you started."

Francine looked at her and put down the popcorn bowl.

"Chrissy, I haven't been totally honest with you. I don't work for Magnacraft anymore."

"What? When did that happen? Today?" Chrissy asked.

"No, it happened in September. I was too embarrassed to tell anyone. I didn't get the promotion I thought. Instead, I was let go," she admitted.

"But these sales orders? I don't understand," Chrissy questioned.

Francine told Chrissy about the employment agency's failure to find her good employment and her good fortune that one of her customers, Specialty Products Distributors, gave her a chance to create a new territory. She went on to tell her about her financial position and the six months' guaranteed income that SPD gave her.

"Oh my, Francine. Why didn't you tell us? We would have understood. Maybe we could have helped you," Chrissy stated.

"Really? Do you think my brother, Gerry, would feel compassion for me? He would just blame me for doing something wrong. So would Mom and Dad. Viv and you would be the only ones who would really make me feel better. So I figured that my best option was to grow a new business, which I did. Now I don't have to feel like such a loser," Francine said while holding back the tears.

"I know what you are saying, but you are underestimating everyone. Gerry loves you, Francine. You should have seen him look at the pictures you posted. He was shocked and so proud. He even showed some of the guys his babe sister in the picture at that gala. I overheard him tell his friends that you were better than all the male salesmen at Magnacraft and that your company entrusted you to build up their business in some low-manufacturing areas. Francine, he showed each and every picture that you posted to them. I even heard him saying something about the rich guy you must have found in Naples."

"Really?" Francine said.

She could not imagine her brother saying compliments to her, much less about her to his friends.

"I think you have the wrong impression of him, Francine. He works hard, but he knows that he isn't a jock anymore. He doesn't have a high position at the university. He's not so cocky anymore," Chrissy said.

"He still called me Fanny Pack when he saw me today," Francine said sharply. "Twice!"

Chrissy started laughing. "Maybe that's a compliment these days. You know, bootie is big nowadays."

Francine took a pillow and gently hit her sister-in-law on the head. They started a pillow fight and knocked the popcorn all over the couch.

"Two-second rule," Chrissy said while grabbing all the kernels to put back into the bowl.

After the popcorn episode, Francine said, "I have something else to tell you that I'm not too proud of."

She decided that her penance for misrepresenting herself was to tell her family the truth, and she started with telling the entire story to Chrissy. Chrissy listened attentively and asked questions along the way. She was fascinated by the story. She couldn't imagine having the guts to try something like that. Francine said that the Naples housewives were so connected to one another. They knew someone for every scenario and mostly led Francine down the path. But she didn't say no. She was wrong and she lied. She admitted that she was afraid to lose her job at SPD today, when she had to talk to her boss. At the end of the confession, Chrissy hugged her sister-in-law.

"You have had a really interesting couple of months. Not many people could do what you did in that time. I don't feel you did anything very wrong. You took advantage of some opportunities, that's all. You're still wonderful in my book," Chrissy said.

"Thank you. I hope everyone else is as understanding as you. The Pacque family is not very adventurous," Francine said.

"Don't be so hard on everyone. I think it will be fine. In fact, I don't know why you have to tell them everything. Just tell them that you work for SPD now," Chrissy advised.

"No, I have to get it off my chest so that I can move forward without guilt," she answered.

"When are you going to tell everyone?" Chrissy asked.

"I think on Christmas. We'll all be together, and I can tell everyone at the same time," Francine said.

"You were going to stay overnight at your mom and dad's Christmas Eve and Christmas night. Aren't you afraid that they'll ask lots more questions when you are alone?" Chrissy asked.

"No, I have some other business to discuss with them. I'm sure that will change their focus," Francine answered.

Chrissy waited for Francine to explain, but Francine smiled and changed the subject. They went back to eating their popcorn and laughing at TV sitcoms. As Francine watched TV, she was thinking about another difficult phone call she needed to make tomorrow.

The day before Christmas was a busy day at the Pacque home in Kenosha. Francine's mother had a tradition of baking cookies and cakes during the day with her children. But as her children had their own families and their own traditions, Francine was the only one to help with the baking. She looked forward to the alone time with her mother as her father enjoyed a book in the living room.

Francine talked about her job successes but steered away from specific topics. She wanted to explain to the family as a whole tomorrow after dinner. She knew that the grandchildren traditionally played with their new toys in the basement after dinner. There would be ample time for her confession.

Christmas Day came, and the Pacque family celebrated by gathering at Bertrand and Gertrude Pacque's home in Racine, Wisconsin. Gerry and Chrissy Pacque came with their three children, Genevieve and Matt Mulvane with their two children, and Francine. Francine had a surprise for them. This year she was not dining alone with the family. She had invited her friend Brian Sherman as her date. The families arrived at the Pacque home about 1:00 p.m., and at exactly 2:00 p.m., the doorbell rang.

"I wonder who that is," said Bertrand as he got up to walk to the front foyer.

"I invited someone as my date," Francine said with a big smile.

Her family was surprised and elated at the news. Brian entered the house, and Francine quickly grabbed his arm to lead him into the family room.

"Everyone, this is Brian Sherman," Francine announced proudly and proceeded to introduce him to everyone in the room. After introductions, Brian took off his coat, and Bertrand quickly took it away. Brian sat down next to Francine on the couch.

Francine was happy to have Brian there. She gently touched his arm and told him that he smelled good. Brian smiled and told her that she smelled and looked good too. They quietly giggled, while everyone was sizing up her date.

"So, Brian, what do you do for a living?" Bertrand asked.

"I'm a civil engineer. I'm running a project in Galena, Illinois, right now. I'm from the Chicago area," he answered.

"How did you and Francine meet?" Gertrude Pacque asked.

Francine had given Brian instructions not to tell her parents about her job change. She was going to announce it to them after dinner.

Francine jumped in with a response, "We met by chance one day in Chicago and ended up going out for pizza. We haven't seen too much of each other since then since we both have been working out of town."

She explained that Brian has a four-year-old son who was celebrating Christmas with his ex-wife's family.

"I thought he might like to join us rather than be alone. Brian's family lives in the Seattle area," Francine added.

"Yes, that's right. I had my son last night for Christmas Eve, so I didn't have a chance to fly to Seattle to be with my folks," Brian explained.

Brian quickly fit in with the Pacque family men, as there was a Christmas Day football game on the TV. Soon they were yelling and jeering at the TV while clearly having a good time.

At 3:00 p.m., the TV was put on pause by Gertrude as she announced, "Who wants some presents?"

"I do! I do!" echoed the five grandchildren, who quickly ran upstairs to the family room from where they were playing downstairs.

The family exchanged presents and later had an exquisite dinner prepared by Gertrude and Francine. The women stayed in the kitchen to clean up the table, while the men relaxed in the family room. Francine could hear the children playing with their toys in the recreation room in the basement.

After cleanup, Francine asked her mom, Viv, and Chrissy if they could go into the family room. She had something important to tell them. He mother took off her apron and looked at Francine questionably.

"Is Francine getting married?" Viv asked Chrissy.

Chrissy shook her head negatively and hooked her arm into Viv's. The women entered the family room. Francine looked at the men who were watching a football game.

She took the remote and said, "I'm taping whatever it is that you are watching. I have something important to tell you."

The guys groaned, but curiosity drove them to settle in their seats and face Francine. Francine took a deep breath and started her story. First, she told them that she did not get a promotion and a new territory but instead got the boot. She shared that she was too humiliated and scared to tell her family. Second, she told them about her time at the employment agency and the lack of qualified sales jobs. She said that the only good thing about the agency was that she met someone wonderful there, Brian Sherman.

She let the information settle into her family's mind and fielded questions about her past job. After a few minutes, Francine continued that she received an opportunity from one of her Magnacraft customers to cultivate a sales strategy she developed. She explained her network briefly to them. She said that the new company she worked for, SPD, only allowed her to try out her strategy in low-market areas, so she chose the South. She said she was working out of her car and staying in the cheapest hotels she could find the past several months.

The Pacque family was very sympathetic, not judgmental. "Why didn't you tell us?" and "We could have given you some money" was repeated several times. Francine was happy and surprised at their reaction. Maybe she had her family pegged a little wrong.

"That's the good part," Francine said with a heavy sigh. "The next part is hard for me to tell you, but I must."

Francine continued telling her escapades in Monroe with the rodeo cowboys and in Naples with the house she stayed at and with the yacht. She left out no details and shared everything with them.

The family and Brian were very quiet through her explanation. They all appeared visibly shocked by Francine's tale. Several more questions were asked along with questions about the pictures she posted on her social network.

At the end of her confession, Francine said, "So I am very sorry for what I did and think I have repaid all the people I may have inconvenienced. But my reputation is ruined, and I almost lost this job too. My boss at SPD and I had a very stressful meeting. For now, he kept me on as a salesperson."

She started to cry. Her mother quickly went to her to console her daughter. The men in the room looked at one another, questioning how they should feel about it. Gerry shrugged his shoulders as if he didn't care, and Matt just smiled at Francine. But Brian looked conflicted. He couldn't believe that the woman he put on a pedestal would do something like this. He didn't think it was so terrible, but his wife lied to him, so being untruthful was a mortal sin in his opinion.

After the discussion, the family went back to watching the game on TV. Brian also watched the TV for several minutes. Unexpectedly, Brian stood up and walked over to Gertrude Pacque.

"Thank you, Gertrude, for the wonderful dinner," Brian said.

Gertrude asked, "You are very welcome, Brian. Are you leaving?"

"Yes, I have to head back to Chicago," Brian answered.

He walked around the family room, saying his good-byes to everyone. Everyone except Francine, that is. As he walked to a bedroom where Bertrand had a pile of coats on the bed, Francine followed him. He turned to face Francine.

"Hey, I'm going to go now. I'm sorry, Francine, but this was a bit much for me," Brian said.

Francine instantly thought of the hurt Brian had endured when his wife lied to him. She hadn't considered the effect her lie might have on him. *Oh, great. I lost him forever.*

Brian walked out the door, and Francine closed it behind her. She stood there motionless when Chrissy suddenly yanked her arm and dragged Francine back into the family room.

"Listen, all of you. What Francine didn't tell you was that her business in the South has taken off! She's been very successful, and I have even been helping her. Yes, Gerry, I have, and I've gotten some money for my work too," Chrissy said proudly.

Her husband, Gerry, looked at her and clapped.

"Thanks, Chrissy. Yes, she's right. I have been successful. Very successful, actually, with two sales zones. I've been able to create a business model for estimating future zones, and I plan to duplicate to a total of six zones," Francine said confidently.

"Francine has other people working for her in those zones too," Chrissy announced.

"Thanks, Chrissy, for the endorsement. Dad, I wanted to talk to you tomorrow about setting up a proper business format so that I can pay my employees properly and supply W-2s and so forth," Francine said.

Bertrand looked at his wife and looked back at Francine. He was clearly impressed.

"You mean you started your own business? I would love to set up a business for you. We can work on it in the morning, my dear. I have to say that I'm impressed. It's not easy to start a business, and it seems like you have done that in record time," Francine's father announced.

Francine's family clapped their hands. Gerry even cheered. *They are clapping! For me! I can't believe it.*

The next day verified Bertrand's pride. Francine gave her father her sales records, with sales dollars and commissions. She also provided him predictive models for the type of manufacturing represented by her two zones, including future predictions for a future six zones based on the type of manufacturing found in each of those zones. The sales numbers were large, even with the wages paid to the zone salespeople.

"I want to supply my employees with benefits, or at least compensation for them to adequately get benefits for their families. I want to give them a vacation plan and incentives if they bring in new businesses into the zones. I plan to have a sales rep in each of the six zones, plus Chrissy, for expediting and special projects. I may need to hire several backups as well," Francine explained.

Bertrand and Gertrude looked at the projections and the sales records. They looked at the extra sales from additional business, such as the commission Francine would get from the import warehouse job in Naples. It was impressive, and her parents commented frequently on the success.

"Francine, you are obviously an exceptional salesperson, and it looks like you are going to have an exceptional business. I have to say that I am astounded with what you have done," Bertrand said.

Francine never remembered such pride being bestowed on her from her parents. She was always in the shadows of Gerry and Genevieve. This recognition left her feeling giddy. Her parents never brought up the issues from Naples, just the success.

Later in the day, Francine reflected back to her brother, Gerry, and the words that Chrissy said about him being proud of Francine. She knew that Viv was always proud of her. She never questioned Viv's feelings toward her. *Maybe I was too oversensitive. Was I?* she questioned as she examined her past memories. She returned to Chrissy and Gerry's house that evening. She was still staying there while Lilly's parents were in town.

When she entered the house, Gerry said, "Well, you got into a little jam there, Fanny Pack. But I didn't see the big deal about it. You didn't maliciously try to get something for nothing. You're still my baby sister to me."

Francine hugged him and wondered why he insisted on calling her that hideous name. But actually, she was comforted by the name tonight. Gerry used it lovingly to her, not mean like she usually interpreted it.

"Thanks, Gerry. But do you think you can stop using that hideous name?" Francine asked.

"Oh, sure, sis. I didn't know it bothered you," he said.

Are you kidding me? I've asked him to stop a million times, Francine thought.

"Thanks, Gerry. It always bothered me," Francine replied.

CHAPTER 19

New Year Surprises

Francine continued living at Gerry and Chrissy's house until after New Year. It had been a fun experience, and Francine loved spending close time with her family. She planned to move back to her townhouse after Lilly's parents returned to Japan, and would be staying there for another week before returning to the South.

She hadn't heard from Brian Sherman. She knew that he was spending lots of time with his son during the holidays, but without even a text or call, she knew any chance for a relationship was over. It was the night before New Year's Eve, and Francine was surprised when her phone rang and it was Brian.

"Hi, Francine. How are you doing?" Brian asked nonchalantly.

"I'm fine. I didn't think I would hear from you again," Francine admitted in a low tone.

"Well, there is a reason for that. Remember, I told you that I wanted to explain why last month when I went to your townhouse, but you were still out of town. I meant to do it on Christmas, but too much drama was going on. The conversation at your parents' house threw me for a loop," Brian stated.

"I understand. You don't owe me anything after what I did, but I appreciate you wanting to explain," she said.

"I was wondering if you could meet me for dinner tomorrow night?" Brian asked.

"Do you realize that tomorrow night is New Year's Eve? It'll be difficult to get in at any restaurant," Francine shared.

"I have to work late, so I'll meet you at Alinea's at seven thirty. Do you know where that is?" Brian asked.

Francine thought about the restaurant. It was one of the hottest restaurants in Chicago. She repeated the restaurant's name to be sure she heard it right. He verified it and the time.

Francine was elated, but something in Brian's voice had her confused. Brian didn't sound like his usual casual self, and he was very blunt with her, ending the call promptly after verifying the restaurant's name. She thought he was angry and wondered why he asked her to dinner. She shook off the feeling and drove to her townhouse to choose a perfect outfit.

Lilly and her parents were sitting in the living room when Francine walked in. They were very happy to see Francine again prior to them leaving back to Japan. Lilly, her parents, and Francine had spent one evening together earlier in their visit, and Lilly and Francine cooked an American meal for them of T-bone steaks, baked potatoes, and baked beans. Tonight, Francine spent an hour talking with them about their thoughts on Chicago. The Lees said they had a wonderful time and did lots of sightseeing and shopping. Finally, she asked if she could go into her bedroom and remove an outfit for New Year's Eve.

The next night, Francine showed up at Alinea's at seven fifteen. She didn't want to be late. She wore a sexy black dress with black nylons and superhigh heels. She had a velvet wrap with fake fur over her dress. Her hair was fashioned into an upsweep, and her nails shined with dark-red polish. Even the hostess nodded in approval when Francine took off her wrap.

"May I help you?" the hostess said.

"I'm waiting for someone," Francine explained and stood against the wall. The foyer was swamped with people waiting for a table, so there were no seats available.

At seven forty, Francine looked at her phone for a message from Brian. She didn't find a message, so she expected he was driving to the restaurant.

At seven fifty-five, Francine tried to reach Brian on the phone. There was no answer. She followed up with a text, "Waiting at the restaurant. Hope you are here soon." Francine watched her phone for a response, which never came.

At five after eight, the hostess asked Francine what the name of her party was. Francine responded, "Sherman, Brian Sherman." The hostess looked at her reservation list and frowned.

"I don't see a reservation under his name. Are you sure you have the right restaurant?" the hostess asked.

"Yes, I'm sure," Francine said disappointedly. "I guess he's not coming. Do you have a table available so I can eat?"

The hostess shook her head no as she said, "It's New Year's Eve, and we are booked until after midnight. We always are booked."

The hostess looked at Francine, who was on the verge of tears.

She said, "I'm sorry. Why don't you at least sit at the bar and have a drink, courtesy of me."

Francine nodded in agreement and went into the bar escorted by the hostess. The hostess muttered something to the bartender and touched Francine's arm as she left.

"I'm sorry, honey," she said affectionately.

Francine mouthed "Thank you." A couple was called to dinner and got up from their bar seats. As they rose, the bartender motioned for Francine to sit on one of the empty seats, much to the dismay of another couple. She ordered a glass of wine and sat there with her head facing down. *I hoped so much that Brian would forgive me. He was exactly like the man I hoped to love. I guess standing me up was his revenge,* she thought. Francine had been seated a few minutes when a hand firmly touched her shoulder.

"Hello there, beautiful," a man said.

Francine turned her head to see who the man was. It was Brian. He was wearing a dark suit and tie.

"Brian! I thought you were standing me up," Francine said as she put her arms around his neck.

"We probably should eat," he said as he gently kissed her neck.

"The hostess said you hadn't made a reservation. She couldn't find your name," Francine exclaimed.

"Hmmm. We'll see about that," he said coyly as he picked up Francine's drink and escorted her into the lobby.

The hostess looked at him and then at Francine.

"Oh! I see your date finally arrived, but we don't have a reservation for you," the hostess shared.

"Really? Look again, Brian said the mayor of Chicago's name, and added, "Party of two," Brian said firmly as he handed a small notecard to the hostess.

She looked at the card and read it thoroughly. Slowly, a smile formed on the hostess's face as she looked at Francine and Brian.

"Yes. Of course. Right this way," the smiling hostess said as she led them to a beautifully decorated table in the center of the room.

Francine was shocked. She didn't know what to think.

She looked at Brian, who leaned across the table and took her hand, saying, "Two can play at that trick."

Francine was more shocked than ever.

"Brian, oh no! Don't say you are someone you're not. I can bear to go through that again," Francine gasped.

Brian laughed.

"First some wine, then I'll explain," he said.

Francine and Brian ordered some wine and an appetizer. When the wine came, they had a couple of sips before Brian reached out for Francine's hand.

"I guess it is time to explain. Then we can eat. OK?" he asked.

Francine nodded.

Brian started, "Well, here it goes. Francine, I've been in love with you since the first time we met. I had a difficult divorce, but I was ready for a solid relationship when I met you. But…I quickly realized how accomplished you were when we were rehearsing our interviews, and I got scared. Then I went to your place that night and saw your home, I knew I was not in your league."

"But, Brian, I just spend my money on those types of things. You have a son to support," Francine interrupted while tightening her grip on his hand.

"I know, but still, a man has to feel good about himself before he can be good for someone else," Brian confided. "I took the engineering job in Galena because I needed the income, but my sights were on another job position."

He took a sip of wine before continuing, "I got that job, and I officially start January second."

Francine was surprised to hear what he said, but she was focused on the fact that he was *in love with her*. She never had another man tell her that before.

"That's so great, Brian. What is your new job?" Francine asked.

"I'm working for a major engineering company with contracts for the city of Chicago. I'm leading a team of engineers. I'm the boss!" Brian exclaimed. "I worked for them before on a contract basis, so they knew my work. They also knew that I could handle a team of engineers from past experience. The old boss is retiring at the end of the year, and they contacted me to take his place. It's my dream job." Brian beamed.

Francine was overjoyed to hear that Brian had gotten the job of his dreams. They toasted to his new job and to his success.

"What about the reservation with the name of the mayor?" Francine asked.

Brian laughed. "I couldn't help myself. I thought you would find it funny."

"Funny? I almost had a heart attack. First, I thought you were standing me up, and then the fake name. You can't do that! Please don't!" Francine pleaded.

"Wait a minute. It wasn't my name, but it wasn't a fake name. The mayor wrote that card. His assistant made the reservation. I had an interview with the mayor because the engineering job interfaces with the city. The conversation got around to my personal life, and I told him my situation with you. I mentioned that I wanted to invite you to a great restaurant for New Year's Eve. He told me to take you to this restaurant but added that I would never get in, so he asked his assistant to make the reservation for me. That was what was written on the note. No joke," Brian confessed.

"You and the mayor are friends?" Francine asked.

"No, not friends, but I did have the interview with him, and he did me this favor. I told him that I walked out on Christmas and wanted to make it up to you. Guys understand stuff like that," Brian said.

Francine was teary-eyed with joy. She stood up and approached Brian, leaning down to give him a long kiss. They had a wonderful dinner and lingered at the table before leaving the restaurant.

"We can pick up your car in the morning," he said while looking at Francine for confirmation.

Francine remembered that Lilly's parents were at her house and shared that information.

"That's even better. Then you can come to my place," he said.

Francine hung on to Brian's arm as they walked to his car, realizing that she was holding on to her dream guy. They drove to Brian's apartment, and Francine did not go home until the morning.

"This is the best day of my life," Francine said to the ceiling before she fell asleep.

CHAPTER 20

New Beginnings

The holidays ended, and thoughts of returning to the South flooded Francine. Francine and Brian Sherman's relationship grew over the next few weeks, but both of them needed to refocus on their careers. They knew that Francine's job would have her traveling much of the time, but they would be together whenever she returned to Chicago. Brian was content with the arrangement because he realized that he would have time to attend his son's various school and social events.

Francine returned to Louisiana, as she had promised Bill Hanson, and they made sales calls together to build zone 1. The zone continued to grow with strong sales as more companies joined SPD's vendor-managed stock.

Francine returned to Naples, Florida, at the end of January. She had lots of work to do with Dominic Pepino's import business, so most of her zone 2 work was being completed by Tom Bender. Tom was a very good businessman, and he was receiving good reviews by the companies in the zone. Francine promised to build up zone 3 in Fort Myers as soon as the import warehouse job was complete. Adding zone 3 would grow Tom's job into a full-time position, and he was anxious for the opportunity.

Francine finished the import warehouse rearrangement with rave reviews. Although her initial contacts with Angie Fratilo were very cold, the two worked together to get Uncle Dominic's import business launched with a gala opening on March 1. Francine asked Noel Noirty to help with the gala as she had personal knowledge of what the Naples crowd would expect. Noel was thrilled to be involved, and soon the three women were going to lunch and to cocktails together as if nothing had happened. The gala was a booming success, and the business launched immediately.

One day, Francine's cell phone rang while she was working. It was a number she didn't recognize.

"Hello, this is Francine Pacque," Francine announced.

"Hi, Francine. I hope I'm not calling at a bad time. This is Karen Warnette," a soft voice whispered.

Karen Warnette! Francine's mind raced. *She got my promotion. She didn't even know how to talk to a client.* Francine's blood pressure rose until she remembered that Karen was let go from Magnacraft in December.

"Hello, Karen. How are you doing?" Francine asked.

"That's why I'm calling, Francine. I'm not doing well. I don't know if you heard, but I'm not at Magnacraft anymore," Karen said. "Francine, I need some help. I didn't have anyone to ask but you. I've been on some interviews, but I really don't know how to sell very well, and no one is interested in me. I don't know what to do."

Francine was stunned and didn't respond quickly. There was dead silence over the phone except for several sobs that Francine recognized. Francine knew how difficult it was to get a sales job. She reflected on the right words to say.

"Karen, of course I will help you. I tell you what. How would you like to take a little trip to Florida?" Francine asked.

"Florida?" Karen asked.

"Yes, Florida. I'm setting up a sales network here in Fort Myers. Then, I'll be going north to the Sarasota area. If you're interested, I can help you develop that area," Francine said.

"Thank you so much. I heard you started a successful company. Everyone at Magnacraft was talking about you. But, Francine, I actually don't know if I can do it. I mean, I've never made a cold call," Karen admitted.

"I'll teach you. That's what friends do, they help each other," Francine said, realizing the greater good she would do by helping a colleague.

Karen's worries melted away as she thanked her mentor and made plans meet Francine soon.

THE END

ABOUT THE AUTHOR

Kathleen "Kathy" Balota was born in Milwaukee, Wisconsin and resided there until 2014 when she and her husband, Dennis, moved to Fort Myers, FL. She graduated from the University of Wisconsin-Milwaukee and received a master's degree from General Motors Institute, now known as Kettering University. Kathy worked for many years in factory management, industrial engineering, and lean manufacturing positions. Although enjoying her retirement, Kathy has found an outlet for her creativity in writing fiction. *The Ethical Business Woman* is her first novel and explorers some of the situations that a business woman could encounter in her career. Kathy looks forward to writing another novel involving some of the same characters introduced in her first book.